Swept Away

By Elizabeth Seckman

Formatting by CookieLynn Publishing Services, LLC

To Jo Wake. The grandmother of dragons.

Prologue

Summer 2010

"Storm's coming, Arie. Please, let me get Troy to help us."

"No." Ariel's answer was quick and sharp.

Maddy shook her head, but said no more. She could see Troy Miller in his yard. The boy could be there in the time it took her to yell his name. He was taller and stouter than either girl, and could probably scale the bank with the dog and be out of the lake before the storm hit. Maddy wasn't so certain about Ariel's chances. The water off Lake Erie grew choppier; its normally smooth waves white-capping, slapping against the jagged rock along its shore. Maddy was beginning to wonder if the stubborn mule would drown herself and the dog.

"Over here," Maddy moved along the edge of the bank to a spot where the land dipped. The ground here was a thickened sludge where the rising water softened the rich, black soil.

First step in, Ariel sank ankle deep. She pulled her foot loose and took another step. "Crap. I lost my shoe."

Maddy was losing patience. With a frown and a head shake, she repeated, "If you'd just—"

"No," Ariel said. Tucking the mud-caked mutt against her hip, she slowly moved toward dry land. Three steps later, Ariel sunk to her knees in mud. She keeled to the left as the weight of the dog threw off her balance. "Good lord, it's like quicksand."

Maddy lay on her belly and stretched her arms out toward her friend. "See if I can get him."

Ariel gave the dog a toss and Maddy grabbed him by the scruff of his neck. He yipped, but quickly quieted as she pulled him up over the bank, safe on solid land.

"You got him?"

"Yeah. You better hurry. It' going to be bad."

Ariel crawled to the drier part of the bank and with both hands free, she was up and over in seconds. Covered in mud, she looked down at herself and frowned. "My mother is going to kill me."

"Tell her you did it…hell, I can't think of a reason she'd be okay with. You're up shit creek. I don't know why you didn't let me yell for Troy. He'd have done it…for you."

Ariel headed for the road, arms swinging. Maddy had to jog to catch up with her. "What gives? I didn't think the date went that bad. You two seemed to hit it off."

"It's not that….it's just…Jeb found out. He wasn't happy," Ariel said.

"Did you tell him your mom gave you permission?"

"It didn't matter. She denied knowing anything about it."

They walked along quietly. Thunder rumbled behind them. Maddy needed to call her mom for a ride, but she hated to leave Ariel when she was in one of her moods.

They walked along silently. The small terrier sniffed every rock and leaf in the road. "What will you name him?" Ariel asked.

"Me name him? You're the one who jumped in and saved him."

"You would have if I hadn't beaten you to it. Besides, I can't take him home. You know that."

The storm-grey light filtering through the leaves gave Ariel a hollow, dead look that made Maddy's skin crawl. There was something different about her friend. Maddy knew something was wrong. Something that wouldn't get better with time, only worse. But she didn't know how to fix it.

"So what's his name?" Ariel asked.

"I don't know," Maddy answered slowly as she pulled herself from her thoughts.

"First name that comes to mind, no thinking."

"Toby," Maddy said

"Toby? Hmm. I like it. Hey, Toby."

The dog barked.

"Cool." Ariel smiled. "He likes it. I suppose a filthy, stinky guy walking with a shoeless girl down a country road would like the name Toby."

Ariel paused at the path that led to the monstrous lake house. She took a deep breath; her shoulders dropped. Maddy hated this part of the day—watching the stress that came over her friend when she had to go home.

"As soon as we turn eighteen, we will get us a place. You, me, and Toby."

"I can't wait," Ariel said.

"You know," Maddy said. "Why don't we do it now?"

"Now?"

Maddy shrugged. "Yeah, now. Come on, we look eighteen. We could get jobs easy. Go somewhere warm…with a beach."

Ariel grabbed her friend's arm. "Are you serious?"

"As a heart attack."

"Oh my gosh. We could, couldn't we? Maddy, I know where Jeb keeps his cash stash. Thousands of dollars. Stacks and stacks of bills in his desk."

"Nuh, uh. Who does that?"

Ariel shrugged. "Jeb. So, here's the plan. You call Devon and tell him we need a ride. He'll give us a lift to the bus stop, and then we take off."

Maddy's face squished. "We can't take Toby on a bus."

Ariel nodded slowly. "Then…what if…we steal Jeb's car. When we get to where we want to go, we ditch it."

"Well there Thelma, how the hell hard do you think it'd be to ditch a car and not be caught?"

"Well, we steal the Porsche and leave it unattended and someone will take it for us."

"You're a freaking genius. I'll go home and get a few things, and I'll meet you at midnight after everyone is in bed."

Ariel squealed, grabbing her friend and hugging her. "This is the beginning of something good. I can feel it."

Chapter One

Summer 2015

Tucker Boone was a peculiar creature compared to the people who raised him. Ed and Marlene Adkins were both short, blonde, and boring. By contrast, at age fifteen, Tucker stood well over six foot with an athletic build, thick dark hair, and a restlessness that was nearly palpable.

When he turned eighteen, the idea of heading to college fit him like a tight suit. Instead, he joined the Marine Corps. Marlene was horrified, certain her only child was headed to Iraq. In her fury, she made a disgusted comment about the apple not falling far from the tree. "You're just like your father," she screamed. "The hell with your family. Go save the world."

Odd thing for a woman who, until that moment, swore his paternity was a credit to a sperm donation from Reproductive Associates, Inc. But there was little time to question the remark, since he was, indeed, headed off to a war zone.

Once his service ended, he was out less than a week before the question began to tingle his spine.

Who was Tucker Boone?

Pressed for the truth, his mother grudgingly admitted his father wasn't donor number eleven-one-five, but a real flesh and blood man. One whom she lived with for years, and who was still listed in the Applewold, Pennsylvania phone directory. Tucker decided he'd visit the man. His mother wasn't happy with the decision, but having lost the moral high ground in her fury, she could only offer a tight-lipped warning about the dangers of turning over rocks. A determined Tucker could not be swayed.

It didn't take him long to realize his mother might be right. Nothing good lived under rocks. On first sight, the ratty old trailer his *father* lived in looked abandoned. Windows were held to the rusting metal walls with duct tape. The garbage-littered yard didn't even have enough space to grow grass. Just tufts of weeds in a square of mud.

Tucker was about to abort the mission when a harried-looking woman with a cigarette dangling from the corner of her mouth hollered to him, asking in a voice as raspy as the tattered screen door her bony arm forced open, "You here about Madison? You with the FBI?"

It wasn't that Tucker, a clean-cut, handsome guy in jeans and a blue Oxford button-up, looked like an agent, he just didn't look like he belonged in that trailer park.

"No, ma'am." Tucker shook his head as he mounted a sagging step.

"You a police officer?"

"No ma'am. My name's Tucker Boone. I'm looking to find my dad, Robert Morgan?"

"Oh." The woman's bony shoulders sagged. "Your old man don't live here no more."

"You know where I might find him?"

"You Marlene's boy?" she asked, ignoring his question.

"Yes ma'am."

"You can drop the ma'am stuff. I'm just Gloria. I suppose I'm your stepmom." Gloria laughed, opening the door wider. "Well, you came a long way; you might as well come on in and sit a spell. I can tell you some of what you probably want to know. I can certainly tell you about your sister. Did ya even know ya had one?"

"No, ma'am. Can't say I did."

"Didn't figure. Your momma did her best to cut ties completely. Not that I'm casting blame, Rob played his part too. He didn't give a fig that she hated military life. When it was time to re-up, he signed on without even asking her. That was it for them. She told him to go to hell, but instead he came to Hooley's Bar and met me." Gloria interrupted the story with her raspy laugh, which ended in a coughing fit. She had to take a minute and a few deep breaths before adding, "My Maddy, she's your age. Let me see if I remember; you turned twenty-two in January, right?"

"Yes, ma'am."

"And Maddy will be twenty-two next month. Born on the Fourth of July in Italy. At the Ghedi Airforce Base. Perfect birthday for a military brat."

"She's the same age as me?"

Gloria nodded. "You two are what my grandma would call Irish twins. Or in you guys' case, a couple of bastards born in the same year."

"I never knew. Is she home?" Tucker felt a rush of enthusiasm.

"No, she ran away five years ago—or so they say."

Tucker's hopes crashed. This morning, he thought he'd meet his dad. Then there was no dad, but he had a sister…briefly. Now he was back to nothing.

"Come on in, and we'll talk."

The air in the trailer was stale, and the floors groaned under his feet with each step.

Gloria made her way through the narrow hall into a living room that was as small as it was gloomy with its faux-wood paneled walls and windows shrouded in heavy brown drapes. The only light in the room was the glow from a table lamp and the muted television. As Gloria moved through the space, she gave her entourage of cats a scratch or a pat on the head and shared each of their stories.

"This is Hercules. I call him Herc. Found him in a dumpster down the street. And Mabel, sweet and able. She nursed Sybil's kittens. Sybil was a rotten mom, weren't you, ya old slut?" Gloria said as she patted a yellow tabby on the head. "And then there's Bonnie. She just showed up on my porch the other day. Heard her meowing in the middle of the night. Last thing I needed was another damned cat, but then I thought of my own girl out there with nothing, and I couldn't help but bring Bonnie in. Guess I hoped if it was my baby crying for help, someone would listen." She made her way to a worn recliner and grabbed a pack of cigarettes on the table.

"That's mighty kind of you, ma'am." Tucker took the seat opposite hers, sinking so far into the broken down cushion, he gripped the armrests to keep his butt from hitting the floor.

Gloria tapped the pack on the palm of her hand and let out a gravelly laugh. "More of that ma'am business."

"It's a habit. I've only been stateside a few days."

Gloria's hands shook as she leaned forward, pointing to Tucker with her cigarette. "And this was your first stop? Poor sap." As she lit up, her eyes crinkled in thought. She frowned as she sucked harder on her cigarette, making it crackle and glow. "Let's see. I suppose you want to know about your dad. Hate to say it, but he's in a nursing home on Baker Street. You can visit him if you want. It's downtown. You can't miss it. Don't know what good it'd do ya. He can't talk no more, and his right side is completely paralyzed."

"What happened?"

"He had a stroke," Gloria said. "I coulda kept him here, but I warned him early on—cheat on me like you did Marlene, and your ass is outta my house. Well, he cheated. Him and Amanda Stone had to *comfort* each other. His daughter was missing and instead of looking for her, he was dipping his wick."

"Amanda Stone?" Tucker asked. Gloria said the name like he should know her.

"Amanda is Ariel's mom. And I will say, though it makes me want to vomit, that Amanda Stone is a looker. I suppose if I was a man, I'd do her before a skinny old gal like me."

"Who's Ariel?"

"Maddy's best friend." Gloria gave him a wide-eyed look. "You never heard of Ariel Stone? Didn't you watch the news? Read the papers?"

"I've been in Iraq, but before that I was in high school and didn't worry too much about the news."

"I see. Well, Ariel Stone was Maddy's best friend. Poor girl was murdered by her stepdad. Seems he was abusing her—sexually. He always did make my skin crawl. Maddy hated him too. I always thought he was too strict with her. Never allowing her to go many places. But I never imagined…that poor girl."

"Ariel? That's the Stone girl?" Gloria nodded. "So, where's Maddy?"

"They say she ran away." Gloria sighed, not at all sounding convinced. She took a deep breath and said, "If she did, I wish she'd come home. I miss her."

"Have you searched the web?"

"No. I ain't got a computer." Then as if an epiphany slammed her tiny body, she nearly jumped in her seat, bringing her close to the edge of the cushion. "Hey, maybe that's why you're here. I know Marlene didn't tell you about your father. Had to be something in your gut bring you here. Maybe it's your sister. Like some sort of blood bond, ya know? You could find her."

Tucker rested his suddenly heavy arms on his knees. All he wanted was a connection. As pathetic as he felt admitting it— when the action stopped, he was numb. In high school, he had sports, and in the Marines, he had a war zone to distract him. Here, in the land of the normal life, he didn't fit in. He moved among people who knew where they belonged, and he had what? A mother who lied to control to him, a dad who was a vegetable, and a sister who was obviously smart enough to get the hell out of Dodge. Even in his messed up idea of ordinary, it was bizarre. Add in the fact that he was now expected to find her? It was too much. Tucker rubbed the back of his head. "If she ran away, maybe she doesn't want to be found?"

"I see what you're saying. Everybody I ask to help me tells me, *'she ran away…she'll come back when she's ready.'* But my heart doesn't buy that story. She wouldn't have left Ariel. And, Rob never believed Maddy ran away either, and there's a couple of things that can be said of Rob Morgan. One, he thinks with his dick. And two, he knows people. He always had great gut instincts. And also, before Ariel died, she swore she saw her stepdad hurt Maddy."

"She saw him?"

"Well, she sort of saw it in a dream, but we all knew Ariel was sort of psychic."

Tucker's eyebrow popped up.

"I know, sounds crazy. But the girl had a way of knowing things that didn't make sense. Rob always teased her about picking him some lottery numbers." Gloria shook her head and stared over his shoulder a moment. "Look, I know logic says Maddy ran away, but there is that voice that bugs me when I try to sleep…did Jeb Stone hurt my girl? Or maybe she run off in fear of him. Maybe she doesn't know he's locked up now. Maybe she doesn't know it's safe to come home."

Tucker rubbed his jawline. He should have listened to his mother. Dead girls, psychics, and a dad who couldn't keep his zipper shut. What a mess. But like any good train wreck, he was drawn in. "What happened the night Maddy disappeared?"

"After dinner, Maddy said she and Toby were going to Ariel's."

"Toby? Was he her boyfriend?"

Gloria laughed. "No. No. Toby was her dog. Her and Arie found the mutt earlier that morning. She was going to take him to spend the night at the Stone place. Rob, of course said no, because he didn't think the Stones would appreciate her dragging the mutt along. Maddy insisted Ariel asked, but Rob wouldn't budge. Of course, neither would Maddy, so it turned into a pretty good fight. They got so loud, a neighbor called the police. The police told Maddy she had to listen to her parents and stay put, so she went to her room. Then like the brat she was, she called her boyfriend and snuck out anyhow."

"Is the boyfriend gone?"

Gloria shook her head. "No, he says he dropped her and the dog off at the bottom of Ariel's driveway. But Jeb and Amanda say she never showed up. Her and Toby disappeared without a trace that night."

"Was she seeing anyone else? Someone who might've picked her up?"

"Well, there was the one boy. She'd dated him a month or so before, but they broke up. He got a little pushy with her. She came home with bruises on her arms and neck, and Rob had to have a talk with him, if you know what I mean." Gloria gave him a wink.

"Was that boy checked out?"

"He was at a baseball camp, so they say he couldn't have done anything. Here," she said, pulling a file folder from a stack of papers on the table. She handed it to Tucker. "It's all in there."

Newspaper clippings of the Stone girl's murder filled the file. There were only a few small articles about Madison—just quick, *if you see her call the police* articles.

"So, Ariel thought her stepdad killed Madison? The same guy who ended up killing her? I hate to say it, but—"

"Don't you dare say she's dead. She may be hurt somewhere or scared, but she can't be dead. And see, I have proof." Grabbing the file from his hands, she clutched the papers, her voice growing more insistent as she explained. "Look here." She pulled an envelope out of the folder. "It's a letter. It arrived a week after Ariel was killed. It looks just like Maddy's handwriting. It's a clue—a clue about where to find her. She probably meant it for Ariel. Those two were like peas in a pod. Looked alike, talked alike. Twins couldn't have been closer."

Tucker pulled the letter out of the envelope and unfolded it. He read the words: *I've gone Mad, Mags.*

"It's a clue, don't ya see? Maddy's alive, and she expects Ariel to find her. But Ariel's dead, so I have no idea what that means. No idea where to look. But I bet you're smart, like your momma. You can figure it out. You can find Maddy."

Tucker stood. "I'll look into it, but I can't promise anything."

That was enough for Gloria. She insisted he keep the file and report back to her with anything he dug up.

He gripped the file in his hands as he walked toward his car. Halfway there, he turned and asked, "If you knew who I was, then evidently my dad knew too?"

Gloria scratched her head and frowned. "By the time he got back to this area, you were thirteen years old and happy enough with your stepdad. Marlene told him to leave well enough alone. He'd just screw up your head— with you thinking Ed was your dad and all. I will tell you Rob went to all your games. He was right proud of you. Though why, I don't know. Not like he had any reason to credit himself for your raising. But still, you were his flesh and blood."

Tucker swallowed the lump in his throat and managed to thank her before driving away. He didn't quite know why, but he wished she'd said his dad knew about him from the beginning, but just didn't care he existed. Then he could hate the man and write him off. Now, he supposed, while he was in town, he owed him a visit.

The nursing home was a short drive from the trailer park. The nurse on duty, a willowy lady with a pinched face, assured him he was wasting his time. As she led him toward his dad's room, she said, "He's a bad tempered SOB. Has a tendency to throw whatever's in reach when he gets tired of being bothered with company. Keep that in mind."

"I'll take my chances," Tucker said.

The nurse pushed a heavy wooden door open and yelled, "Knock, knock, Mr. Morgan. You have a visitor."

Tucker frowned and stuffed his hands in his pockets, wondering why people assumed everyone in a hospital was deaf.

"Well, I'll leave you two to visit. Remember to duck if he gets mad," she whispered as she took off down the tacky mauve hallway.

"Mr. Morgan?" Tucker announced, entering the room slowly. The meeting seemed like a great idea in the parking lot, but as he ventured into the darkened room, he lost some of his nerve.

Rob Morgan sat slumped in a wheelchair. Turning it with a single foot, he slowly faced Tucker.

Tucker kneeled in front of him. The man was a frail shell with gray hair and shaking hands.

"Sir, I'm Marlene Adkin's son, Tucker? Tucker Boone?"

Rob grunted and pointed toward the door. Tucker looked over his shoulder, but he wasn't sure what Rob wanted from him.

"I, uh, went to your place and talked to Gloria. She told me about Maddy, asked me to find her."

Over and over, Rob slapped his hands on his legs, seeming more agitated with each blow.

"I don't understand. Is it Maddy?"

Rob yelled as his clumsy hands cleared his lunch from his hospital table.

A carafe of coffee landed in Tucker's hand, but the plates and utensils clattered to the floor. Within seconds, the nurse returned, carrying a hypodermic needle. She had his dad stabbed and drugged quicker than she could say, "Now, Mr. Morgan, there's no reason to be rude."

"I think he wanted something," Tucker said.

She flashed Tucker a disgusted look. "He's a cantankerous pain in the who-zits. And getting visitors always unsettles him. Don't make so much of it, Mr. Boone." Standing upright, she pressed the call button on the side of his bed. "He'll take a little nap and hopefully wake in a better humor. You remember your way out?"

Rob's head dropped to his chest as the drug coursed through his body. Tucker backed out of the room.

Chapter Two

A gull cried overhead. The Ocracoke Ferry was approaching land. Tucker wasn't sure what he thought he'd find on the quiet North Carolina island, but it was this or another tour in Iraq.

After meeting with Gloria and then his dad, logic told him the girl probably did run away, and that she'd return if and when she wanted. But then there was Gloria. That crazy cat lady got under his skin. How could he add his name to the list of people who advised her to give up without even following a single lead? Besides, what else did he have to do right now? Without the mystery of Maddy—he had no other diversion to life other than a war zone, and the idea of re-enlisting without Ash was like a knife to the gut. It seemed trite to say the man was like a brother, but he was the best friend Tucker ever had.

The boat slowed. People moved from the railings and the viewing deck to their cars. As Tucker sighed and headed toward his own car, his phone rang. His mother. "What?"

"No need to be snotty. I'm just checking in."

"I'm fine. Just arriving on the island. And you?" He unlocked his door and climbed in.

"Also fine, though worried sick over the sanity of my only child."
Tucker laughed.

"It's not funny, Tucker. You realize you didn't even unpack before running off on this little adventure?"

"Shove it in my closet. I'll deal with it when I get back."

"And when will that be?"

"No idea, but I'll guarantee I'm in no hurry." Tucker started his engine and flipped on the AC.

"It's Holly, isn't it? That bitch was crazy; even your dead friend knew that."

Tucker moved the phone from his ear and stared at it. His mother was amazing, and that wasn't a compliment. Putting it back, he said, "His name was Ash."

"Ash, that's right. Bottom line is—you are jumping out of the frying pan into the fire. What happened with Holly isn't your fault. Running away won't change anything."

"That's ironic coming from you."

She was quiet a minute, before she said, "So, that's what this is about? You're still mad at me about Rob? How was I supposed to know he'd have a stroke before you could meet him?"

"I'm not discussing this anymore. I need to try to find Maddy."

"She's probably a hooker somewhere, given her environment and gene pool."

Rubbing his chin, Tucker didn't answer.

"Fine. Whatever." His mother's words were clipped. "You never listen to me anyhow. I just hope you don't regret this. Trust me. Anything that has to do with Rob Morgan is bad news."

"You started it, not me."

"It wasn't my idea for you to track him down."

"But it was your idea to have sex with him."

There was a weighted silence that Tucker had to break. "I don't want to fight. I have to do this."

She sighed. "Fine. Scour the globe for a white trash runaway."

"That's the positive spirit I know and love," he said with a laugh that was far from merry. "If it makes you feel better, it's beautiful here. It's more like a vacation."

"God knows you could use one of those. This was a bad year, sweetie. It'll get better. If I could take your pain, I would. I swear."

The banging and clanking of the stewards removing the wheel blocks grabbed his attention. "I know you would. I need to go. The ferry is unloading."

"Okay. Love you. Be careful!"

Tucker shifted into drive and slowly rolled his grey Fusion onto land. He'd planned on getting a Mustang or a Corvette when he joined the military, but ended up listening to his mother and getting the smaller, more economical car. It was one concession he could make, considering he'd ignored her advice about everything else, from joining the Corps to Holly.

The image of a feisty blonde tried to nudge its way back into his thoughts, but he shoved it out. Instead, he tried to think about Maddy. His only clue was the cryptic, *I've gone Mad, Mags* note.

At first, the only stories his internet search popped up were satirical *Mad Magazine* articles. He spent an hour or more wading through page after page of comic links before he finally stumbled onto a different sort of Mad Mags: a restless spirit that supposedly haunted the family graveyards of Ocracoke, North Carolina.

A ghost story. Tucker knew it was a stretch, but it was all he had.

Driving down Highway Twelve, he took in this new world. Fresh and foreign felt good. The two-lane blacktop ran straight down the narrow island. The green of home was replaced by the beige of sand and sea oats. Gulls gathered in puddles along the road, squawking indignation at passing cars. Tucker couldn't blame them. Humans could be so intrusive.

He was beginning to think there was nothing on the island but trees, sand, and birds, when the land opened up and a town appeared. Grey-sided stores and restaurants lined the road. The towns along the Outer Banks boasted little color, unlike other coastal towns that flaunted Caribbean flare. This place conformed to nature, allowed itself to be carried along with it like the tides surrounding it.

Tucker pulled into a general store that promised free saltwater taffy and AC. The door chimed as he walked in, and the lady behind the counter looked him over with a smile. She had an athletic, slender build that belonged to a twenty-year-old, not to the middle-aged, graying woman in front of him. "Hey there, handsome. What can I do you for?"

"Pardon?" Tucker nearly stuttered.

The woman laughed. "Relax soldier, I'm too experienced for a young pup like yourself. You vacationing or just passing through?"

Telling people he was on a quest to find a runaway sister felt a bit dramatic, so instead he said, "Just got out of the Marines. Was feeling cooped up, so I thought I'd try a change of scenery."

"Was it bad over there?"

"It's war."

"Hard to come home? My uncle was a Vietnam vet. He had a hard time adjusting to civilian life."

Tucker shoved his hands in his pockets. "Nothing like that. I'm just glad to be stateside and need a place to relax."

"A sojourning soldier, eh?"

Tucker smiled and nodded. "I suppose so."

"Well, you came to the right place. Salt heals wounds, and you can't escape the salt in this place. That's how I ended up here. Got set aside for the younger model and needed to find a place I could breathe. My original intention was to write a book of all the people who travel here from wanderlust—The *SoJournal*. Get it? Sojourn? *SoJournal*?"

"Yeah, that's clever."

"Evidently not. Couldn't find a publisher to buy it no matter how many trees I shook."

"Sorry about that."

"It's all right. I met a lot of people writing it—got a lot of stories from people passing through."

Tucker's eyebrow shot up, and he stepped forward, leaning across the counter. "You've met a lot of people here?"

"Most certainly. We're the first stop and only full service grocer on the island. Isn't anyone here that stayed for any amount of time that I don't know."

"When I got out of the service, I, uh, looked up my biological father. He's gone, but I was told I had a sister—Madison Morgan." He pulled her picture out of his pocket and showed the smiling blonde teen to her.

She looked it over. "She looks a bit like Murray Bank's niece, Josie McCoy. Only Josie has brown hair. And she's a bit older. I'd say about your age."

Tucker nodded, excited that it could be this easy. "Do you know where I could find her?"

"And what? Go up to Josie and ask her if she's your long lost sister? Seems her and Murray are pretty sure she belongs to his sister." She took the picture from him and looked more closely. "Though the resemblance is uncanny. Eyes may be a little different, but then I've never seen Josie smile like that. You know, I always thought it was weird that Murray suddenly had a niece come live with him."

Tucker looked down at the picture. "If it's not her, it's not her. No harm in asking."

"We'll see if you think that after meeting Murray. The way I see it, you drive down there and ask outright, you're going to get a firm no. If you want information from a guy like Murray, I wouldn't ask any questions at all. Here," she said as she ripped off some register tape and started writing an address. "You said you needed a break anyhow, so what's your hurry? You go to Murray and tell him you're looking for work, and Ella sent you his way. He's always needing summer help. Then you snoop about for dirt on Josie. I mean if she is this Madison, she's evidently hiding from someone, right? Why else would she change her name?"

Tucker took the picture, the address, and thanked her as he backed out of the store. Ella leaned a hip against the counter as she said, "You better tell me what you dig up. Nothing I love better than a good story. Even if I can't write one and sell the damn thing."

"Will do. Thank you, ma'am."

"Ma'am? Pah. I'll let that slide since you're a soldier. But I'm too damn young to be a ma'am."

Tucker grinned and offered her a wink before the door closed.

Chapter Three

Murray's place was a bit harder to find than Tucker expected. Half hidden behind a grove of small cottages was a peeling yellow house. Seems Murray Banks was willing to do battle with nature and paint his house, though he was obviously losing ground. Nature always won. The heat, wind, and salt spray could scrub a house back to grey in a season, but other than the peeling paint, the house looked sturdy. The driveway was in better shape than the pitted sandy road he took to get here, and there was a large garage peeking from around the side of the house that looked almost new.

As Tucker climbed out of his car, a man emerged from the house. He was a short, stocky guy dressed in jeans and a button-up. His shirt had stains and sweat marks under the armpits, but the sleeves were creased like they had been freshly ironed. The man gave him a nod. Tucker read a lot of respect and snap in that head nod. Tucker suspected he was former military. With a fresh burst of hope, Tucker moved forward.

"Mr. Banks? Murray Banks?"

"Yes, sir. I'm Murray. Can I help you?"

"Sir, my name's Tucker Boone. Ella sent me. She said you may be able to help me find work?"

Murray nodded as he pulled a rag out of his pocket, wiping his hands clean before reaching out to shake Tucker's. "Always looking for a good worker."

A smile spread across Tucker's face. "That's good news for me."

"You got any experience with motors?" Murray asked.

"No, sir. Graduated high school and went into the Marine Corps. That's pretty much the extent of my skills."

"I figured from the haircut. Well, I suppose an old Airman can teach a jarhead all he needs to know," Murray said with a grin. "Come with me to the shop. We'll get your information and get you started."

"Yes, sir," Tucker said as he followed the man down the short drive to a room off the garage. A window air conditioner hummed and blocked the view to the outside, making the room dark. Murray flipped on a light, revealing a room filled with neatly lined rows of worktables. Each table had an engine or appliance on it. Attached to each table was a swing arm lamp and a clipboard hanging from a nail. It was like a mechanical surgical center.

"This is where I fix most of the engines. No sense battling the bugs and the heat, just pop them off and bring them on inside. I'll teach you how to do it. Guess that means you'll mostly be out in the heat. But shoot, you're young."

"Heat doesn't bother me, sir."

Murray laughed. "That sir stuff will wear off. How long you been out?"

"Two weeks tomorrow."

"Well now, no wonder. I've been out over twenty-five years and still haven't shaken all the habits. You're probably still gulping your dinner like a black snake."

"Yes, sir." Tucker nodded with a grin. That habit bugged his mom and Holly, but dinner while deployed wasn't a social affair. It was done as efficiently as you made your bed or polished your boots. His mother had gone so far as to insist he set his fork down on the table after each bite. And she wondered why he didn't want to stay at home. "But I do chew with my mouth closed," Tucker informed Murray.

It was Murray's turn to laugh. He opened a file cabinet and pulled out a sheet of paper. Tucker looked over the standard employment application, filled it out, and handed it back. After a quick glance, Murray filed it in the cabinet. "You got a place here on the island? I see you're from Ohio. I assume you don't own land here."

"No, sir."

"The cottages out front are mine. I can let you have one of the small ones as part of your wages. Say instead of twenty dollars an hour, I'll give you twelve and lodging. Used to offer room and board, but my wife, Hetty, ain't well enough to keep up anymore. Or if you need, I could ask Josie if she'd cook for you. She's one helluva good cook."

Tucker's heart sped up. "Josie?"

"My niece. She lives in the cottage by yours. Sweet girl—don't you go getting any ideas."

Tucker thought about Josie being the possible runaway Madison, and therefore his *sister*, and he almost cringed. "No worries of that, sir."

"Well, you don't have to be so quick to say that. Just 'cos I'm an ugly son of a bitch doesn't mean Josie isn't a looker," Murray said with a snicker. "Come on, I'll show you the cottage. You're in the Fig Tree. Hetty named them all. She's not overly creative. We have Fig Tree, Atlantic Shore, Sunset, ah shoot...look around you. If you see it close by, that's one of the names of our cottages." Murray led him out of the garage. The garage and personal residence were separated from the cottages by a tangle of wild vines, pine shrubs, and crooked-trunked trees. A packed sand road wound its way through the cluster of rental cottages like a community of small, look-alike homes. They were all grayed cedar with a nameplate on the porch. Only the doors were painted different colors.

At the back edge of the property, nestled in the woods, were two tiny rectangular structures. They were no bigger than lawn sheds and sat only a few feet apart. They couldn't offer much more than a few hundred square feet of living, but for a guy who spent the last year sleeping in a hole he dug in the desert, they looked as good as mansions.

The isolation of the cabins also appealed to him. A mini jungle, similar to the one providing Murray's house with privacy, surrounded the cottages. He could sit out on the porch and almost feel like he was alone in this wooded sanctuary. There was even a porch swing. This place was perfect.

As they moved closer, Tucker could smell fresh paint on the breeze. The front doors of the cabins were a crisp marine blue. Large pots of pink flowers flanked each blue door. A bit girly, but nice after spending the last year surrounded by brown.

"Josie maintains the cottages. Makes 'em right pretty if you ask me,"

Murray said as he fished a key out of his pocket. He unlocked the door and handed the key to Tucker. "I'll let you make yourself at home today. Put you to work in the morning. I start about ten in the summer. I'm too old to wrestle myself out of bed with the damned rooster."

As Tucker stepped into the cottage, Murray flipped on the light. The living area and kitchen area were all one space. It took Murray two strides to reach a narrow doorway covered with a shell-splattered curtain. "Here's the bedroom," Murray said, pulling back the curtain to reveal a solid wrought iron bed. The bed took up most of the room. But it looked comfortable, covered in a colorful quilt and stacked high with pillows.

Nodding as he scanned the room, Tucker was satisfied. Nothing was perfect, from the mismatched furniture to the miniature appliances in the kitchen, but it was all good. This place offered nothing more and nothing less than exactly what he needed.

"AC unit is in the bedroom. Keep the curtain pulled back, and it will keep the whole place cool."

Tucker pulled back the navy blue curtain of the north facing window and found himself staring into what had to be Josie's place. The structures were so close, he could open his window and tap on hers. He could easily see that her cottage had the same layout as his, but hers was decked out in yellows and pinks, with pictures on the walls and plants and flowers in every corner and on every table.

Movement inside the cabin caught Tucker's eye. A woman walked into view. Tucker sucked in a breath. Yes, she was pretty. She had all the necessary parts—cute little nose, big eyes, silky-looking hair that curled in wisps around her ears. Dressed in cutoff denim shorts and a tank top, she had a style that promised a lack of complication. Her eyes widened when she spotted him, and an immediate blush stained her cheeks. Nothing coy in her response. No rehearsed smile or suggestive stare.

Tucker wasn't one to brag, but being all-state in three sports and having a face that wasn't hard to look at got him quite a few looks and frequent offers from women, even a few from his teachers and once by a friend of his mom's. Such an honest, clumsy response was refreshing after the whiplash changes in his love life.

"Told you she was a pretty girl." Murray gave him a nudge.

"And you're sure she's your niece? Was she adopted?"

"Dang boy." Murray laughed. "Damned but if you don't just put it right out there. I told you she doesn't look like me."

Tucker's cheeks burned, and he felt hot. "I didn't mean that. It's just…well, your coloring is different."

A good-natured grin spread across his face as Murray scratched his ear lobe. "It's all right, son. I own a mirror. Josie is my sister's girl."

"You're sure?"

"Hell, boy, I think I know my own family."

"I'm sorry. I'm sure you do. It's just…well, this is going to sound crazy, but my mom just recently told me I have a half-sister I've never met."

Murray's laugh nearly rattled the windows. "Oh Christ, you poor kid. That's got to put a damper on dating."

"It doesn't make it any easier, that's for sure."

Murray shook his head, his laugh reduced to a chuckle he seemed unable to stifle. "Damn if I couldn't use this to my advantage, but hell, you look like a good sort, for a jarhead. I promise you, Josie ain't your sister. She's an only child."

Tucker breathed a sigh of relief. Sure, finding Madison would have been nice, but he couldn't help but be glad as hell Josie couldn't be her.

Chapter Four

Tucker offered to start work that afternoon, but Murray wouldn't consider it. Suggested Tucker do some sightseeing, maybe spend a day at the beach. Murray even suggested Josie show the new employee around the place, but she professed a headache and practically slammed her door. Tucker was almost offended, but he noticed she kept peeking from behind the lacy curtains. He pretended not to notice.

Murray wandered home, proclaiming it was past time to fish. Tucker unloaded his bags from his car. He'd packed clothes, laptop, and toiletries, but he never thought to bring towels, sheets, or food. Shopping was his first order of business. Unpacking his things took him all of five minutes.

First stop was back at Ella's. She smiled as he came in the door. "My favorite soldier is back. Murray give you a job?"

"In a heartbeat. The guy that desperate for workers?" Tucker said as he leaned against the counter.

"Nah, you just have the look of a lost soul, and Murray collects 'em. Have you met his wife, Hetty? She's the prize in his collection."

"No, I didn't meet her. I think Murray said she was sick?"

"Yeah. She's sick most days." Ella wiped dust from the counter with her hand.

"Anything wrong with her?"

"Yeah, she weighs about four hundred pounds."

Tucker didn't say anything about that. He'd learned long ago not to comment when women and weight were mentioned in the same conversation. "You know where I could buy sheets and towels? Stuff for the kitchen?"

"Closest K-Mart is back up on Kitty Hawk."

"You're joking? That's more than two hours away."

"Yeah, it sucks." Ella thought a minute. "Let me call a friend. She's head of housekeeping for a cottage cleaning company. Maybe she has some old rentals you could buy."

A call later and Tucker had another name and address.

"I appreciate all the help. I hadn't meant to stay here for long, and I sort of assumed I'd stay in a hotel."

Ella gave him a wink. "This place will grow on you. And I figure if you're going to get any answers about Josie, it won't be easy. She's lived here for years, and I don't think the girl has said more than ten words to me."

"You're right. Murray is pretty adamant that she's his niece."

Ella nodded. "That's what he says. And it could be true. Murray does have a sister who left the island years ago, and she's never returned. It's just that the Banks family are all so…well, let's just be honest. They're ugly as a dog's ass, but Josie is cute as a button."

Tucker thought of his short, pale mother and his own tall, dark frame. The other parent offered genes to the mix too. "Maybe she gets the looks from her dad?"

"I suppose. Just can't imagine overriding those genes so easy."

Tucker shrugged. "So, is this the best place to get groceries?"

"Sure is. Just get what you want, and I'll ring you up. I'll even give you the resident discount."

Tucker loaded cans of food, bags of chips, and packages of cold cuts into his cart. He laid it all on the counter and went back for paper plates, napkins, and plastic silverware. Then he grabbed a gallon of milk and a box of Life cereal.

Ella rang him up and bagged the food. He asked, "What do you know about Mad Mags?"

"The ghost story?"

"Yeah."

Ella shrugged. "It's this island's version of the Lady in White. I think every town has one. She's said to walk the path down near where you're staying. People say they've seen her. Hear her sea shells tinkling in the middle of the night."

"Sea shells tinkling?"

"Yeah. Don't ask me what it's all about. I've never really paid much attention to the ghost stories. I'm more into the stories about the living."

"The ghosts were once people too, I guess."

Ella laughed. "If you say so, soldier. Here." She flipped his receipt over and wrote down a phone number. "Give this lady a call. She's a bit of a nut, but she'll be able to tell you all about Mags."

Tucker gathered up his groceries, visited the housekeeper for his bag of sheets and towels, and headed back to the cottage. Josie was curled up on her front porch rocker reading a book when he pulled up. As he stood there, staring and debating what to do, she looked up at him and blushed.

"Hey," he said.

"Hey to you too." Josie carefully tucked a folded sheet of paper into the book before setting it down on the table next to her chair.

"I had to get some groceries," he said, feeling stupid as he hugged the paper bags.

"You go to Ella's?"

"Yeah. She said it was the best place to shop."

"She wasn't lying. It is the best place, even if she does ask a lot of questions," Josie said with a little laugh.

"She is curious. Says she's a writer."

"Really?" Josie sounded intrigued.

"Yeah, says she has some book she couldn't get published."

"Well, that's sad. She's never mentioned it to me, but then I try to avoid her as best I can. I mean, she's nice; it's just all those questions." Josie rolled her eyes and grinned.

Tucker was sure she had the prettiest smile he'd ever seen. He wasn't done admiring it when she said, "See you later, Mr. Tucker."

"It's Boone. Tucker is my first name."

"All right. Mr. Boone." She grabbed her book and an empty glass from the table and opened her front door.

"It's just Tucker...I mean, call me Tucker. Not Mr. Boone."

She nodded and was gone. He had the urge to follow, but he fought it and made a mental note to never bug her with questions.

Chapter Five

Tucker settled in, laptop on the dining table, notepad to his right, and a cold beer on the left. Turning on the laptop, he quickly realized he didn't have any internet. "Shit," he said aloud to the empty space.

He went to the workshop to find Murray and see if he needed a password or something, but the old man was nowhere to be found. Tucker went outside and looked around. The shop was unlocked; surely Murray was here somewhere.

A screen door squeaked open, and a woman yelled, "What the hell you snoopin' 'round for?"

Tucker turned slowly. The woman addressing him was huge; dressed in a bright red muumuu, she leaned heavily on a cane as she stood in the door of the house. "Name's Tucker Boone, Ma'am. Murray hired me this morning."

"He did, did he?" The woman sighed and shook her head. "You're not here about the girl, are ya?"

Tucker's brows drew together, but he didn't have a chance to open his mouth before she added, "Last guy had to be fired. He never did a lick of work, too busy trying to chase the girl all over the property. She's a good girl. Minds her own business. She doesn't like to be bothered much, and we respect that. I suggest you respect that too."

"Ma'am, I can see where a guy would want to chase your niece around, but that's not what I'm here for."

Pointing to her eyes, she assured him. "I'll be watching you, remember that."

"Yes, ma'am. You have anything you need done? I can't seem to find Mr. Banks."

"Oh, he's probably down at the dock fishing. He's put in an hour or so of work, time to play." The woman wiped her brow with a handkerchief. "I suppose as long as you belong, I can get inside. I can't handle this heat. You may as well relax and have a look around the island. Murray will put you to work when he feels like it."

With that, the door slammed, and she was gone.

Tucker made his way back to his cottage. He'd ask Josie if there was a password. He knocked on her door. She didn't answer. Looking in the window, he could see her in her kitchen. He knocked again. She ignored him. "Josie?" he shouted through the door. Still no answer.

He turned to leave when he heard her door open.

"Uh, hi," she said, blushing.

Afraid she'd lose her nerve and slam the door, Tucker asked quickly, "Hey, I was trying to get on the internet. Didn't know if there was a password?"

"Sorry. No internet."

"No internet?"

Josie shrugged. "Nope. Hetty says it's a luxury."

"I just met her, and I'm not shocked she said that," he said, trying to make conversation.

"Hetty?" Josie grinned. "She was that nice, huh?"

"If by nice, you mean rude and bitchy, then she was a total sweetheart."

Josie laughed. Her shoulders rolled forward with the effort, and she covered her mouth with her hand. "She's crusty, but sweet in her own way."

"I can see that. She made it clear she wouldn't tolerate any bull from me. Says she fired the last guy?"

The color washed from Josie's face. "Yeah, he didn't work out."

Tucker nodded. "Well, I'm glad for my sake he didn't. I'll have to keep my nose clean."

"Oh, I have a feeling you'll do fine. You have the look of good people."

Tucker nodded. A smile twitched at his lips. "That's a plus. I like to think I'm good people."

"Hetty is good people too. She's grumpy, and you never know what she'll say. But she's very kind, she and Murray both."

"It's not Aunt Hetty and Uncle Murray?"

Josie's eyes widened. "I didn't meet them until I was sixteen. Calling them aunt and uncle feels awkward. It's like consciously, I know they're my family, but they don't feel like my family." She leaned back against the doorframe.

"I understand that," Tucker said. "I grew up never knowing my real dad. If he was in my life starting now, I wouldn't call him dad either."

Josie nodded. "I never met mine either. To be honest, my mother wasn't ever really sure who to blame. She had a few guesses…there was her high school gym teacher, her senior prom date—" Josie stopped mid-sentence and bit her lip. "I'm sorry, I don't usually admit that. I'm not sure what came over me."

"It's all right. My mother told me my father was sperm donor eleven-one-five my whole life. Turns out, it was an old boyfriend of hers."

"Did you ever find him?"

"Yeah, right before I came here. He had a stroke and is in a nursing home. It was a waste of time."

"Oh, I'm sorry. That must have been very disappointing."

"It was, a little." Tucker stuffed his hands in his pockets. The tiniest twitch of guilt told him it was wrong to use his dad to get her sympathy, but it worked so well, he had no intention of stopping. Should he add in the long-lost sister?

"So, what brings you here?" Josie asked.

"Just got back from Iraq and needed….wanted something different."

Josie nodded slowly.

A quick internal debate nixed the idea of telling her about Maddy. If the Mad Mags clue was a dead end, she'd expect him to move on, to keep looking for his sister. But standing here, looking into a set of eyes he could only describe as hypnotic; in a place he could only call perfect—he knew—he wasn't going anywhere else.

"This is the perfect place for different," she said. "There's so much history and beauty. And when the tourist season is over, it's quiet—a true sanctuary."

"So, it won't stay as crowded as it is now?" Tucker figured as much, but any way to keep her talking.

"Oh no. It will begin to slow in August. But there are still quiet places here, even with the crowds. If you know where to look."

"Maybe I could get you to draw me a map," Tucker joked.

"I suppose I could show you." She let her head rest on the doorframe. "I'm sorry. I was rude earlier. I was just embarrassed. You're so…and I'm so…"

"So what?" Beautiful? Alluring? Mysterious?

"Boring. You've seen the world. You've been to war."

Tucker's face scrunched up. "I don't know that any of that makes me interesting."

"You're, like, a hero."

Tucker laughed. Josie grinned and said, "I'm serious. You're handsome and have that GI Joe look going on. Only you're not an actor—so what branch?"

"Marine Corps. First Division."

"See? That's something. You did something. You saved people."

Tucker's smile died on his lips. "Sometimes. Sometimes not."

"I'm sorry to hear that. I know how bad it hurts to lose someone." Josie straightened. "I better get going. I have a couple of cottages to tidy up for some renters. Hetty said they'll be checking in this evening. And I need to get the midweek linens washed and delivered."

"Let me change, and I'll help you."

"No, that's all right. You get yourself settled."

"To tell you the truth, I'm going a little nuts with nothing to do. It's like being in the Stone Age here without the net. Hell, we had internet in war zones."

"You're really going to be crushed when you hear we don't have cable."

"No cable?"

"We get the basic. About twenty channels, nothing overly exciting."

"What the hell do you do?"

Josie smiled and shrugged. "I suppose you have to get creative."

Chapter Six

In an instant, Tucker's brain was more than creative. A red flush crept up his chest staining his cheeks a blood red. Thankfully, Josie didn't seem to notice his embarrassment. With a slight tip of her head, she said, "I better get busy. I'll see you later."

Tucker was more than disappointed she didn't take him up on his offer of help. He stood, frozen to his spot on the porch until she was long gone. Thoughts of a girl he hardly knew completely distracted him from his original purpose. Mad Mags. And Maddy. He came for Maddy. Sort of.

Phoning the lady Ella suggested, Tucker was told to come on over to her home.

Jane Carson met him at the door of her small bungalow's screened-in front porch. Dressed in white from her flowing skirt to linen blouse, she seemed to be channeling the ghost she was a reported expert on. "Tucker Boone, I assume?" she asked holding the door open for him. Tucker nodded, offering the appropriate greetings and small talk.

"Come on inside. I'll get us some iced tea, and we'll chat."

"Sounds good." He followed her inside. Her home, like so many houses on the island, was built by amateurs using scrap materials and imagination rather than blue prints. The ceilings were so low, he had to lower his head to maneuver past hanging light fixtures. Shelves and shelves of books lined the walls on their walk to the long, narrow kitchen at the back of the house. This room greeted him with light that poured in from a line of windows overlooking the smooth, grey waters of the Ocracoke Inlet.

Jane moved past the view with barely a glance. Tucker came to a halt, his attention drawn to a Coast Guard cutter passing through the channel.

"So, you're from Ohio, huh?" Jane asked as she pulled glasses from her cupboard and filled them with ice and tea.

He pulled himself away from the window sat at the table. "Yes, ma'am.

From a little town on the Great Lakes."

"I've never been any farther north than Roanoke. How do the lakes compare to our ocean?"

Tucker thought a minute. "The lakes are more like small models of the real thing."

"I see," she said, handing him his drink before sitting cross-legged across from him. "It sounds like you've caught the ocean bug. It happens to some. Salt water has a primordial lure, much like returning to the womb."

Tucker scratched at his ear. He had zero interest in returning to the womb, but he did like it here. He said politely, "It is pretty here."

"Oh, I love it. I've no desire to even look around other places. Ocracoke has history, beauty, nature, and crazy-assed people galore. Have you been to Springer's Point? Seen the grave of Sam Jones and his horse? That looney buzzard loved the beast so much, he had it buried in the family plot."

Tucker shook his head. "No, I just got here today."

"Did you really come all this way to find out about Mad Mags?"

"I was mostly looking for a change of scenery, and found the story of Mags intriguing. Especially since she seems to be linked to a mystery in my own family. You see, I have a sister who ran away, years ago, and the only clue she left behind was this note." Tucker pulled the note from the file folder and handed it to her. Jane pulled a set of glasses from on top of her head and looked the note over.

"Hmm. She did capitalize both M's. I suppose that could mean our Mags."

"It's the only connection I can make. Her mother swears she knows no one named Mags and doesn't have a clue what the note means. I found the ghost story on the net, so I thought I'd check it out."

"I'm surprised you found anything on her at all. Blackbeard gets all the press. Even ghosts suffer from gender bias. But trust me, Mags's story is just as bloody and sexy as that beastly villain with the midnight hair."

"Ella said it was like most lady in white stories?"

"Pah. What does Ella know? Bait and propane are her specialties."

"I'm sure she meant no—"

Jane ignored him with an eye roll and a hand in the air. "Ella fails to see because of her own practicality. I take no *real* offense, though Mags *is* special. She's hardly *just* a ghost story. In life, Mad Mags was Margaret Eaton. A beautiful young girl, with a countenance so lovely, she drew suitors like stars to the moon. Men swooned on sight. Can you imagine?"

Josie popped into his head, and Tucker couldn't stop the heat that moved up his neck. Yesterday, the idea of falling for a girl based on a look would have sounded insane, but not today. Though, it wasn't simply a pretty face that compelled him. There was something in Josie's eyes…her smile…he couldn't quite put a finger on it, but when she looked at him, he recognized a sensitivity, an understanding…

"Hello? I'm taking that far-off look as agreement that you can imagine a face that could launch a thousand ships, so to speak?"

Tucker squirmed in his chair and cleared his throat. "Yeah, I guess I can imagine that."

"Good. Well, that face was young Margaret's gift and her curse."

Settling into his seat, Tucker reached for his iced tea, cleared his mind of the girl next door, and listened.

"Margaret Eaton was originally from a port town in Maine. She was smart and talented, with a big heart and a spirit that just seemed to glow from within. I'm sure poor Mags thought she'd live a happily-ever-after. I mean, she could pick a rich man, or a sweet man. They were hers for the asking."

Jane's voice went from excited to hushed. She leaned closer to Tucker, placing a cool hand on his warm arm. "But sadly, she caught the attention of a much older ship captain. And when I say older, I mean older by decades. Mags was probably fifteen and he was over fifty. I'm sure to a girl that age, he just seemed ancient. So, the captain asked for her hand, but Mags's father was quick to say no. He sent the sea captain on his way. Now, most men would have sailed away, broken-hearted. But not the captain. He was an arrogant lout. Probably a bastard child of a pirate, or in the very least, one aligned with their take-what-they-want thinking. He wanted the girl, so he snuck into her

room in the middle of the night, and he stole her."

"He kidnapped her?"

Jane nodded. "Yes, he did. Dragged her onboard his ship and sailed back to Ocracoke. He told everyone she was his wife…that she was a little crazy…and they accepted it."

"She didn't tell anyone she was kidnapped? Get help from someone?"

"Nope. From what I hear, she didn't exactly make friends with the islanders. Personally? I think the girl was too ashamed. And who knows, even if she had asked for help, who would have gone against Captain Howard? He was a very prominent man in the Ocracoke Village. If you haven't noticed how many things are named after the Howard family on this island, well, you haven't been reading anything. If Captain Howard said the girl was his wife, the girl was his wife."

"That's awful. How could they—"

"Oh, now, imagine it from an 1800's perspective. This island was barely settled. It was a wild spot that harbored pirates and miscreants galore. And by the time Mags made it to the island, she was acting more than a little off. I suppose the isolated voyage, the homesickness, and probably the revulsion of being *married* to a man against her will, drove the girl crazy. Folks say she chopped off her toe with a meat clever and branded her own forehead with a hot iron. And then, there's the story of her cooking her new husband his beloved cat for dinner."

"That definitely qualifies as crazy."

"It sure does. And every year, she got a little crazier and crazier. As an old woman, she wore a long white dress and wandered the sandy lanes of the town, often ending up in the graveyard where she would stand for hours."

"Did she ever make it back to Maine? Maybe after the captain died?"

Jane shook her head. "No. She died here, but never moved on. She wanders some nights. You might mistake her ghost for a bit of fog, but if you look closely, it's shaped like a woman. And you can hear her shells tinkling. That's when you know Mags is visiting you."

"What's up with the shells?"

Jane shrugged. "A lot of people made necklaces out of them, stringing together pretty things they found along the beach. Perhaps she just wanted some beauty in her life."

"If I wanted to find this ghost, where would I look?"

"Paddy's Holler. You said you're staying at Murray's?"

"Yes, ma'am."

"Why, that's smack dab in the middle of Paddy's Holler. As a matter of fact, at the end of Murray's Lane, is Mags's favorite graveyard, as of late."

"Of late?"

Jane nodded. "She's been seen all over Paddy's Holler, and there are more graveyards on this island than there are tourist stops, so she has plenty to visit. But for the last couple of years, she's mostly been spotted near that graveyard."

Tucker rubbed his head. None of this helped a damn bit. He was beginning to question whether or not the letter meant anything. If Mad Mags was supposed to help him find Maddy, he didn't know how.

"Well, ma'am, I appreciate the information. It's been real interesting."

"I hope it's been at least a little helpful. I mean if a runaway was hiding here, I suppose it'd be easy enough to go unnoticed during the in season. But during the off season, it's pretty quiet here. Hardly anything goes unnoticed by folks."

"And you've not noticed any northern girls in their early twenties hiding out here?"

Jane laughed. "No. No, I can't say that I have. Murray's niece, Josie, and a Korean girl named Susan are the only ones who are recent additions to our permanent young population in the last few years."

Tucker left with an uneasy feeling. Josie did fit the bill perfectly. She arrived at the right time, and he couldn't help but admit, she looked a bit like Maddy. No, Murray promised. Hell, he practically approved of him showing an interest in his niece. If there was even the slightest chance—no, it was a coincidence. Josie was Murray Banks's niece.

Thanking the woman, he left. Back at his cottage, he looked through his clippings, focusing on the newspaper picture of the two girls.

Comparing them side by side, he could see why Gloria said Ariel Stone and Maddy could pass for twins. They both had similar features, though Ariel had lighter hair and was a little heavier than Maddy. It was tough to tell them apart, especially in a newspaper photo, heavily shadowed and pixilated. Tossing the pictures on the table, he wondered what Maddy expected someone to find here. If anything. Why did she send that note?

Tucker didn't know. But then a thought occurred to him—what if she wasn't leading him to a place? What if she wanted to let someone know what was happening to her?

If Stone was abusing his own stepdaughter, what would've stopped him from doing the same to Maddy? What if he had kidnapped her?

Tucker sat up straighter. He read through the clippings trying to make out a timeline. The night Maddy disappeared, Ariel attempted suicide. That was two weeks before Ariel was murdered. The letter arrived a week after Ariel's death. That would also have been a week after Stone was arrested.

If Maddy had been kidnapped, what the hell could he do to help her? He didn't know anything about law enforcement. Where the hell would he start?

David Santos.

Aside from Ash, Santos was the best friend Tucker ever had, and he left the service for a job as a sheriff's deputy.

Santos answered on the first ring. "If it isn't my favorite cracker."

"Cracker?" Tucker laughed. "What the hell?"

"I'm living in the deep south now. I'm trying to pick up the lingo."

"Racist prick. Someone will grab your fajita-eating ass and use you as a piñata."

"Fajita eater? Did you get your smack talk from a Taco Bell packet, or what?"

Tucker laughed. It felt good. He hadn't laughed in months. "Where you at now?"

"Alabama. Got a transfer from Galveston to Birmingham."

"Wasn't hot enough for you in Texas?"

"You could say that. No, it was part personal, part better career move. Here, I get to be full-fledged detective."

"I see there's no damned standards what-so-ever in Alabama."

"Ha ha. Well, screw you. What are you into, lately?"

"That's actually why I called." Tucker squeezed his eyes closed as he imagined how stupid this was going to sound. "You near a computer?"

"Yeah, always."

"Still haven't beaten that porn addiction?"

"Hey, why fight it? It's not a problem until I get carpal tunnel."

"You're such a freak. Look up Ariel Stone. A-R-I-E-L Stone, like the rock."

"Okay." Tucker could hear keys clicking. "Murdered girl?"

"Yeah."

"Damn shame. What the hell's wrong with these sick bastards? I'd like to say this shit hardly ever happens, but it happens way too often. Here's a video clip. Have you watched it?"

"No, I don't have any net access. I have to use my cell data, so I've been keeping it to email and websites."

Santos clicked and Tucker could hear a woman talking. She had a silky-sexy voice that sounded like a porn star trying her hand at drama. "Who is that?" Tucker asked.

"Amanda Stone, the murdered girl's mom."

"Start it over. I want to hear it."

"*...I, uh, I came home early from dinner. Some friends asked me to go...I didn't want to...I just had a feeling.*" There was a small pause for whimpers and tears. "*When I got home, I went to Ariel's room to tell her good night, and...and I found Jeb.* More tears. *He was strangling her, holding her down. She had no clothes on, and I screamed. I screamed for him to get away from my daughter. I shot at him, but I missed. He charged at me and wrestled it from me...shooting me...here...I passed out, and when I woke...my...my...little girl...was gone.*"

The woman's voice annoyed him, which made him feel like shit. Poor woman lost her kid and Tucker couldn't get past the woman's voice being

annoying. "I've heard enough."

"She doesn't sound all that damned torn up, does she?" Santos said as the sound went off. There were more clicks then Santos said, "You realize they convicted Stone without ever finding her body?"

"They can convict without a body?"

"Get enough circumstantial evidence, it's doable. Seems they had the mother's testimony. Sheets soiled with the girl's blood and his semen. And her blood was found all over his car. And she was the second girl to go missing that month, with Stone being the common denominator."

"That second girl, seems she's my sister, and she's missing. The police have her down as a runaway, but a letter about Mad Mags arrived about a week after the Stone girl died. Maddy's mom swears it's from my sister. Swears the girl was trying to send her a message. Mad Mags is the ghost of a kidnapped girl here on Ocracoke, so I came to check it out. Now, I'm thinking it's meant to reveal a what, not a where."

"I hate to say this, but the more I read on this, Stone seems to have been getting away with molesting the stepdaughter for years. Maybe he was molesting the friend too. Hell, he could have had countless victims. Maybe someone else sent the letter?"

"Hard to tell. It's just—this girl's mom—she's convinced it's Maddy."

"And she wants you to find her baby?"

"Yeah."

"Well, hero, you're the shit, but even you can't work miracles. My money is on both of these girls being dead. Probably a hundred feet deep in Lake Eerie."

Tucker sighed.

"Tell you what, send me the letter. I have a friend at Quantico. I'll see if he can have it analyzed and get anything from it."

"That would be great."

Tucker hung up the phone. He was about to grab a beer and find out what all wonders general cable had to offer, when his phone rang. Marie. Ash's widow.

"Hey, Tucker! I told David he didn't give you an address. You can just send it to my house. David's here all the time.

"David?"

"Santos? You were just talking to him."

"Our Santos? He's there? With you?"

"He stops by when he can. He came over tonight to mow and I talked him into staying for dinner. He told you he moved to Birmingham, right?"

"I never put the two together. So, Santos is hanging around your house, huh?" Tucker ran a hand through his hair. Tucker hoped he wasn't plugging their buddy's widow. Ash deserved better than that.

"Some. You got a problem with David? Something I should know about?"

"Not at all. I'm just surprised. You and Ash were perfect together, and this…hell, this sounds pretty damned cozy."

Marie was quiet. He could hear a puff of breath. "Tucker, we're just…friends."

"Just friends?"

"Uh, yeah. Mostly. I--"

Tucker's chest hurt, and he wasn't sure why. Marie was young. Of course she'd move on. And Santos was trustworthy. He loved Ash almost as much as Tucker did. How could Santos move so quickly? It'd only been what—six months?

Marie took a deep breath. "Look, Tucker, no matter how much I miss him, I can't bring him back. David is a good friend, and I need that. It's scary, you know? I never imagined life alone."

Tucker closed his eyes. Who the hell was he? It wasn't like he was the one raising a three-year-old alone. And hadn't he spent his day trying to hit on the hot girl next door only a few weeks after Holly died? He knew he was being selfish not to let Marie off the hook, but he couldn't do it. He couldn't tell her it was all right to move on.

There was an awkward silence until Marie took a deep breath and asked, "So, the rumors about Holly? They true?"

"Afraid so."

"I am so sorry. I know things were crazy between you two, but still…I know you loved her."

"Don't worry about me. I'm fine."

"David said her mother refused the flowers you sent to the funeral."

"Yeah, well, that's their right."

"It's rude. I can't believe they blame--"

"Look, I'm fine. You don't need to worry." Tucker tried to sound light, but it came out with more than a little bitterness.

"Tucker, you know I love you, so I mean no offense, but you sound like hell."

"I swear. I'm fine."

"Holly's death wasn't your fault. Neither was Ash's."

"Shit Marie, there's someone at my door."

"You liar. Okay, fine. Go drink your beer, but remember, I'm here for you."

Tucker hung up. Snatching a couple of beers from the fridge, he took them to the couch. He was done talking. And thinking.

Chapter Seven

Tucker woke stiff and achy after curling his six-foot frame into a five-foot couch for a night. Twisting his neck left then right, he tried to work out the kinks. After a hot shower and a thorough scouring away of beer mouth with his toothbrush, he was ready for work.

Murray was waiting on him at the shop with his list of work. Trim the trees near the cabins and deliver the day's repaired appliances. Tucker finished before four, but Murray assured him, "When you're done; you're done. I give you a list, you get done…the day's yours." Adding with a wink, Murray said, "Might want to get you a fishin' pole."

But Tucker had no pole and no real desire to sit on a dock and wait for fish to bite. Instead, he lounged on his porch swing. Lost in thoughts that were far more uncomfortable and unsettling than a pleasant day deserved, Tucker tried to shut his brain down and enjoy the sunny skies, but it was impossible. The conversation with Marie ruined what small level of comfort he'd found in this place.

"Hey," Josie said, stopping in front of his porch. "You look a million miles away."

Tucker jumped, sitting straighter in his seat. "Nah, just relaxing."

"I usually look happy when I relax. Anything wrong?"

"No. I'm fine."

"You're a terrible liar, Mr. Boone." Josie wagged her finger at him.

"I'm not lying." He grinned. He suddenly wasn't lying. Having Josie walk up on his porch was a game changer. Today was turning out to be a good day.

Josie settled herself on his porch, leaning her back against the rail post. "You can tell me, if you'd like. I'm trustworthy, I swear."

"It's not that. It's just a stupid thing."

"Nothing's stupid. Not if it bothers you."

"No, this is stupid."

"Let me be the judge." She grinned.

He took a deep breath. "A friend of mine died, and his widow seems to be moving on—

you know dating another guy."

Josie thought a minute before she said, "It's till death do they part."

"I know. That's what I keep telling myself. So, why does it bug me?"

"Do you have feelings for her?"

Tucker's body pulled back at the thought. "No. Nothing like that. And the guy she's talking about, he's a good guy. One of the best. What the hell's my problem?"

"How long has your friend been gone?"

"Six months."

"That's not a very long time. You're still grieving. Any change while you're hurting feels like a new wound."

Tucker nodded. He gripped the swing until his knuckles turned white. "I guess part of me wonders why she isn't grieving any more. Like he's dead and gone, but that doesn't matter to her anymore." His nose burned, and his eyes stung. He shouldn't have brought this up. "Oh well, hell. What do I care? None of my business."

In a heartbeat, Josie was beside him. Her hand was small, but warm against his arm. "You're a good friend. He'll always have you. Even if everyone else forgets, you won't. He has that."

When she looked up at him, he was startled by her eyes. He'd assumed they were brown, but in the afternoon sun, he could tell they were as dark blue as an evening sky. In a moment, he felt understanding and hope—a levity he hadn't felt in years, if ever. "I should tell her it's all right?"

"I think," Josie said, the pressure on his arm increasing as she spoke, "you should take care of yourself for a bit. This is her decision, not yours."

He nodded. She was right. He'd have to accept whatever Marie chose to do.

"Thanks, Josie."

"You feel better?"

"I do."

"Good." She patted his arm, then stood to leave.

"Can I get you something to drink?" he asked.

"No, thanks. If you need anything else, you know where to find me," she said as she stepped off his porch.

Tucker jumped up and followed her. "Before you go, would you mind telling me how to get to that beach you told me about? Murray says I'm done for the day, and there's still a hell of a lot of day left, especially for a guy without cable or internet. Pretty soon, I might start reading books."

She chewed on her lip, but a grin tugged at the corners of her mouth. "Would reading a book kill you?"

"I don't know. I haven't done it since I graduated. It could. My brain might reel from shock."

Josie laughed, unleashing her smile on him. It was the kind that wrinkled the corners of her eyes and made her face glow. She shook her head slowly as she said, "You remind me of someone I used to know."

"Not a prick of an ex, I hope?"

"No, a friend. A really, really good friend." Josie's eyes sparkled with unshed tears.

Tucker opened his mouth to ask her more about her friend, but he could read in her eyes, she was done.

"Let me go change and I'll take you."

"Excellent," Tucker said as he watched her walk away.

Eager as a fourteen-year-old on his first date, Tucker was dressed in his swim trunks and waiting on her porch in less than ten minutes. When Josie opened her door, Tucker almost fell off the step. Her hair was loosely piled on top of her head, the front shoved back by sunglasses. Her skin was shiny, and he could smell the sunblock. She'd traded her tennis shoes for flip-flops, and her pink toes matched the straps of the bathing suit circling her neck from under her tank top.

"Ready?" she asked.

He broke out of his stupor and nodded. Oh hell yeah, he was ready.

"It's a long walk," she warned as she pulled her sunglasses off her head and slid them on.

"I've done all-day hikes through deserts in my play clothes. Walking in the sunshine with a towel as my only gear…life is damn good."

"Play clothes?"

"Battle rattle? It's when you head out in full gear—gas mask, gunny sack, IMTV."

Her face scrunched up. "IMTV?"

"Improved Modular Tactical Vest. Previously known as an armored vest, but that's so first Iraq War. IMTV is fully updated with removable plates and iPhone holder."

"Really?"

Tucker laughed. "No. I mean yes to removable plates, no to the iPhone dock."

"Why would you remove any plates? I'd wear them all, or does it get too heavy?"

"It's not too bad. The towel, though, is a hell of a lot better."

She smiled, reaching out and giving his arm a squeeze. "I bet it is." As quickly as she touched him, she pulled away.

They wound their way through cottage-lined roads. Paved roads quickly gave way to rutted, compact sand. As they walked, crickets chirped from clusters of oleander, and mosquitoes buzzed in his ears. He slapped at them, though Josie didn't seem to mind the bugs or heat. She pointed out historical houses as they passed. "Isn't it just amazing how long these have been here?"

"Impressive how they've withstood so many storms. Makes you wonder what they did differently when they built them."

Josie nodded. "When storms hit, they used to drill holes in the floor, so the water could rise in the house. If they didn't drill the holes, the water could lift the house off its foundation and it'd float away. And the families rarely evacuated. Instead, they'd go as high as they could, like to the attic, and wait out the storm. Can you imagine?"

"No. I'd be all for evacuation."

Josie laughed. "I'd have to agree. I've weathered a few nor'easters since I've lived here, and they were enough to make me think this little island was going to get blown off the map. But some of these houses have been here for more than a century. Like the house up ahead. It was built in 1883. It's for sale, so I toured it during an open house. It's just amazing. If I only had a few hundred thousand, I could own a piece of island history."

Tucker looked over the grey-shingled house raised off the ground by squat, brick columns. A tire swing hung from a solid though twisted-looking oak tree in the grass-covered front yard. "Not worried about ghosts?" he asked with a grin.

Josie looked at him like he was still twelve. "Oh geesh, there are no such things as ghosts."

Embarrassment crept up from his collarbone to his cheeks. Usually picking up women was easy for him. Why did this one shove him all the way back to puberty?

Josie smiled at him. "Sorry if I burst your bubble."

"No, I was joking. Making conversation."

"You have to make conversation?" She chuckled and pointed to a path. "Here's our turn. The beach isn't too far. And the walk is gorgeous. See those flowers?"

Tucker looked down at the white sand. Clumps of yellow and red flowers were scattered among the sea grass.

"Farther up the islands, they call that Indian Blanket. Here on Ocracoke, they're Joe Bells. Legend says Joe Bell came to the island to mend a broken heart, and he brought the flower with him to remind him of his lost love. Now, they grow all over the place."

"So, this is where to go to mend a broken heart too? Seems the island is good for a lot of things." Tucker muttered as he allowed Josie to take the lead down the narrowing path.

She asked, looking over her shoulder, "Still making conversation, Mr. Boone, or did you come here to heal a broken heart?"

Tucker grimaced, but didn't offer an answer. Thoughts of his ex brought a bead of sweat to his brow and a hole in the pit of his stomach.

They walked the rest of the way in silence. When they arrived on the shore, Tucker had to take a minute to absorb the vastness of the place. He'd never get over the rush he felt when he saw the ocean. White sand and sea green water topped in foam-tipped waves that spread as far as the eye could see. Above that was a porcelain blue sky dotted here and there with thin, wispy clouds.

Josie set her beach bag on the sand and kicked off her flip-flops. As she dug a sheet out of the bag, she cleared her throat. "I didn't mean to pry back there. Whatever, whoever, broke your heart is none of my business."

He took a corner of the sheet and helped her spread it out. Then he sat, knees bent, with hands busy snapping bits of dried sea grass scattered around him.

She sat next to him, cross-legged, and turned toward him as if getting comfortable for a long story.

"No one broke my heart," he said, glancing at her a moment and quickly turning his gaze back to the sea.

"But someone hurt you?" Josie asked quietly.

His heart sped up as he turned to her. She looked certain, like she would know if he lied. "I was engaged to a girl from my hometown, but it didn't work out. Seems being in college and having your guy overseas was too lonely."

"Lonely for her?" Josie's forehead wrinkled.

"That's what she said. Anyhow, we broke up, which was fine. I'm fine."

"But you don't seem fine."

"Seriously," Tucker said, looking back to the water. "I'm fine."

Josie leaned closer to him. "You sure it's over? Maybe you'll get back together?"

"No chance of that," Tucker said. This wasn't a conversation he wanted to have. He stood. "I say we check out the waves."

Josie didn't budge. She sat, the wind moving through the curls on her head. He could see himself in her sunglasses. He wanted to pull them off so he could only see her. Turning away, he rubbed the back of his neck.

"I'm sorry," Josie said. "I hate it when people get in my business. I don't know why I'm doing it to you. Come on." She jumped up and grabbed his hand. "Let's hit those waves."

His legs felt like lead. Thoughts of Holly physically wore him out like he'd been on night patrol. Josie laid a warm hand on his cheek. Her thumb caressed the bit of whiskers he hadn't shaved since yesterday. "I'm sorry," she said.

"It's fine. Don't worry about it."

"You want to go back?"

"Oh, hell no. I came to swim. I'm swimming." He plastered a smile on his face and threw his towel on the ground.

Giving him a silent smile, she went about stripping down. As she unbuttoned her shorts and slid them down over smooth, creamy legs, Tucker forgot all about his ghosts. Mindful not to ogle her, too much, he took a deep breath and looked away. When he turned around, she was in nothing more than a pink bikini. Breasts not too big or too small, perfect amount of soft flesh teasing from the edge of her suit. He almost said, "Wow", but he didn't think she would appreciate it as a compliment.

Pulling his tee shirt over his head, he tossed it on the ground. She gave him a double take. A satisfied grin tugged at the corners of his mouth, especially when a blush crept across Josie's cheeks. He knew she knew she got caught.

Heading toward the crashing water, they moved quicker and quicker until they were running. It felt good to feel free as a child. The soft dry sand yielded to the pressure of his feet then became almost as firm as concrete where it had met the water. The firmly packed sand barely left a trail of where their feet landed. The first splash of rolling waves brought squeals from Josie and a deep belly laugh from Tucker. A few yards out, the water was swifter and deeper than what he was used to along the Atlantic mainland. He didn't have any problems navigating the harsh waves, but Josie was much smaller, her legs not nearly as well-muscled.

He stayed close to her as they jumped each swell. The feeling of unbound buoyancy made his soul feel light. He knew Josie felt it too. Each wave she swam over left her with smiles so big they lit up her face. During a lull, Josie floated on her back. Eyes closed, chin tipped toward the sun. As the water moved and rippled under her, Tucker craved to grab her, hold her, and kiss her. Taste the salt water on her lips.

Lost in those thoughts, he didn't notice until too late, a monster wave was building. He yelled for Josie, who quickly flipped onto her feet and let out a scream as the wave curled over her head. Tucker saw her go under as the water swirled around him. He lunged to the left, trying to grab her around the waist, but she slipped out of his hands. Panic hit him. People got rolled in the surf all the time, Tucker knew this. But in that instant, when she disappeared under the water, it felt like life or death. It was the same as the moment he told Ash to watch out. When he told Holly to get it together. Neither listened. Both were gone.

Panicked, he dove under the water. The salt and stirred up sand burned his eyes, but he saw a flash of pink. Reaching out, he made contact with flesh. Grasping, he pulled her toward him and wrapped his arms around her waist. Her arms circled his neck and she laid her cheek against his chest as he carried her to shore.

Setting her on the ground, he wrapped a towel around her shoulders and pretended not to notice her bikini needed adjustment. She sat, laying her head against her bent knees. "I got rolled. That's so embarrassing."

"Technically, you didn't get rolled. I caught you before you bit the sand."

"That's true. Thank you."

"Damn, that's a rough sea," Tucker said rubbing his face with a towel.

"Must be a storm brewing. That always makes the waves bigger."

"You sure you're all right?" He tried to look at her, but his eyes still burned and the sun wasn't helping. He tried rubbing them one more time.

She blotted her face with the towel as she watched him. "Your eyes are blood shot. Did you open them under the water?"

He nodded. "I think they still have sand in them." He rubbed at the corners.

"Lay back," she said picking up her bag and pulling out a bottle of water. She removed the lid, warning him, "This is going to be cold, but it will help."

She leaned over him, her hands soft and cool on his hot skin. He had to remind himself to breathe. As she came closer, he could smell her. Laundry soap and sweetness.

"You smell good," he said, swallowing past the lump in his throat.

"Salt and sea weed?" She gave him an odd look.

"No, something else, I smelled it earlier." *Smooth Tucker. Real smooth.*

"Honeysuckle body wash."

Honeysuckle body wash. Sexiest words he'd ever heard, and he'd been offered some hot pick-ups in his life.

Cold water splashed in his eyes. *Shit, was it iced?* The thought ran through his head, but he never flinched. She doused him thoroughly, carefully wiping his eyes with her tee shirt. "There you go," she said. "You did very well."

"You're much better at it than a grunt."

Josie laughed. "You guys do that to each other often?"

"Mostly training. In case we ever get caught up in chemicals. In basic, the guy who did mine about ripped my damned eyelids off."

She laughed as she wrapped her hair into a knot at the back of her head. With her arms above her head and behind her back, her breasts were pushed out. The tiniest bit of rounded flesh worked its way free from the side of her top to tease him. Aware he was fully ogling her, he tried to shake it off and make conversation.

"So, where do you hang out around here? Are there any clubs or bars?"

Josie laughed. "There's nothing like that on this island. Even if there were, that's not really my thing. Most everything I do, I do alone."

Tucker nodded as an ornery grin tugged at his lips. "And yet you came with me. I guess I'm pretty special."

Josie matched his grin, rolling her eyes at him. "You're the first to actually live in one of the cottages. The rest are tourists who rent them for a

week and leave. A few come back year after year, but they're mostly retired and not really the *hanging out* type."

"Hetty told me about the guy she had to fire. Don't try to deny it. I'm special."

Josie laughed as she settled herself back against the sand. Lying there, knees bent, she sighed. Droplets of water rolled from her stomach down her sides leaving a mesmerizing trail. Digging her toes in the sand, she said, "I suppose you are pretty special." Then she closed her eyes, turned her face toward the sun, and smiled.

It was the most beautiful smile he'd ever seen.

Chapter Eight

Lying next to her soaking up a drenching sun, Tucker broke the peace. "I'm starved. You want to get some lunch?"

Josie cupped her eyes and looked up at the sky. "I'd say it's well past dinner time."

"No wonder I'm so damned hungry." Tucker rose to his feet and offered her a hand. She hesitated, but accepted his offer. Her fingers felt small and fragile. He'd have gladly kept hold, but she pulled her hand back as soon as she was on her feet.

Grabbing the sheet, she shook off the sand, quickly folded it, and stuffed it in her bag. Then she slipped on her shorts and tee shirt.

"Ready?" Josie asked. She bent forward to pick up her bag, but he reached it first and slung it over his shoulder.

Josie laughed. "Looks good. It matches your eyes."

Tucker looked down at the pink bag covered in daisies and smiled. "Go ahead, you can tell me how pretty I am. I won't be insulted."

Josie shook her head as she laughed. "You're very pretty."

"Thank you. But I hope you're still interested in my mind."

"I'm beginning to think your mind is a little demented."

"A little?" He scoffed. "It's a whole lot, baby."

Her smile came fast and easily, and her laugh carried on the wind, mingling with the crash of the waves and squawks of the gulls on shore. Damn, he'd forgotten how good life could be.

Tipping her head slightly, she said, "You're prettiest when you smile, Tucker Boone. Happiness suits you."

He'd like to say he took her appraisal real cool, like a mature man could, but he felt the heat crawl up his neck to center on his cheeks. Walking beside her, he asked, "Anywhere good we can eat?"

"I usually cook."

"All I've got are cans of food and cereal. I had some frozen pizza, but I ate it all. Let me take you somewhere."

"I don't really feel like dressing up and going out." Her voice dropped lower, as if she was embarrassed.

"Me neither. How about I pick up a pizza? We could watch a movie." *Calm down, Tucker. No sense letting her know she's making you insane.* He gripped the flowered bag tighter.

"At my place?" She stopped in the path and turned to look at him. She chewed her lip.

"I'm being pushy. I'm sorry."

"No, no. It's just that…well, I mostly have old black and white movies."

"Like Casablanca?"

"Yeah, and the *Maltese Falcon*. I have the entire Hitchcock collection."

"That's great. I've been wanting to see them all."

"Really?" Josie didn't look convinced.

"Really. Every single one is on my bucket list." *As of right now.*

Josie's face lit up. "I can't believe you like old movies. I can make sandwiches."

"No, let me get the pizza."

"Okay. Then tomorrow, I'll make dinner," Josie said, her body giving a little bounce as she talked.

"Awesome," Tucker said, hoping to hell he wasn't headed to the friend zone. But sadly, he admitted to himself, if she asked him to spend an evening highlighting their hair, he'd agree.

He showered and drove into the cozy town for a pizza. Then over to Ella's to buy drinks. He debated between picking up beer, wine, or cola, but instead grabbed a pack of fruity flavored wine coolers. He wanted everything to be perfect. He almost asked Ella if his shirt looked all right, but he squelched it. It was just a movie with a girl. Even if she did make his palms sweat and his brain lock up, she was just a girl.

Arriving back at the cottage, he knocked on her door. She answered, wearing a pair of yoga pants and an over-sized tee shirt. Her cheeks were pink from the sun, her hair a riot of untamed curls piled on top of her head. Her hair looked soft, tempting him to reach out, wrap a curl around his finger, and see if he was right. But the thought of touching her made his heart race like he'd run a mile. He suddenly worried he was going to break out in a sweat. The idea of ending up with wet arm pits made him feel even hotter.

"I, uh, brought wine coolers." He lifted the brown paper bag as evidence. "I wasn't sure if you liked them or not."

Josie pulled one from the carton and looked at it. "I've never had one. I drank a beer at a party once, but I hated it."

"One beer? Slow down there, tiger."

"Yeah well, my mother was strict. I didn't get out much."

"It's all right. I'm more than happy to be your bad influence. Try one. They're much better than beer. Or so the ladies tell me. I'd never admit to drinking them myself." He took the bottle from her and twisted. It hissed as it opened. He handed it back; she hesitated a moment as if deciding if it was beverage or poison.

After taking a small sip, she smiled. "It's good. I like it."

They each made a plate. Josie carried hers to the couch and sat with her feet tucked under her. Picking up the remote, she flipped on the TV. "I put in *Psycho*. I mean, you may as well start with the most famous. If it's the only one you get to see, then at least you're less culturally deprived than before you met me."

Her words made his heart sink to his stomach. *If? Another movie wasn't a sure thing?* Tucker sat beside her. In his nervousness, he left more than two feet between them. He realized that was a newbie move, and he couldn't help but think drunk girls in clubs were a damned sight easier to pick up than shy girls who liked black and white movies. He suddenly wasn't sure he was capable of closing the deal with a girl like her.

She hit play, and the movie started. Josie was engrossed in the story, but Tucker couldn't keep his eyes off her. His brain was on fire obsessing about the things he'd said and the things he should say. Catching his gaze out of the corner of her eye, she turned to him with a blush and said, "You're not

watching the movie."

"Sure, I am. Sort of." He set his plate on the coffee table in front of him.

"I can pick another one if you don't like it."

"I like it."

"You're not watching it."

"Well, no. But I mean, yes, the movie's fine. I was just…oh hell, it's your fault."

"My fault?"

"Yeah. Holy shit, Josie. You're too distracting. I can't watch a movie when all I can think is what can I say to impress you and try really, really hard not to break out into a sweat."

"I can turn up the air conditioning." Josie started to get up. Tucker grabbed her arm.

"Sit. It's fine. I could be at the freaking Arctic, and I'd still be sweating." His cheeks felt like they were on fire. This had to be his most humiliating moment. With his cool gone, he only had his dignity left to trample, so he figured what the hell. "Damn Josie, you're beautiful."

Poking him with her naked foot, she laughed. "Oh hush, Mr. Don Juan."

"I wish." He rolled his eyes and took a deep breath. "Now, watch your movie." He turned his attention back to the TV. He could see Josie watching him from the corner of his eye.

After a few minutes, she said, "You're pretty good-looking yourself."

Tucker felt like a complete idiot. He couldn't remember a time when a date made him feel so inept. He was pretty certain that when she looked at him, she saw through him, and he worried she'd find the nothingness he worked so damn hard to hide.

Unable to look at her, he rubbed his chin. He finally managed to say, "Thank you."

Josie turned off the TV. "The name on your tattoo? Was she your girlfriend?"

Touching his shirt where the anchor and globe tattoo would be, Tucker said, "No, Ash was my buddy."

Josie scooted closer to him and held his hand. "He the friend you lost, with the wife?"

"Yep, that's him."

"What happened?" She looked at him, but he gazed at the floor.

"He went to war, and he died."

Her words were quiet, her tone patient. "How?"

Finally making eye contact with her, he thought about telling her the whole story, but he couldn't say the words. Over and over he saw his friend's last minutes. Saw the blood bubble from his mouth. Shaking off the nightmare montage that replayed continuously in his head, he said, "He died. That's what happens when you fight a war. People die. End of story."

Josie's hand tightened around his. "I'm sorry, Tucker."

Words choked him, so he nodded.

Josie leaned closer, pressing her cheek against his arm.

They sat there, neither moving, neither speaking until Tucker picked up the remote and turned the movie back on. Clearing his throat, he finally said, "Now, where were we on putting an end to my cultural depravity?"

Chapter Nine

At the end of the evening, Tucker wanted to kiss her good night, but he couldn't gather the courage. Instead, he stood there like a moron on her porch, making more conversation while he tried to grow a set big enough to close those few feet between them.

All he had to do was take one step. One step and he'd be close enough.

It never happened. He walked home feeling like he'd lost a big game. As he opened his door, his cell rang. He'd left it on the table, not wanting any distractions while he was with Josie. Picking up the phone, he answered it. "Hello, Mom."

"Why haven't you called or answered your damn phone? I was worried sick."

"I was busy." Thoughts of Josie flashed through his head. The smell of her hair, the feel of her skin…her smile. He felt lighter than he had in years; his mother was barely annoying.

"What was her name?" His mother didn't sound the least bit impressed.

"Josie." He grinned as he said it. Sitting on his couch, he kicked off his shoes and put his feet up on the table.

"Josie what? I'll google her."

"Holy shit, Mom. We watched a movie."

"Oh. *Watched a movie*, huh?"

Tucker rolled his eyes and pressed his head against the back of the couch.

"So, find out anything about your missing sister?" she asked.

"No." He sighed. "It was a dead end."

"Then you'll be coming home?"

"No." His scalp started to itch. Scratching his head, he said, "No, I'm sticking around a while."

"You're what?"

"I'm staying here. I got a job."

There was a long pause before his mother asked, "You still mad at me for not telling you about Rob? That you never got to know your real dad?"

"I'm not happy about it, but—"

"I'm sorry. I hated him for hurting me. For cheating. And he didn't just cheat on me, but on you, too. I just wanted him to do things my way for a change. Instead, he married Gloria, and they went off to Italy to live happily ever after."

In that moment, Tucker realized his mom had loved his dad. He imagined being young and pregnant, loving a guy who moved on. He knew from Holly's cheating that it also made you look and feel like a fool, shattering your pride. "If you'd ever let me finish a sentence, I was going to say, I'm not happy about it, but that's not why I'm staying. I'm over the past. I'm just not ready to come home."

She was quiet a second before asking, "Is it Holly?"

He stood and paced the room. "No, it has nothing to do with her. I met a guy down here. He rents cottages and fixes engines and appliances, and he needed summer help and—"

"I think that'd be good for you. Do you need some money?"

Tucker's mouth dropped open and he felt momentarily speechless. It took him a full second to respond, "No, I'm good."

"Well, I think a summer at the beach after all you've been through is a good idea. So, this girl? She work there too?"

"Yeah, she does."

"She in college?"

"I don't know. Like I said, I saw a movie with her. That's it."

"So, what's her last name? Josie what?"

"McCoy."

His mother laughed. "Josie McCoy? You realize she's a Pussy Cat doll?"

"A what?"

"The Archie and Jughead comics? Josie and the Pussycats was a band.

Josie McCoy was the lead singer. I think there was even a movie in the nineties. Doesn't that seem strange to you?"

"No." He paused his pacing. "I went to high school with Bo Jackson."

"Bo Jackson? He's not famous."

"Yeah, he was a pro athlete in the 90's. Wasn't that your era?"

"Oh well, I never followed sports much."

"Really? I'd never have guessed."

Tucker could hear his stepdad shuffle into the room. "Have you seen the remote?" Ed asked real low, but not quite a whisper.

"Probably in the side of the recliner. I don't use it. I don't know why you ask me. I got you the remote holder. How hard is it to put it back when you're done?"

"That Tucker?"

"Yes. He's staying down there."

"That all right with you, dear?" Ed asked.

"Yes. He could use a vacation."

"Well, then good. Hey Tucker, have fun," Ed said, his voice coming closer to the phone. "I'm going to go find the remote." Ed sounded farther away. He was probably trying to escape back to the TV room.

"Hold on a minute, there Mr. Neilson. Have you heard of Bo Jackson?"

"Yeah, he went to school with Tucker."

"No, a famous athlete Bo?"

"No. Oh wait—there was that guy on the Nike commercial…or was it Gatorade…that Bo knows this and that campaign?"

"Hey Mom, look, you and Ed go google him. I need to get to bed."

"Of course. Certainly. Love you, sweetie. Keep your pants on."

"Love you too," he said before he hung up the phone.

Tucker grabbed his beer and took it to the couch. He opened the email on his phone. Santos sent him police reports. He had to give his friend credit; he was diligent.

The information in the police reports was much the same as the news articles. The only new interesting information was Jeb Stone's statement. He denied raping his stepdaughter…swore it was consensual. That he loved the girl, and she loved him. A real Woody Allen sort of asshole. He also swore Amanda Stone shot her own daughter and himself in an attempt to frame him. Tucker flipped through the pages. Jeb Stone wasn't asked a single question about Maddy. What the hell? Maddy was simply chalked up to a runaway? After a murderous pedophile was the last one to see her?

He shut off the phone and switched on the TV. The local newsman predicted a storm brewing in the Caribbean. The island would have some heavy rains in the long-range forecast. Josie was right. A storm was coming.

Going to the kitchen, he grabbed more beer.

Something moved outside his window. Pulling back the curtain, he saw her. Evidently Josie couldn't sleep either and was going for a midnight stroll. He dropped his beer on the table and followed her. "Josie?" he called. She didn't turn or even seem to notice he was behind her.

Walking as if in a trance, she made her way to a small graveyard. The white rounded head stones were ancient, the writing rubbed smooth and unreadable by time. The once-white picket fence surrounding the graves was now a weathered mildew-gray with peeling paint and rotting boards. On the crooked gate hung a dead flowered wreath adorned with a tattered bow. The constant sound of chirping crickets seemed louder in the dark, and the wind blew in low, warm gusts.

Josie opened the gate and stepped inside. Moving gracefully around the stones, she finally knelt. Bowing her head, she sat still a long time before standing and turning, nearly bumping into Tucker.

"You're up late," she said.

"I saw you through the window, and wondered where you were going?"

Laying a hand on his cheek, she brushed her thumb across his skin. "I needed to think some things over."

Looking around at the creepy place, he asked, "Here? You come here to think?"

"Sometimes." She walked slowly toward the gate, pausing a moment as if waiting for him to follow.

They left the graveyard wordlessly. Once they were on the road, she turned toward him, taking his hand in hers. "You're troubled. I feel it. The pain I deeper than losing a friend."

His mouth went dry and the muscles on his shoulders tensed. He had no clue how to respond to a revelation this insane by a chick, albeit a hot one, who was just meditating in a grave yard.

"I'm sorry." Josie sighed and gave his hand a gentle squeeze. "You have such a good heart." Then she stopped in the middle of the road and kissed him—just a slight brush over his lips with her own cool ones. She was so close he could smell the honey suckle, feel the warmth from her body. Proximity so enticing his mouth watered, but still, hanging out in graveyards was crazy. "What's in the graveyard?"

"Dead people." She grinned. Her eyes sparkled with mischief in the moonlight.

Tucker couldn't help but smile back. He decided maybe it wasn't all that odd. "Wow. A comedienne too. You're freshly amazing at every turn."

Josie laughed, her body dipping toward him, nearly touching her chest to his. Tugging on his hand, she pulled him along with her, explaining as she walked slowly back toward the cabins. "Most graves are blessed. They're sacred ground, so it's a peaceful place. No interference. I can think best there."

He wanted to pretend that wasn't a weird answer. Tension moved up his spine, causing every snap and rustle in the dense foliage to be amplified. When they arrived at their cottages, Josie kept hold of his hand as she turned toward him. "I wish you weren't troubled. You were so happy today."

His laugh was dry. "I'm not troubled. I just saw you walking and I…"

"Well, I couldn't sleep. And I suspect you don't sleep very well either. We may as well be up together, right?" She smiled and led him to her place. Inside, the hum of the air conditioner was the only sound. Soft hands moved up his arms to rest on his shoulders. He caught her by the hips, his fingers inching their way around her waist until he had her wrapped in his arms. Then leaning down, he kissed her. She pulled back ever so slightly as if she'd never been kissed. Tucker wasn't ready to let her go, not when he'd finally made it this close. Moving his hands from her waist to her cheeks, he held her, tilting her head, allowing his lips to explore hers. At first he worried he'd gone too far as her breath caught in her throat, but then with a sweet sigh, she relaxed against him.

Taking a step back, she pressed her hands to her reddening cheeks. "Wow."

Tucker smiled.

Josie slid her hands to his upper arms, squeezing the heavy muscles as they roamed. "Now, will you tell me what happened to your friend?"

The warmth of her next to him made him feel calmer, and as if reading his mind, she stepped even closer, wrapping her arms tight around him.

He closed his eyes, breathing in the sweet smell of her. "It was a Monday morning...typical day at the office..." His chuckle was brittle. She gave him a patient look.

Taking a deep breath, he explained, "Our platoon was on a transport, you know one of those Humvees with an open top?" Josie nodded. "Anyhow, we were riding along this narrow city street. We thought the area was cleared, so we were kind of relaxing, joking around. Suddenly Ash jumps up. I thought he was goofing off, but then I heard the pop." Tucker held her tighter. "A bullet doesn't really go bang, it makes a pop. I heard it- pop, pop...a shooter in a window." Tucker took a deep breath. "Ash had his arms up, covering me, and that's where the bullet got him...right through his raised arm into his damned heart." Tucker was quiet a minute. His voice cracked, so he cleared it. "There is one weakness in the vest where the plates dip under the arm pit. What were the son-of-a-bitchen odds that shooter hit that exact spot?"

Josie shook her head as she hugged him tighter.

"I often wonder if it was a fair trade. That bullet was meant for me. If he hadn't gotten in the way, he'd be alive. He had a kid. A little boy who will never know his dad. For what?"

Josie pressed her cheek to his chest. After a long silence, she said quietly,

"For you. Personally, I'm glad it's you right here right now."

He relaxed his body into hers. Buried his face in her hair.

She kissed his cheek and pressed her hand to his heart. "None of it is your fault. Not your friend, not Holly. You have to let it all go."

Tucker tried to remember what he'd told her about Holly. He was pretty sure he'd not said anything. As he was about to ask her what the hell she was talking about, she moved her hands down his arms and led him to her room.

Chapter Ten

Waking him with a light kiss, Josie stood above him, smiling down at him. Tucker stretched and tried to snuggle deeper into the soft sweet sheets and pillows that were more like fluffy clouds than the thin bags of polyester he used.

"You better get up. I don't want Murray to know you slept here. I'm not sure he'd approve."

"Shit." Tucker nearly pulled a muscle rolling out of bed. Murray would never believe they didn't have sex. Hell, he barely believed it. He remembered snuggling in, her kissing him and brushing soothing fingers through his hair, and then he woke up. Had he even tried to make a move? He knew it had been a long time since he'd slept well, but to crash that close to the red zone?

Josie sat on the edge of the bed and grinned. "I wasn't going to have sex with you, no matter how good your moves were."

He almost tripped over his jeans as he pulled them up naked legs. "I wasn't..."

Josie laughed and walked from the room. When he emerged, she kissed him on the cheek. He damn near had to bite his tongue in half to stop from saying, "I love you." Instead, he offered an almost intelligible promise of getting together later.

As he stumbled out into the harsh morning light, he wondered—was she some sort of witch? Looking back over his shoulder, he saw her in her window. She waved at him, and he smiled. If she was, he supposed it didn't matter.

He practically ran to get to Murray's shop by ten.

He got his list of work: a washer to pick up, unclog a sink in cabin four, and so on. He started at the top of the list and finished as quickly as he could. The whole time he worked, thoughts of Josie occupied him. Last job done,

Murray told him to go find Josie and help her spruce up the door on one of the cottages. Some ignorant renter used it as a dart board, which was fine with Tucker because it gave him an opportunity to be with Josie. Time spent with her, even over a can of paint, suited him just fine.

He found her hard at work, humming a tune he didn't recognize. Stepping up on the porch, he asked, "You need some help?"

"You have perfect timing. I'm just about done."

He took the brush and bucket from her. "Then I better work fast, so I can remind you I helped when I ask you to spend the evening with me."

"Giving up charm for guilt?" The smile she gave him made his heart swell.

"Whatever it takes," he said, smoothing yellow paint across the grains in the door.

Josie sat beside him, her arms wrapped around her legs. "What did you have in mind?"

"Grab a bite and hit the beach?" he asked.

"Sounds good to me. I'm starved. And hot."

A truer statement was never made, Tucker thought as he glanced at Josie, swiping paint across the window.

"Oops," Josie said, hopping up and cleaning the window with a rag she had tucked in her back pocket. "There," she said, "door looks good." She grabbed the paint and stuck the lid on it. "I just need to clean these, and we're done."

They walked back toward their cottages. There was an outside spigot next to his garbage can. Tucker took the brush and started cleaning, and Josie wiped the paint from the side of the can with a paper towel. Finished, she pulled the lid off his trashcan and said, "Holy cow, these all yours?"

Tucker felt his skin turn red from his collar to his scalp.

"That's a lot of cans. That's a lot of beer," Josie said.

Tucker looked in the trash. A few nights' drinks made a more impressive stack when gathered together. "It's almost a week's worth. And I'm recycling."

"Three days. You've been here three days." Her words dripped with worry. He was about to throw out some justifications, but she stopped him. "Come on," she said. "I want to show you a special place."

Tucker agreed, happy to be moving away from his garbage. She led him down their road, past the cemetery, and down a shady valley into a thicket of woods. In the center was a small pond. The grass around it was lush and tender, the air thick with the cool moist scent of moss and earth. Warblers, mousey palm-sized birds, sang their sweet sing-song soprano from the trees overhead. It was a melodic change from the bold, near-bitchy squawks of the gulls on the shore.

"Isn't it beautiful here? It's a sanctuary. A long time ago, there was a lady who owned this land, and there was a little house. It was sort of dug into the side of that hill, like a Hobbit hole without the cuteness, so no one could see it unless they were looking for it." Josie pointed to the area where the place would have been. "Pirates would raid ships and towns, and they'd take women as spoils. Since there are hundreds of hidden coves on this island, Ocracoke was a popular pirate haven. Sometimes, if the women were lucky, if they made their way here, she'd help the captured women escape."

"I've never heard that."

"It's not in any of the written history. She didn't exactly advertise it, or it wouldn't have been a secret place."

"So, how did the women find it?"

"The lady who lived here would hang strings of shells from the trees, and the sound called to those in need."

Tucker scratched his head as he thought of tinkling shells and wondered if this woman and Mags had anything else in common.

Josie turned to him and smiled. "I'm not completely crazy, I swear."

"I wasn't thinking that."

She moved closer, stepping into him as easily as if she'd done it a million times. The sunshine filtered through the trees, making lacy patterns on her skin. Yellow paint speckled her hair, and a smidge of it was smeared on her cheek. His lips pulled into a smile as she looked up at him. She looked innocent. Gullible. He wrapped his hands around her waist and pulled her closer. When she didn't resist, he kissed her. He was much taller, but she fit perfectly into him. She seemed far more comfortable around him than she did the first day he met her, but he could still feel some hesitation.

He couldn't risk making a wrong move, and honestly, he didn't have much experience with girls like Josie. Most of his *relationships* started with a pick up and ended a few hours later. Well, there was Holly, but their hot-and-cold train wreck started and stopped so often, he couldn't remember how it first began.

No, Josie was different. He'd play it smart. So, with a final, light kiss on her lips, he pulled away.

Pink-cheeked, she cleared her throat and said, "We probably don't have time for the beach now."

"That's all right. I'm glad you brought me here. This is an interesting place."

Josie looked around. "It's one of my favorite spots. But I'm still hungry, and I bet you are too. How about I make you dinner?"

"Sounds perfect." They shared one last kiss before walking back silently. When they reached their places, she turned to him and smiled. "Give me twenty minutes. I just need a quick shower. I painted more of myself than the door."

"I noticed." He brushed his thumb across the smear of paint on her cheek. Pulling her toward him, he kissed her. "I must say, you look delicious in yellow."

"Such a flirt." With a wink and a peck on his cheek, she was gone. He stood in the shared lawn and watched her until her door was closed. With a sigh, he headed to his own place. Logically, he knew the girl was a bit weird. But there was something about her, beyond the irresistible body and a smile that made his heart stop. When he was with her, he felt content, peaceful. When she walked away, the shadows returned. He had a feeling a relationship with Josie was never something he'd be able to control. Like the waves in the ocean, he was best to just roll with it.

Showered and changed into clean shorts, he headed over for dinner. She had on cutoff denim shorts and a v-neck tee. She was dipping stir-fried chicken and vegetables over rice.

They sat together at her little table and ate. She asked him questions about Iraq. Was there much color, because it looked so brown on TV? Was it scary? Were there really fleas in the sand?...and so on.

"So, have you always lived here on the island?" he asked, turning the questions on her.

"No. I've only been here a few years."

"Where did you live before here?"

"Here and there," Josie said as she dropped her fork on her plate and scooted away from the table. "Nothing memorable. This is home now." She gathered her dirty dishes and washed them, straightening up the place with an efficiency that would have impressed a drill sergeant. Tucker was so absorbed in watching her movements, she was almost done before he thought to hop up and help. Wordlessly, he took over the job of washing while she dried and put everything away.

"About how many people live here in the off season?"

Josie brows raised in thought. "I really couldn't say for sure...a lot less?"

Dishes done. Tucker pulled the drain stop and wiped out the sink. "Did you go to school here? Was it very big?"

"I didn't technically graduate," Josie said.

Tucker nodded. "Home schooled?"

"Uh, yeah. I didn't want to start a new school for the last two years, so Hetty hired a tutor—a retired professor living on the island."

"You get to go to prom? Stuff like that?"

Josie set the potted plant back in the center of the table. "No, but none of that stuff mattered much to me. I was just happy to be here and away from home."

"Was it that bad?"

"Oh, it wasn't so much bad," Josie said, her hands trembled as she gripped the back of the chair. "Let's just say my mother and I didn't see eye to eye."

"Sounds like your mom and Murray aren't anything alike."

Josie laughed, but it was far from good humored. "Oh, no. They're night and day. No one would ever believe they're related."

Tucker nodded. "I can understand that. To be honest, one of the reasons I asked Murray for a job was to avoid a summer with my mother."

"I'm sorry to hear that, though I'm glad it brought you here."

For the first time he could remember, Josie made full eye contact with him without blushing and looking away. A warmth spread though him that was so foreign and so intimate, he suddenly felt the need to look away.

"Maybe tonight we could watch *The Birds*," she said, taking a step closer to him.

It felt good to make plans. It felt solid. He closed the space between them, leaned forward, and brushed a kiss across her lips. Her eyes fluttered closed, and she didn't pull back, so he wrapped an arm around her waist and pulled her close. He kissed her again. Her breath was warm against his cheek, her lips soft and pliant.

He could have kissed her all night, but he didn't want to push his luck.

Pulling away, but not letting go, he said, "So about those birds..."

"It's actually a stupid movie."

"But it's iconic, right? How can I say I've never seen *The Birds*?"

"True," she said. He held her hand as they made their way to the living area. She didn't pull away until she went to set up the movie. Once it was over, Tucker had to admit, the movie was lame compared to today's horror standards.

"I told you it was bad," Josie laughed.

"Hey, I thought it was awesome. I mean how Tipi Hedren made her car peal out on gravel was pretty impressive."

"Tipi Hedren?"

"Melanie? The main—"

"I know who played Melanie. I'm just shocked you know who she is."

"I lived with my mom and grandma without any sort of manly influence until my mom married my stepdad. I know all sorts of things a guy my age shouldn't have to know."

Josie took his hand and gave it a squeeze. "You never cease to amaze me."

Tucker tried really hard to think of something clever to say, but his brain wouldn't comply. Instead, it was stuck in a loop like Sally Field at the Oscars, *you like me; you like me. Shit*, his mind finally jolted awake. *What the hell? Sally Field?*

As if she could read his melting mind, she leaned close to him and whispered, "I haven't had this much fun in a long time. Thank you."

"Anytime," he said. The A/C hummed and the clock ticked. Tucker finally said, "I guess I better head on home."

"Yeah, I suppose," Josie agreed. As she stood, the soft skin of her legs brushed against his knee making his brain run away with ideas he'd best consider when she wasn't around. His heart raced, and his palms sweated. Trying to fake calm, he tripped over his own feet as he stood, stumbling into her, planting an awkward kiss on her lips.

On his walk home, he chastised himself for his lack of mojo. He had better moves than that. He shouldn't have offered to go home. She practically invited him to make a play for her. If he had, he'd probably be wrapped in her arms right now. He'd never met a girl who made him feel so comfortable and inept at the same time.

Chapter Eleven

The next morning, Tucker met up with Murray in the garage. He got his list of pick-ups and drop-offs and finished before noon. He'd worked quickly, assuming when he was done, he'd be working with Josie. Instead, when he told Murray he was finished, Murray sent him over to the main house to do some work for Hetty.

Tucker knocked on the metal screen door with the fancy *B* in the center, the kind popular in the seventies. He supposed the Banks liked to keep it old school.

Hetty yelled, "Come on in. I'm in the kitchen."

Tucker wasn't sure where the kitchen was exactly, but after a few wrong doors he found her. The kitchen was at the back of the house, secluded from all the other rooms. When he saw her, it took effort, but he managed to stifle a grin. She had her hair tied up in a kerchief and a white apron fastened around her thick middle, like a pasty, less friendly looking version of Aunt Jemima.

"Morning, Mr. Tucker." She clapped her meaty hands together like she was excited to get started.

"Morning, Ms. Hetty. Murray said you have some work for me?"

"Yes, sir," she said. "I'm looking to clean this place out a little. And I thought, since you're spending so much time with our Josie, I ought to get to know you a bit better." Hetty looked around the cluttered room. "Dear God, this place looks like an episode of *Hoarders*."

The place was stacked with stuff, crammed from floor to ceiling with boxes, totes, and odds and ends. Tucker blamed Hetty because he'd seen Murray's work space, and neat and tidy was his style.

"Life has a way of pulling a body under. You don't even realize you're drowning until you can't see the sun anymore."

Tucker nodded, at a loss for what to say.

"Here's my plan. I want to start in the kitchen; that way I can get back to cooking. I used to be an amazing cook. Now you can't even move in here. We're going to clean it out. Then I'll start making some healthy grub, and hopefully by the end of summer, I'll be able to walk my fat ass to the beach."

"I think that's a fine idea, Ms. Hetty."

"Just call me Hetty. Now, let's get started," she said, then stopped. Her shoulders sagged.

Tucker recognized that look. He'd helped young athletes weight train. They'd come in their freshman year and watch seniors lift huge amounts. They'd sometimes take one look at their beanpole skinny arms and lose hope they'd ever make it. One step at a time. One day at a time. That's what he'd tell them.

"We can do this. It's just stuff. My mom used to tell me to start at the door and work to the left."

"From the door to the left, eh?"

"Yep."

"All right. Let's start."

There was a shelf of dishes left of the door. Hetty dusted the shelf as she handed Tucker the glassware to wipe down.

"So, I hear you been spending evenings with Josie?"

"Yes, ma'am. I didn't bug her. It was her suggestion—"

Hetty laughed. "Don't get so nervous. Made my day to hear the girl was doing something normal. I love her, but she's a bit bizarre. Spends all her time reading and working and whatnot."

"She is different, but good different. She told me you had her home schooled?"

"Mmm hmm. A friend of mine is a retired college professor. He tutored her so she could pass the tests she needed to get a high school degree. She's a bright girl. Shame she'll never go to college."

"What makes you say that?" Tucker rubbed the dust off a rooster-topped dish.

Hetty turned and looked at him square in the face. There were beads of sweat above her lip and on her forehead. "Haven't you noticed? She lives like a hermit, avoids almost everyone. The girl totally hates crowds. And don't tell her I told you this, but she *feels* people."

"Like walks up and—" Tucker held out his hand like he was touching someone. He imagined shy Josie going up to people and feeling their faces like a blind person. It was absurd.

Hetty hooted. "No. My goodness, no." She laughed a bit more. "No, she senses people. She can tell you what you're feeling. She can tell if a person is good or bad. She *feels* people. She doesn't talk of it much. She's sensitive 'bout being called crazy."

Tucker thought of all the times he felt like Josie was reading his mind. But that was nonsense.

"Hah!" Hetty pointed a finger at him. "She's done it to you, hasn't she? Guessed all the stuff you try to hide?"

"She is very acute." Tucker set the rooster dish on the now clean shelf.

"She's freaky. And if she's around someone she senses is dark, she loses it. Given that, can you imagine her on a college campus? She'd have a panic attack within an hour. That's why I'm happy she's spending time with you. I want her to have a normal life."

Hetty plopped her weight down in a chair and sighed. "And that's why I'm doing this. If I expect Josie to face her demons, I can at least kick mine in the shins." She fanned herself. "Oh dear lord, I am one fat woman. This shouldn't be so hard, child."

"Take it slow. You'll get there. Might feel like you'll never make it, but you will. You just have to focus on what you have done, not what needs done. See?" he asked, looking at the now sparkling shelf. "It looks good. We'll get this wall done today. That only leaves three more. Get all that done; I can teach you how to spit shine your boots."

Hetty laughed. "I don't wear boots, but I like the way you think. I suppose Murray does something right every now and again."

Tucker nodded. He gave Hetty his spray cleaner and dust rags so she could stay seated and dust the knick knacks he handed her.

"So, how did you meet Murray?"

"Oh hell, we grew up together here on the island. Our families go way back. Aren't too many of us left. Hard for plain folk like fishermen to make ends meet here anymore. Murray and I just got lucky that we have the cottages. Rentals from the summer keep us afloat. Can you believe there was a time not too long ago when life here was all about fishing, fig trees, and family? It's sort of sad. Most of the islanders have sold out and moved onto the mainland." Hetty sighed. "I suppose that's progress. Hard to tell what it will be like in twenty years."

Tucker shrugged. "It's pretty perfect right now. I love it here. This is a beautiful place."

"You have natural island thinking, Tucker. I'm surprised you haven't taken up fishing with Murray."

Tucker laughed. "I'm too busy chasing the girl."

Hetty let out a hoot as she slapped her knee. "Well, I give you my approval. You keep on chasing. I must say, our wall looks pretty good. Those boxes there on the floor—they're filled with old beauty magazines. Why in God's name I thought I needed to keep years of old fashions is beyond me. You take them on out of here, and we'll call it a day. That will give you plenty of time to chase the girl."

Tucker stacked the boxes three high and lifted them off the floor.

"You sure we're done?"

"Yep. I'm doing like you said. I am going to sit here and stare at this pretty-looking wall and imagine how nice this place will be by the end of summer."

"You're a wise woman."

Tucker carried the boxes out and returned for the rest. Six boxes in all. He tossed them on the back of the truck, planning to take them to the dump for recycling.

"You running away?" Josie asked with a laugh. She was dressed in paint-splattered shorts and white tee with her hair piled sloppily on top of her head.

He couldn't imagine her looking any cuter.

"Nope. Helping Hetty clean out her house."

"Really? Wow. I'm shocked. She never throws out anything. What's in the boxes?"

"Old magazines."

Josie nodded. "You taking them to the dump?"

"Yeah, you want to go?"

"Oh my, Mr. Boone, you certainly know how to offer a girl a good time."

Tucker laughed. "I could throw in lunch, just to make it more impressive."

"No need, you had me at trash dump," she said with a laugh.

Tucker pulled the keys out of his pocket and waved for her to follow. They drove along with the windows down. Unloading the truck only took a few minutes, and then they were back on the road. Josie told him to take a right. The road quickly turned from packed sand to a soft, barely traveled road. Fortunately, the truck had four-wheel drive and slowly climbed the rutted sand. At the crest of the road appeared a wide band of powder blue sky. Below that was mossy green grass and brackish water covered in copper-colored algae.

"Stop here," Josie said. "It's a bird sanctuary, so we can't go any farther."

Tucker shut off the engine. "Are we looking to get attacked by birds?"

Josie giggled as she shook her head. Chewing on her nail, she turned bright red.

"What is it?" Tucker reached out and grabbed her arm, pulling her toward him.

"Promise not to laugh?" she asked with a grimace.

"Promise," he said, laying his forehead against hers.

"Well, I've never gone parking. All my friends did, but I never got a chance. So, I want you to kiss me, so I can say I made out with a guy in a car."

Tucker slid his hands into her hair and laughed.

"You promised not to laugh," she said, draping her arms over his shoulders.

"I'm definitely not laughing at you. Totally a laugh of pleasure and delight. Of all the requests I've had today, this one is the best."

"Considering the other was cleaning with Hetty, the bar wasn't set very high."

"Well then, let me clarify. That is the best request I've had in a lifetime."

"Really?" She made a pouty face. "Here I thought I was the one with the boring life."

Chuckling, he kissed her, happy to help her cross *making out in a car* off her list.

Chapter Twelve

They ate dinner while watching another movie. She seemed relaxed, sitting with her back against his chest, looking up at him to share a laugh or a snarky movie comment. Perfect position for teasing kisses. At the end of the evening, he kissed her good-bye and headed home.

Back at his place, he lay down on the couch. Today was a good day. Kissing was natural, perfect. His mind wandered to more intimate situations, but he was quick to rein it in. Josie was different. She wasn't some barfly he wanted to nail. He wanted to make her smile, hear her laugh...

In the quiet of the cottage, he heard her door close. Hopping up, he looked outside as Josie stepped off her porch. She was only wearing a little nightgown, so Tucker immediately worried she was sleep walking. He grabbed his shoes and followed behind, whispering her name. She didn't seem to hear him.

She went down the road, past the cemetery, back into the thicket of woods she'd led him to earlier. Tucker got more nervous with every step. He tried to remember what he knew about sleepwalkers. Should he grab her? Yell at her? In the middle of the clearing, she turned to him. The moonlight made her skin glow. She smiled at him and said, "Did you hear them, Tucker?"

"Hear what?" he asked.

"The shells."

He shook his head as he stepped toward her. "Come on, Josie. I think I better take you back."

"No, I heard them. I heard the call. They called you too. You're here for me."

Smiling, she backed to the edge of the water, turned, and dove in. It seemed like she was under forever.

"Josie?" He kicked off his shoes and dove in. The water was so dark, it mirrored the moon. He couldn't find her anywhere. He called her name again. No response. Diving under the black water again and again, he reached out with his hands feeling for her body. He took a gulp of air as he broke the surface. "God damn it, Josie," he said, panicked. Then she emerged, her hair slicked back, eyes closed. When she opened them, she seemed shocked to see him there.

"Tucker," she said. "Why are you here?"

"Better question is, what are you doing? You scared the hell out of me. Do you sleepwalk?"

"I was dreaming. And I felt hot, so I came for a swim."

"You weren't following shells?"

Tipping her head to one side, she looked confused. "No, just needed to cool off."

Swimming toward her, he said, "Then turn up your AC. It's not safe for you to be out swimming by yourself."

"I'm a good swimmer."

Tucker thought of the many men visiting the island. Any one of them would follow a half-naked chick into the woods. He started to tell her that, but something made him stop. Frustrated, he swam to the bank and climbed out. The grass was tender and cool, a nice contrast to the heat of the night air. He sat, knees bent, arms around his legs and watched her swim toward him.

"You mad at me?"

He sighed. "You scared me. I'm not mad."

"Good," she said, stepping out of the water. The thin nightgown was soaked—clinging to her body, nearly transparent.

"No way," he said, forcing himself to look to the moon. The cosmos was screwing with him. That had to be it. She couldn't be this clueless.

Sitting beside him, she untangled her wet curls. "It's sweet of you to worry."

He looked back at her. Her smile was guileless. She wasn't even trying to turn him on, yet every red blood cell in his body had traveled south of his belly button.

"I suppose we should get back," she said.

Thinking of her near nakedness and a boner he could never hide, he shook his head. "No, we should stay here a bit."

"And talk?"

"Yeah. Talk."

Crossing her legs under her, she leaned back, throat exposed along with everything else.

"Josie," he said looking her up and down.

She looked down at herself. With a squeal, she sat straight up and hugged her knees to her chest. "I'm sorry. Oh my God, I didn't realize."

"That's why I mentioned it."

Laying her cheek against her knee, she squeezed her eyes closed. "That's so embarrassing."

"Don't be," he said. "You're beautiful."

She smiled. "Thank you…did you see very much?"

"No." He lied. He'd seen everything. He wouldn't need porn ever again.

Tucker couldn't formulate thoughts that didn't involve scooping her up and laying her back on the grass. They sat in silence for quite a while. His pulse was headed back to steady, and he was about to suggest they go when she said, "Tucker? Can I ask you a question?"

"Sure," he said.

Biting her lip, she was quiet a minute before asking, "You ever have dreams about *it*?"

"It? As in *it*, like sex?"

"Yeah," she said, tucking her legs tighter to her chest.

"Shit yeah. Two, three times a night."

She laughed. "Seriously?"

"Okay, so maybe not that often, but it's hardly a rare occurrence."

She was quiet a while, like she was thinking over what he said.

He took a deep breath and asked, "Have you ever…you know?"

She ignored the question. He was about to ask again, but she looked at him and asked, "Would you kiss me again? Like earlier?"

Cupping her cheek, he tilted her face until she was looking up at him, and he kissed her. Deliberately lingering, teasing her lips, until she was pulling him closer. Gradually, he eased her back until he was lying beside her on the bed of soft grass. Her hands felt hot on the naked flesh of his shoulders as she clung to him. Kissing the hollow of her throat, he could feel her pulse quicken against his lips. When he swept his lips across the swell of her breasts, she gasped but held his head to her chest, pulling him closer.

Trailing kisses back to her lips, he savored her, tasted her. Her body arched against him as he ran a hand down the curve of her waist to the hem of her nightgown. Her thighs were silky smooth, spreading for his touch. Tucker wasn't an amateur. He knew from the feel of her he could take her. Or he could finish her with a touch.

She never answered his question, and if she was a virgin, they should probably talk it over. A girl didn't wait as long as Josie had, and not have some moral or relationship convictions. Was Josie the kind of girl he'd want for the rest of his life? His body screamed yes, but he needed a clear head. He couldn't come up with an honest answer while her body moved against him. He increased the intensity of his hand. Her body stiffened, a leg wrapped around his, and then the shudder.

Kissing her throat, he pulled his hand away and tucked her body closer to his.

"How did you…why…oh my goodness…I don't think I was breathing."

He couldn't help but smile. His body wasn't satisfied, but his ego was.

He kissed her, unhurried and teasing. She looked at him for a long moment, her hands gripping his forearms. "Could you…love me like that?"

His voice caught in his throat, his confidence suddenly put to the test. Her breath against his neck might be enough to end him. Propping himself on an elbow, he looked down at her. She looked nervous and doubtful, like she thought he might say no.

She kissed him. It was a hesitant, nervous graceless attempt at seduction. Pulling back, she bit her lip. "I'm making a fool of myself, aren't I?"

He pulled her close. "The hell you are. You're killing me. Damn Josie,

what are you doing to me?"

"I'm sorry," she said.

He kissed her and wrapped a hand around the back of her neck. He could feel her warmth against his skin through the thin fabric of her nightgown. A battle raged between his mind and his flesh. He wanted to tear the fabric from her body and make love to her right here in the moonlight. But his mind said he should make her wait, make sure this really was what she wanted.

She looked at him and said softly, "I know what I want."

"It's not that..." he hesitated. *Why was he talking her out of this?*

"Is it protection?"

Heat surged through him. They were definitely on the same page. Josie was obviously aware of what she was asking for. Tucker felt his back pocket to make sure he hadn't lost his wallet in their midnight swim. It was there. "I've got that covered. I just need to know this is really what you want."

"I can't explain why I need this. I just need you to trust me."

"I do. Tell me what you want, Josie. I'll do anything."

She pulled her nightgown over her head and tossed it on the ground. Gathering her close, he held her naked body against him. She felt warm, slick with sweat from the heat and the quickened pulse. Kissing her, his hands roamed down the smooth contours of her neck to the perfect curve of her shoulders.

His soul knew her a million times over, even if it was their bodies' first time. He caressed her flesh like a devoted addict, satiating his tangible understanding of her. He relished in the feel of her legs, smooth as velvet wrapped around his hips; he delighted in the taste of her moistened flesh as their bodies heated up; and his heart melted with the little gasp in his ear as his body joined hers. He understood it all in that moment. She was everything, and he was nothing without her.

Chapter Thirteen

The sun filtered through the crack in the curtain, casting a line of light across the scuffed hardwood floor. Tucker rolled onto his back and stretched. There was a foreign feeling in his chest—a levity of spirit, possibly even an eagerness to roll out of bed and start a new day. Throwing back the covers, he swung his legs to the floor. He snuck a peek out his window. Josie's silhouette moved about her kitchen. His lightened heart easily picked up speed.

Skipping breakfast, he headed to Josie's and knocked on her door.

"Tucker," she said, opening the door only wide enough for her head to poke out.

"You all right?"

"I, uh, I think I may be coming down with the flu. Or something."

She sounded fine. A bad feeling crept up his spine, but he shook it off. "Can I get you anything?"

"No, I'm okay. I just need sleep."

"I could keep you company." He leaned an arm against the door frame.

"That's all right. I'll be fine in a few days."

He nodded, but didn't move.

"I think I better go lie down." Josie took a step back, closing the door.

Tucker placed his hand against the door, stopping her. "Josie, about last night…"

Josie's hand flew to her mouth and her face drained of all color. "Please don't. Not now."

She did look like she was about to vomit. Tucker began to think maybe she was sick. "You have my number, right?"

She nodded.

"You call me if you need anything."

"I will," she said, shoving the door closed. He heard the lock turn, then the sound of footsteps as she ran through her house.

"Well, hell." He headed to the garage and got his work done. Afterward, he visited Ella and picked up soup and ginger ale for Josie. He planned to make it for her, but she took the bag from him with a "thank you" and nearly slammed the door in his face.

He gave her three days, then returned, knocking on her door.

She answered looking like hell. Her curly hair was fuzzy, sticking out all over as if she'd been electrocuted, and she had large shadows under her eyes. He shoved the door open before she had a chance to hold it closed against him. Stepping into her cottage, he saw that the bag of food was still on her table. He looked inside. She hadn't even unloaded it. There were no dishes in the sink. Turning to her, he asked, "Have you been eating?"

"Of course."

Tipping her chin until she had to look him in the eye, he studied her. Her eyes were rimmed in red and her skin was too pale. Her hand wrapped around his wrist and her eyes sparkled with tears. His thumb brushed the tender skin of her cheek. "What is it, Josie? What's wrong?"

She swallowed and tried to back away, but he wouldn't let her go. Wrapping his hand around the back of her neck, he held onto her.

"You're going to tell me what's going on. No more I'm sick bullshit, either."

She bit her lip. Her chin quivered, and a tear rolled down her cheek. Tucker's own eyes stung and his chest tightened. Pulling her close, he wrapped her in his arms. As if exhausted, she sighed and laid her cheek against his chest.

Tucker kissed the top of her head. "Is this about the other night?"

She nodded.

"Then we should talk about it."

She shook her head.

"It was special. The two of us—"

"I don't...I think you're reading too much into it. I shouldn't have...done that. We were better as friends."

"I see." Tucker didn't know what to say. He felt like he had a bit of the flu. So, she was out of sorts because she had regrets. That happens. Girls did shit they wish they hadn't all the time. He just never expected he'd be one of them. Like an idiot, he'd completely misread what was between them. He let go of her.

"I think you should go. I need time," she said.

"You're joking, right?"

"No. I…I'm afraid you need more from me than I could ever give."

His eyes narrowed. He hadn't asked her for a damn thing.

"Don't be mad. I just…" She stepped toward him, but he backed away. He didn't need her pity, so he left, slamming the door behind him. He expected her to follow, say she didn't mean it and ask him to come back, but she didn't.

So, he avoided her. For eight days, he barely looked in her direction, much less spoke to her. He didn't need some crazy chick messing with his head. He worked for Hetty with a fury. Throwing things away was good for his soul. Then in the afternoons, he drove to Ella's. She gave him full use of her office and internet to make searches and phone calls for any clues on Maddy.

Finding information on his sister was what he came here for in the first place. He never should have let Josie distract him. Unfortunately, that search frustrated him too.

Madison Morgan had zero online presence—not a single profile on any of the social media sites, not even on the ancient *My Space*. Ella worked right there with him. She was full of ideas, thinking of things he surely would have missed. Like, registering Maddy's profile with the National Missing and Unidentified Persons System. There was no match. With Gloria's help, he ran a credit check to see if Maddy's social security number was ever used for a loan or a credit card. Nothing. He even ran her information through the welfare system and Public Record Finder. Maddy was either deep in hiding, or dead. As a last resort, he even called the boyfriend who dropped her off the night she was last seen. The boyfriend, Devon Riggs, now a young man, was surprised he called. Tucker apologized for the intrusion.

"Hey, no. Not at all. It's bugged me for years that no one seemed to care about Maddy's disappearance. She was a sweet girl. A bit of a hothead. I mean, we had our share of fights and all. You didn't tell Maddy no, and you did things her way," Devon said with a chuckle.

"Police reports say you were the last person who admits to seeing her. The night she disappeared, did she seem normal?"

"She was pissed at her mom and dad for not letting her go to Arie's. She had to crawl out of a window and meet me at the end of her street for a ride to the Stone's."

"So, she was mad?"

"Yeah. But that's typical Maddy. She was always bitching about her parents. Always threatening to run away."

"She said she was running away?" Tucker rubbed the top of his head.

"Yeah, but like I said, she was going to run away all the time. I never thought she'd actually do it. I figured she'd get to Arie's and calm down."

"Evidently, she didn't calm down."

"I don't know what happened. Honestly, all things considered, I think Stone killed her. Just like he did Arie."

"But she told you she was running away."

"Yeah. But you had to know Maddy. She was all talk, and she was real high-strung that night. Talking a mile-a-minute. One second she was slamming Gloria. Next minute, she was talking about getting even with the Stones. She was more hyper than that damn dog she dragged with her—what the hell was his name?"

"Toby?" Tucker offered.

"That's it. Toby. She said her and Ariel were taking the dog and skipping town."

"And you didn't warn anyone?"

"No. Looking back on it, I realize I should have. But back then, I never dreamed she'd be in danger at that house. I thought the Stones were perfect. When my dad lost his job, Jeb Stone hired him. When my little sister needed surgery, the Stones paid for it. I figured Maddy would get to Ariel's and Ariel would talk some sense into her."

"I take it you don't trust them anymore?"

"Nope. Maddy and that dog got out of my car, walked up the drive-way, and went into that house. Then no one ever saw them again. *I saw them go in.* So, where the hell did she go?"

"And that was the last time you saw or heard from Maddy?"

"Yep. Not another peep."

"And no one questioned the Stones?"

"Nope. Everyone assumed she ran away. But I'll never buy that. You've got to understand, those girls were tight. Maddy wouldn't have left Ariel in a million years. I swear. I knew her. Maddison Morgan didn't run away."

Tucker sighed into the phone. "I appreciate the information. If you can think of anything, no matter how trivial, give me a call?"

Tucker thanked him and hung up the phone.

Ella sighed, slapping her hands on her knees. "Well, I'm plum out of ideas."

"Me too." He powered down the computer and spun away from the desk. "I appreciate the help. Even if we didn't find shit."

"You know the storyteller in me hoped like hell that one of these bites would've turned up something." Ella took her place behind the counter.

"I wish it had too. I suppose I'll buy another twelve-pack and head home."

Tucker stepped out into the sun. There was a group of shoppers coming up the steps, so he went right, down the wooden ramp to a shady breezeway between the grocery store and the bait shop.

His phone buzzed with a call. Pulling it out of his pocket, he stared at it. Santos. He'd avoided talking to him since he had his conversation with Marie, instead leaving their interactions to emails and messages. But it was time to put that to rest.

"Hey, *David*," Tucker said when he answered.

"So, Marie did call you, eh? She wouldn't give me a straight answer." Santos' laugh was tight.

"Yeah. Hell, I didn't even know you had a first name. Thought you were just Santos, like Madonna and Cher."

"Oh hell, mi hermano, I'm way better looking than them. Got bigger tatas too."

Tucker couldn't help but laugh. "I miss you, buddy."

"Then come see me. You're probably only a few hours away."

Not being able to leave Josie was his first thought. His second was how full of bull his first thought was. She evidently had no more use for him. Why the hell would he stick around? "I may take you up on that. Make sure you're keeping it real down there."

Santos was quiet. Then he said, "I hate myself for this, man. I came here to help. I mean I've got nothing holding me anywhere, so why not? And then, the more time I spend with her, with Tom-Tom. I love them. It's wrong. You don't know how bad I wish she was someone else's widow."

Tucker thought of Josie. She left him feeling hollow. Tucker leaned against the store watching families unload from cars. Happily vacationing. Santos and Marie could have that. Both of them being miserable wasn't going to bring Ash back, or make the pain in his chest any better. "Look," Tucker said. "Don't overthink it, all right? You love her; you guys should be happy. Ash would want that. I'm sure if another man was going to raise Tommy, he'd want it to be you."

"I appreciate that. I'm not going to lie and say I'd have walked without your blessing, because I'm in deep. But it means a lot. And we're taking it slow. I plan to talk to Ash's mom too. I won't disrespect his memory."

Tucker nodded. "I trust you, brother."

"That means a lot, man. So, will you come down here? I could probably get you hired on."

"Me, be a cop?"

"Why the hell not? What else you got going on?"

"Nothing, really. Still trying to find that sister."

"Oh yeah, the sister. That's actually why I called."

Tucker stood up straight, suddenly feeling a spark of hope. "You find something?"

"I watched the interrogation tapes of her friend, the one who ended up dead?"

"Yeah?"

"She swears she saw her stepdad kill Maddy."

"And nothing came of that?"

"Well, it seems the girl was suicidal and more than a little crazy. She witnessed this *murder* during an out-of-body experience after an attempted overdose."

Tucker groaned. He remembered Gloria telling him Ariel Stone was psychic. How had he gotten caught up in so much insanity? Murdered girls, psychics, and pedophiles. This shit belonged in Hollywood. Add in the cold shoulder he got from Josie, and he was ready to hop in his car and head to Santos's house tonight. "This is a total dead end, isn't it?"

"Seems that way. Even the letter you sent me got us nowhere. That lady? Your, uh, stepmom? She says Applewold PD took the envelope the letter came in, and it's now gone. If we had that, or if the letter wasn't handled over and over, we might have been able to get prints or DNA. Hell, even a date stamp would have been great. Gloria swears the letter arrived after Ariel was murdered, but there's no proof, and for all I know it's a grieving mom grasping at straws."

"I appreciate you trying. I owe you one."

"I'll call in that favor. Get on down here."

"I think I will. But I'm working for a guy. He hired me when I needed a job, and I don't want to leave him short-handed. I'll talk to him this evening."

"All right. Keep me posted."

"Will do," Tucker said, then hung up.

The gravel crunched under his feet as he made his way back to his car. He tossed his twelve-pack and a bagged sandwich in the passenger seat and headed back to his cottage. As he drove, he thought of Josie. Should he go talk to her? Be up front with her—was there any reason for him to stay on this island? Pounding the steering wheel with the heel of his hand, he detested

being *that* guy: the desperate son of a bitch begging a woman who wanted nothing to do with him. Screw her. Walk away. Keep some pride.

By the time he arrived, he had himself broiled into a seriously bad mood. He slammed his door as he got out of his car. First step he took, his foot sunk into a puddle. He was so distracted with his soggy shoe and the litany of colorful curses he was spewing, he didn't notice Murray standing in his yard.

"Bad day, Tucker? I came to ask for a favor, but now, I'm not so sure."

Chapter Fourteen

Tucker shook his head. It wasn't Murray's fault his niece was making his life miserable. "Hey, Murray. No, I'm fine. What did you need?"

"Hetty's niece is getting married, and she's bringing some of her girlfriends to the island for some sort of bridal stag party, or whatever in the hell women call it." Murray swiped his forehead with a handkerchief. "Hetty promised them *The Big Cottage* would be move-in ready by tonight for the weekend. So, I have a list of things that need done and some groceries they asked for." He pulled the list out of his pocket. "And she wants firewood in the pit in the backyard. I know it's a Friday night, and you put in a full day already. Doggone Hetty."

"It's no problem. I don't have anything planned." Tucker grabbed the list.

"Thank you, son. Josie is over there putting on clean sheets and turning on the AC. She'll go with you to the store. I already told her."

"That's not—"

"Oh shoot, she can go to the store. She's been moping in that cottage for days. She needs to get out. If not, she'll end up like Hetty. Can't even get the damned woman to come out in the yard. I know this shindig was her way of getting out of going to the wedding. This all-inclusive- weekend-getaway is her gift to the bride. I told her to get her a damned crockpot. When she got the invite, I thought she might actually go. I mean she's been doing great work with you in the house. Life was beginning to feel like it could be normal. But with the wedding a week away, she says no and comes up with this. Damned ridiculous. She won't leave that house, much less the island."

"Give her time. She seems happier every day. Josie—I'm not so sure about. I think it's me she's dodging."

"That's bullshit. She may be mad at me too. I told her I wanted the night visits to the cemetery stopped. I put up with it for years because I knew the

girl didn't have any sort of mom, but she's an adult now. Time for her to quit consulting a dead woman with her troubles. She's been hunkered down in her place since I said it. Did she tell you she talks to her guardian angel in the cemetery?"

Tucker tried to convince himself he was lucky she dumped him. Consulting angels in the cemetery? That had to be certifiable insanity. Logic offered him a high five, but his damned heart still ached. "No, she never mentioned that. She said she went there to pray."

"Yeah, well…whatever she calls it, it ain't normal. I want some damned normal in this place for a change."

Tucker nodded. "Sounds like a good day to fish?"

Murray pulled off his straw hat and nodded. "Sure does. It's good having you here, Tucker. Refreshing to have a sane man among the weird women."

Murray thanked him and headed back to the garage. Tucker put his food and beer away and walked across the gravel drive to The Big Cottage. Nestled behind shrubs and fig trees, the two-story, four-bedroom place was the biggest rental on the lot, hence the name, The Big Cottage. Tucker yelled for Josie from the wide open door. She came out of the downstairs bedroom looking harried and sweaty. "I can't get the AC to come on. I tried to call Murray."

"I'll check it," he said. She looked skeptical, making him all the more intent on getting it working. He went to the side of the cottage where the large grey unit sat idle in the sun. Pulling off the control panel, he changed the fuse. Within seconds, it was humming and spinning.

When he went back inside, Josie was nowhere to be seen. He assumed she was the one opening and closing drawers in the downstairs bedroom. Tucker went to the backyard, grabbed a hatchet from the shed, and started gathering fallen tree limbs from the woods around Murray's property. He wasn't sure how far Murray's land went back, but he didn't have to go far before he had enough to burn a campfire for the evening.

Josie came out on the porch and watched him as he finished. When he looked up, she blushed and said, "I'm done. Murray said they needed groceries too?"

"Yeah, but I can get them if you don't want to go."

"I, uh..." she stammered.

"I'll make it easy on you. I don't want you to go. I'd hate for you to have to spend more than ten minutes with me." He walked past her into the house.

"Tucker, I..." She followed him, grabbed his arm and opened her mouth to speak, but stopped. A sound at the front door caught her attention.

The house was open-concept. The living, kitchen, and dining area was one large space. From their spot in the kitchen, they could see the front door as it swung open and a gaggle of women poured in with overnight bags and loud, happy voices. Josie looked about as comfortable as a nun on a stripper pole. Tucker stepped closer to her.

There were six women in various shapes and sizes. A tall blonde with short dark nails and blood red lipstick stepped forward and grabbed Tucker's arms. "Oh, you guys got me some man candy. How sweet."

Tucker pulled away with a laugh. "No ma'am. We're the help. Just getting the place ready. Looks like you guys got here faster than Murray expected. I'm headed out for your groceries. Josie?" He turned to Josie. She took a step forward, but the blond blocked her progress.

"Oh no! You don't have to do that alone. I'll go with you," the blonde said.

"Marcia!" A red-haired woman squealed with delight. "You little slut. Hitting on the help a week before the wedding?"

"Thanks for the offer, but I have Josie. Josie?"

"You don't mind, do you, hon?" Marcia asked Josie.

Tucker expected her to step up and save him, but she shrugged and said, "Tucker's a big boy."

Marcia grabbed Tucker's arm and dragged him out of the cottage. "Shall I drive?" she asked.

"Fine by me," Tucker agreed. And off they went to Ella's for groceries and ample amounts of alcohol. Marcia couldn't keep her hands off him as they shopped. She was pretty enough, but damn was she loud and forward.

She was like a skinny, happy, and excessively horny Hetty.

Shopping done and delivered, Marcia asked him to build the fire. By the time that was done, the noise from the house was at a boisterous hum. The women had evidently picked up a few men from the local hotels while he and Marcia were shopping, so the place was in full party mode. Marcia met him at the fire and rubbed his back in slow, sensual circles. "Now, since you worked so hard, let me get you a drink."

"No, but thanks. I still have work to do."

"So, when you're done, you'll come back?"

"I'll see."

Marcia slapped his ass as he walked away. He was beginning to feel like a party favor. Heading back to his cottage, he was happy to see Josie sitting on her porch. He leaned against the column. "That's quite the crowd over there. You going back?"

"No way," she said.

"Aren't they your cousins?"

"Huh? Oh, no. She's Hetty's niece. I've never met her before."

A voice yelled from behind him, "Tucker! You said you had work to do. You don't look so busy to me." Marcia had changed into the shortest dress he'd seen in a long time. She was carrying her sandals as she walked across the grass. "I'm taking a walk on the beach; want to join me?"

"Maybe later. I need to talk to Josie about some stuff."

"Okay. I'll walk slow," she said, wagging her shoes at him.

Once she was gone, Tucker banged his head against the column. "I swear, she's relentless. I don't know how to shake her."

"Why shake her?" Josie asked, pulling her legs up and crossing them. "She seems like she'd be fun for you."

Tucker took a step off the porch. "So, that's it? You really don't give a damn, do you?"

"I didn't say that," Josie said, her voice was quiet, shaky.

"But it wouldn't bug you at all if I hooked up with the wedding tramp?"

"You'd probably be happier with her. She's pretty…and vibrant."

"What the hell, Josie? I swear to God, you are the most aggravating woman I have ever met. I thought we had a connection. I've been wracking my brain trying to figure out what's going on, but I come up with nothing every single damn time. And you know what? I don't need this shit. I don't need the complication." He took two steps toward the beach path and then turned back around. "I don't need you screwing with my head or my life."

Josie leaped from her seat with a small whimper and ran into her cottage. Tucker thought of following, his gut screamed for him to, but he didn't. He turned and followed Marcia down the path.

He found her sitting at the top of the beach looking down over the water. "Hey," he said. "Why aren't you enjoying your party?"

Turning to him, she smiled. "I needed to call Gary, my fiancé. I didn't want him to hear the party. He doesn't trust me."

Tucker sat beside her, laughing. "You don't say."

"Oh, my God," she said, poking his ribs. "Don't you judge me. Gary has screwed more women than I can count. I've only had two. Men, that is. Not women. Though there was the one time in college with my roommate's bi cousin, but I don't know how you count that, so I guess, maybe three. Compared to the girls back there, I'm a saint. I don't think one last fling is that horrible."

Tucker wanted to ask her if she even loved the guy, but he suspected he knew that answer, and quite honestly, he didn't care. If she wanted a fling, he could use the distraction.

"So, tell me, Tucker." She ran her finger along the collar of his shirt, grazing his skin. "You as good as you look?"

Tucker grabbed her by the arms and pulled her close. "I'm better."

Growling, she wrapped her arms around him, practically jamming her tongue down his throat. She tasted like cigarette smoke and beer. Just like Holly. Nothing like Josie. Not that Josie gave a damn about him. Hell, she'd been just as eager to get laid as Marcia was now. Maybe he was just lucky enough to find horny women who only wanted to use him. Why should he care? He would have loved this problem when he was sixteen. Women. They

were all alike—horny and conniving.

You know damned good and well Josie didn't use you.

The thought flowed through his head making him jerk away as if he'd suddenly realized he was kissing a snake. Josie was nothing like other women, and she hadn't been looking for quick sex. She loved him that night; he felt it. He didn't have a clue what the hell was wrong with her since then, but it wasn't because she used him. He wished she was as easy to read as Marcia, who he guessed was planning to screw him to get even. Curious to see if his gut was anywhere near correct, Tucker asked, "Gary didn't happen to cheat on you, did he?"

Marcia's face fell. Her lipstick was smeared across her cheek and now, the onslaught of sudden tears made her mascara run. "He…he…found his ex online and took her to Bermuda during a business trip. God, I hate her. But I need him. If I dump him, I'll lose everything. I can't even confront him. I'm scared to death he'll admit he loves her." Burying her face on her hands, she cried, "Oh my God, I am so freaking pathetic."

Tucker pulled her in and hugged her. "You're not pathetic. Love sucks."

Laughing, she wiped away a tear. "It does, doesn't it?"

"Yep. Seems relationships are the quickest route to heartache."

She nodded and rested her cheek on his chest.

Tucker rested his chin on the top of her head and sighed. "I know my life was much less complicated when all I had to worry about were hook-ups and one-nighters."

Chapter Fifteen

Walking back from the beach, he said good-bye to Marcia and headed to Josie's. He decided he had nothing to lose; Josie owed him answers. Looking in her window, he could see her on the couch. He knocked on the door, but she ignored him. Her arms crossed over her chest, she looked pissed. He banged on the door until it bowed. She continued to ignore him, putting her hands over her ears like a child. Furious, he rammed into the door, shoulder first. On the third try, the casing splintered and the door flew open.

Josie jumped from her spot on the couch and squealed. "What the hell are you doing?"

"I wanted to talk to you."

"Who says I want to talk to you?" she yelled back.

Her eyes were puffy and her nose red. His walk to the beach with Marcia bugged her. He knew it. He pulled her close. "Why are you doing this to me?"

"Doing what?" Her eyes were narrowed and lips pressed into a petulant bow.

"I miss you, damn it. I don't understand why you're avoiding me."

"I am not avoiding you," she screamed at him as if he was yards away instead of inches.

"The hell you aren't. That night, in the woods, you said it was what you wanted. You wanted me—"

"I don't want to talk about it. I told you…it was a mistake." Her eyes sparkled with tears and she tried to squirm out of his grip, but he wouldn't let go.

"No, it wasn't. If having sex with me that night was just something you regretted…something that *complicated* our friendship, you wouldn't be so pissed off that I went with Marcia. You wouldn't care if Marcia and I had—"

"Shut up." She pounded on his chest. "Don't you dare say it."

"Say what? That Marcia wanted me to screw her right there on the beach?"

"I hate you. I hate you, Tucker Boone. I wish I'd never met you."

"Do you? Do you hate me enough for me to walk out of here, go find the bride, and find out what tricks she can do with—"

A haymaker she threw with her left caught him completely off guard clipping his chin and making his jaw sing.

It took a minute for his brain to register what happened. She punched him.

Looking down at her, he could almost feel her eyes burn through him with her rage.

She loved him.

Taking another step toward her, he secured both her hands in his. "I love you, Josie. I love you, and I only want to be with you. No one else."

A fat tear rolled down her cheek.

He lowered his head toward her. His words were soft. "You love me, Josie. I'm not just a complication, and it scares you. Admit it."

"No," she said.

"Then what?"

"I…I think we were better as friends."

It felt like a stab to his heart, but he kept his cool. "Friends?"

"Yeah. Friends."

A battle waged in his mind. Did he want to stay here and be her friend? Look at her every day and know they were over? Maybe she was scared and needed time…

Josie interrupted his thoughts with a question that made her voice quiver. "Did you, you know, with her, like you did with me?"

"Who? Marcia? Hell no." He moved closer, his voice barely above a whisper. "And that night? What was between us wasn't about sex. It wasn't some physical attraction out of control. It was more. Do you understand that?"

She nodded. "But it was a mistake. We never should have done it." He offered her a heavy shrug. "You mean a lot more to me than sex. I won't lie and say I didn't love doing it. That it probably ruined me for all other women, but if you regret it, then I suppose we're friends."

"Really?"

"Really."

A tear trickled out of the corner of her eye. She quickly wiped it away. "I've missed you."

"I've missed you too."

She gave him a hug. He held her, not wanting to let her go. It was like sweet torture, but at least she was right here, right now. He'd worry about tomorrow later. Josie was the first to pull away. "Will you stay? I could make you food?"

A small amount of relief washed over him. "I'm starving. I had a sandwich from Ella's but stuck it on the fridge to get the cottage ready."

"I can't compete with that. But I do have pancakes?"

"Sounds perfect."

Josie walked to the kitchen. Tucker followed her. As she worked, he leaned against the counter and watched. Tendrils of hair brushed against her slender neck. Her eyes were still puffy, and it tugged at his heart.

Flipping golden pancakes over in the skillet, she asked, "So, what happened with the wayward bride?"

Tucker crossed his arms over his chest as he debated how much to tell her. Should he tell her she kissed him? That he considered having sex with her…to prove Josie didn't control him, and then admit that she did? That he stayed and talked with Marcia until she was cheered up and laughing?

As she reached for a plate, she looked at him, brows drawn slightly as if she knew he was hiding something from her. She buttered his pancakes and handed him the plate. Licking some butter off her finger, she asked again, "So? What happened?"

Tucker felt nervous discussing another woman with a girl who trusted him about as much as a mouse trusted a ravenous cat.

"I told her it would be a mistake."

"I saw you two walking back. She didn't seem like a girl who got rejected."

"You saw me coming and still made me kick down your door?"

"I asked my question first," Josie said, adding an eye roll. "I still can't believe you beat down my door. Kind of caveman-like."

"It was a cheap door anyhow."

"Evidently." She laughed. "Now, back to the question. Why was she so happy you rejected her?"

"How do you know she tried anything?"

"Oh, my gosh, seriously? She may as well have mounted you in the house. In front of everyone."

"Okay, yes, she made a play. But I didn't reject her."

Josie's eyebrow popped up.

"No, I didn't have sex with her. I just explained to her she could ruin her marriage before it started, and if she was smart, she'd keep her nose clean for at least ten years or she wouldn't get any of Gary's big bucks." Tucker grinned. Marcia loved the idea of getting even with the man where it really mattered to him—his wallet. Maybe at some time during those ten years, they'd work it out and have a happy marriage. Or not.

"Oh, you didn't."

"I did."

"Poor Gary."

"I figure he's a douche. He cheated on her first."

"Somehow, I don't feel any pity for her." Josie frowned as she turned her attention to pouring him a glass of milk and making herself a cup of tea.

Tucker enjoyed her obvious jealousy. With a grin, he added, "She was mostly just pissed at the fiancé for cheating. That's the only reason she hit on me. Wasn't my charm after all."

"Poor baby."

"I'm recovered, trust me." He grabbed his plate of food and dug in.

Josie fiddled with the handle of her mug for a minute, then took a deep breath and said, "In the future, if a tramp asks you to pole dance with her, I'd appreciate you saying no."

Tucker's laugh reverberated off the close walls.

"I'm not joking, Tucker."

"Joke or not, it's still funny as hell. I never wanted her in the first place. You practically threw me at her."

"I did not."

He poorly imitated her words, *"Tucker will go with you, won't you, Tucker?"*

"I didn't."

"You did."

She chewed on the side of her cheek. "I was mad. I don't remember what I said."

"Oh well, it's over." He took his plate to the sink and washed it and dried it.

"Can we watch a movie?" Josie asked the question like she wasn't the one who pulled the rug out from under their relationship.

"I'd like that," he said. "And I suppose I should warn you, I'm staying over. I'll take the couch."

"You're staying over?"

"Yeah, spending the night. I'm not sure if you noticed, but some jackass broke your door. I'm sorry about that."

She wrapped her arms around his waist and hugged him. "It's all right. I'm a basket case; you're a crazy man. We'll be the best of friends"

Damn. That hurt.

Chapter Sixteen

Murray called him bright and early the next morning. The bridal crew got out of control and broke a window. Tucker agreed to fix it.

"On the upside, they're leaving today instead of tomorrow. Seems the groom is pretty pissed off about the party. Throw in Marcia fawning over you like her best party gift and her friend catching it on video—the wedding may be off. I told Hetty we shoulda went with the crock pot."

"Oh shit. I swear, I didn't do anything."

"Don't worry none. That was pretty obvious in the video Hetty's sister sent her. You have some damn good self-control boy. Or has Josie got you on a leash?"

Looking into the room where Josie slept, he sighed. "No, just trying to use my head."

Tucker started walking toward the garage as he finished his conversation with Murray. He loaded everything he needed onto the truck and headed to the cottage. It was relatively quiet compared to the day before. A curly-haired woman was packing her bag in the back of the SUV when he arrived. She nodded at him as he got out of the truck.

Grabbing the replacement glass and his tool kit, he headed into the cottage. He heard dishes clanking and smelled freshly brewed coffee. He made his way to the kitchen. A woman with black hair gave him a smile. "Why, if it isn't the wedding wrecker in the flesh."

Tucker frowned, ignoring her remark. He turned to a small blonde sitting at the table and asked, "You know what window is broken?"

She nodded. "Marcia's room. Big room with all the windows, top of the stairs."

Tucker nodded and headed up. The door to her room was wide open, and Tucker was a little disappointed to see she was sitting on the bed. He knocked on the doorframe. She turned, her face lighting up when she saw him.

"Tucker," she said, coming toward him, arms out for a hug. She was wrapped around him before he could block her.

"Oh Tucker, I had the shittiest night. Mona, that whore, sent Gary the video of me teasing you about being my stripper. And of course she added that we disappeared to the beach. Gary didn't buy for a second that all we did was talk. Can you believe that?"

Tucker tried to push her away, but she held tight.

"He's just upset. He'll calm down," Tucker said.

"I don't know. I've never seen him this mad."

"I'm sure it was humiliating for him. You were rowdy."

That made her step back. Hands in the air, she paced, her voice rising as she explained. "I swear, I just wanted to have fun. I was hurt that the son of a bitch cheated on me. I've never cheated on him. Ever. Have you ever been cheated on Tucker?"

He nodded.

"Makes you feel like shit, right? Like some sort of idiot? And I don't know about you, but it made me feel like I wasn't good enough. I mean, I give it up whenever he wants it, and I try to shake things up and make it good. Why did he have to go screw his ex? So, when I got here, with my freaking guts ripped out, I was trying to find some way to forget...to feel pretty and wanted. That's why I hit on you."

"Did you tell him that?"

Her feet stopped pacing while she wiped away tears. "He called, all high and mighty, and gave me hell. I tried to tell him my side of the story and he hung up on me. Now, he won't talk at all. All of my calls go to voicemail."

"Go home. Talk to him. Make him listen."

"He doesn't want me."

"What the hell do you have to lose? Bug him until he hears you out. Then if he still says it's off? Screw him. Is a cheating prick really who you want for the rest of your life?"

His words brought her flying back into his arms. He had to hold onto her to keep from toppling over.

"Oh Tucker, you are the best. I swear my biggest regret in life will always be not making love to you on the beach. I can't believe I walked away. If I'd have known I was going to be crucified for it anyway, I would have done it for sure."

"Oh well." Tucker peeled himself away. "I guess life is all about regret."

"Maybe…" she said, running a hand up his chest.

He was about to say no when a sound on the steps caught his attention. Shoving Marcia aside, he turned to the sound. He recognized the top of her head as she disappeared down the steps. Josie. Tucker ran after her.

He caught her at the bottom. Grabbing her by the arm, he spun her toward him. "I can explain."

She slapped him as she jerked her arm away. "Leave me alone. I hate you."

Noticing the kitchen crew was making their way into the hall, he let her go, and she ran off.

"Son of a bitch," he said, taking after her. Outside, in the glaring sun, he couldn't see her anywhere. He assumed she went to her cottage, but the place was quiet. She wasn't in any of the rooms. His next guess was the cemetery. Also nothing. He checked the pond, the beach, and Hetty's. She was nowhere to be found. He tried to call her, but she never answered. Frustrated and feeling like an ass, he went back and finished the window. He was happy to see the entire wedding party gone. Window fixed, he went back to the shop to put everything away.

Murray was seated on a stool, a pair of reading glasses perched on the end of his nose as he slumped over a motor with a screwdriver. Tucker offered a good morning, and Murray gave him a harrumph as a greeting. Tucker cleared his throat and asked, "You seen Josie anywhere?"

Murray swiveled toward Tucker. Leveling him with a look over the rim of his glasses, he said, "My niece isn't a toy. You understand that, right?"

Tucker's palms were immediately sweaty. "No, she's not. She saw me talking to Marcia, but it was nothing."

"Hope not," he said, turning back to his motor.

Tucker moved closer. He might as well let the man know he had more interest in Josie than just the horizontal hokie pokie. He leaned his elbows on the table so he could look Murray in the eye. "Look, Josie is special to me. I didn't mean to get myself in hot water with Marcia. I just tried to be nice to the woman. Her fiancé dumped her, you know?"

"I'm the one who told you," Murray said, still working on the motor.

"And last night, Josie made it clear she didn't want a relationship. That she only wanted to be friends. I honestly don't know how to deal with her."

Murray pulled his glasses off and rubbed the bridge of his nose. "She's an odd sort, son."

"Well, so now she's pissed. Any other time, I'd say she's jealous and that's a good thing, but with Josie, all things normal are off the table."

Murray nodded.

"I need to talk to her. You wouldn't happen to know where she went, would you?"

"She was planning to go to the thrift store out the road a ways. Seems she busted all her dishes throwing a temper tantrum. Toppled the cabinet. I was headed over to check in on her and heard the commotion. I asked her what was going on and she said she hated you. Then she left."

"You didn't stop her?"

Murray put his glasses back on and picked up the screw driver. "No, I didn't. I learned long ago not to get between a fool woman and her fits. I asked her where she was headed, and she said she needed new dishes. So, off she went."

"Shit Murray, I better find her." Tucker headed to the door, then stopped. "Seriously, if she's that upset thinking I might have something going on with Marcia, that has to mean she's into me, right?"

"Got to give you credit for positive thinking. Never knew a woman destroying half her kitchen was a good sign. If you're fool enough to want to approach a mad woman, the store is to the right at the end of the road, then

left. Follow that road, and you'll drive right into it."

"Thank you."

Tucker nearly ran to his car.

He found her walking, arms swinging, fists clenched. He pulled up to her and got out, talking to her over the roof of his car. "Josie, we need to talk."

"No," she said and kept walking.

"Come on. It's not what you think. I can explain."

"I don't care. Go away."

"Come on, Josie. Let me explain. Are you really going to judge and convict me without hearing my side of the story?"

She turned slowly toward him.

"Come on. It's hot, let me give you a ride." He pulled the handle and shoved the passenger door open.

Without a word, she climbed in his car.

"I was only there to fix a broken window."

She stared straight ahead. "I don't care. You can do whatever you want."

"I want you."

"You've done me. Feel free to move on."

The muscle in his jaw twitched.

"This is the place," Josie said, pointing to a converted two-story house nestled into a shady corner lot on an otherwise busy street. The lawn was covered in large items set out for sale. A weathered bench welcomed uninterested shopping sidekicks to relax and wait under a yawning, scraggly oak. A hand painted sign welcomed customers to enter from 9:00 AM to whenever the owner felt like leaving.

"Thank you for the ride. I'll only be a minute, wait if you want, or go. It doesn't matter to me."

He grabbed her arm and held her there. "We need to talk."

"No, we don't. I need to buy some dishes. That's all I need right now."

"Ah, come on. You said let's be friends. You can't shut me out for this."

"No, you come on. I can do whatever I want. You lied to me. The only reason you didn't screw her is because she told you no. Which is just fine, because you don't owe me anything."

"It wasn't anything like that. And I told you I convinced her she didn't want to cheat on Gary. Her thinking she told me no made her feel better."

Glaring at him, she said, "Aren't you just the most noble of all heroes."

"You know what? I don't deserve this shit. I haven't done a damn thing."

"Fine," she said, pushing her door open.

"Fine," he echoed, letting go of her arm.

She got out and slammed his door. The curse words flew as he pounded on the steering wheel. He told himself he should leave her. Let her walk home. Why was he working so damn hard on a woman who was obviously bat shit crazy?

"Damn it," he said, getting out and slamming his door shut. A group of guys made it to the entrance before him. Laughing and joking, they took their sweet time filing through the door. Tucker was steps behind them as they approached the girl at the counter. The largest in the group slapped his hand on the counter making the clerk jump. "Hey Natalie, aren't you glad to see us?"

The girl flushed and said, "Barely containing myself."

Tucker gave them a closer look. His guess was frat boys vacationing on mom and dad's money. Four in total. One large guy, the big mouth, and three others who looked like they were cloned from a prep school catalogue. Polo shirts, in varying colors, the same baggy khaki shorts, and all in desperate need of a haircut. Tucker rubbed his stubbly high and tight military cut as he gave the guys a nod hello.

They ignored him and made their way through the store.

Tucker was weaving the aisles looking for Josie when he realized the guys found her first. Or at least he assumed the *pretty lady* they were taunting was Josie. He followed the sound. He found her in the back of the store in a small room that said *Clearance* on the open door. Josie had her back to them, pretending she couldn't hear as they hit on her. Tucker's heart pumped faster. His muscles tightened.

"Come on, baby girl. Sweet ass like that. How have we not met?" the big guy asked.

Josie did a sort of slide to the right to try to slip out of the back room, but the big guy caught her by the arm and spun her around to face him. Josie was white as a sheet. Her body shook. She looked as though she might pass out. He had seen that look of sheer panic plenty of times. In battle. From soldiers who had seen or experienced things no human should ever have to. That realization that someone might have hurt Josie that badly sickened him for a moment, but that feeling passed and fury took its place.

Tucker charged, grabbing the guy by his pastel blue collar. Almost in a single motion, Tucker lifted the man off his feet and into the shelves next to him. There was a crash of glass and clatter of metal. "Who the hell do you think you are? You don't touch her; you don't talk to her. Do you understand me?"

The guy was wide-eyed as he stuttered, "Hey man, be calm. I didn't know she was with you."

Josie clutched Tucker's arm. "Stop it. It's all right."

Tucker's jaw clenched. "No, it's not all right." Glaring at the guy, he added, "Stop being a prick. You need to learn some respect."

"I will. I swear."

"Tucker! Stop it!" Josie sounded pissed as she pulled at his arm. She seemed madder at him than she did the son of a bitch he was nearly strangling.

He let the guy go as Josie stormed off. He looked around the room at the broken shelves and shattered glass. "Clean this shit up," he said and walked away. Stopping at the counter, he said, "I'm staying at Murray's. Once they get that cleaned up, see how much I owe you for the damages, and I'll come by and pay it."

Natalie grinned. "No charge. I'm sick of them. Every day this week…same bullshit. I told my boss, and he said it meant they had a crush on me. Hah. Sure. Do I look like their type?"

"Like someone who'd be interested in a dumb ass prick? Not at all. They just enjoy being assholes."

"Exactly," Natalie said with a grin. "You scared them pretty good. I doubt they ever come back."

That was the sort of response Tucker expected.

Not Josie's fury.

Chapter Seventeen

Tucker and Josie drove most of the way in silence. Josie stared out the side window, as if she feared looking forward would put Tucker in her peripheral vision. As they got closer to Murray's, Tucker said, "I'm sorry. I was only trying to help."

Josie nodded, but maintained her study of the passing scenery.

Tucker sighed. Pulling up next to the cottage, he parked the car. He looked to Josie, but she didn't seem to be any closer to talking. "Hell with it," he said, slamming the car door as he got out.

He made his way to his cottage, fully intent on packing and leaving. A voice behind him made him turn.

"It's not your fault." Josie stood there. Trembling from head to toe. "They scared me. I…I'm glad you were there." Taking a deep breath, she said, "I'm sorry I'm driving you crazy."

Tucker shook his head. He didn't know what to say, so he said nothing.

Josie took a step toward him. "I don't know what's wrong with me. I don't know why, but it's like I can't control my emotions around you. If I'm irritated, I want to smash things; if I feel attracted, I want to strip your clothes off. I don't understand. I've lived a quiet, peaceful life for years. Then you show up, and I'm on this insane roller coaster. You make me want things I can never have. I feel like I need to set boundaries to keep us under control, but then I feel so lost when you're not with me. I am trying to find some solution, and I know…" Her voice cracked, and she had to pause to blink back tears. "I know I'm hurting you. I feel your pain."

Holy hell, what had he fallen in love with? Like Holly wasn't crazy enough.

Tucker dropped himself on the kitchen chair. "So stop it. It's not that complicated."

Josie moved closer. Her eyes were glassy as she kneeled in front of him, her hands gentle on his knees. "My life is far more complicated than I can explain."

"Then tell me. What's going on?"

Pressing her lips together, she shook her head. "I can't. That's one of the problems. How can I be close to you when I cannot be honest with you?"

Sitting straighter, he leaned closer to her and brushed a wisp of hair from her cheek. "You can tell me anything. You can trust me."

A tear rolled down her cheek. "I do trust you, but I still can't. There are things I can barely think about, much less talk about it."

Of course he wanted to know everything, but more than that—he wanted to protect her. Whatever haunted her couldn't be her fault, and he wanted to assure her of that. But for now, her secrets were her business. "It doesn't matter. Tell me when you feel comfortable. If that is never, then I don't give a damn. I don't need to know your secrets to know you."

She cried. He lifted her off the floor and settled her onto his lap, tucking her head under his chin. Arms wrapped tight around his shoulders, she took a slow, shaky breath. "I don't want to lose you. And I don't want to be your friend, but I don't know what else I can be…and if I keep pushing you away, one day there will be a Marcia, someone who will love you. Someone normal."

"I only want you. You're very special to me." He kissed the top of her head.

"But I want to be normal. I want to be rational. I want to love you and be loved by you, but I don't know if I can."

"Can or will?"

She took a suck of air and asked quietly, "What do you mean?"

"Stop pressuring yourself so much. Forget about the sex. I'm not some kind of animal who needs to get laid constantly. I just want to be with you."

Her eyes were glassy, and her lips trembled.

Wrapping his hands around her waist, he asked, "Do you even want me to be in love with you?"

"More than anything I've ever wanted in my life. I just don't know how

it could ever work."

His jaw twitched. It made no sense. Any rational guy would run from this situation. Pack his shit, get in his car, and go. But as long as she would have him, leaving wasn't an option. His thumbs found the separation between her shirt and her jeans, and her flesh called to him. All he wanted to do was touch her. And as he looked into those clear, blue eyes, he wanted to make the world go away and forget all about what made sense. Yes, he did love her, he just didn't know if that was enough to make her trust him.

Josie sighed. "Right now, I don't know if I should kiss you or cry for you. You're confused, and it's my fault."

"Hell yes, I'm confused."

"I'm sorry."

"Don't say that. You haven't done anything wrong." He looked at her, locking his fingers around her waist. None of this made sense, but she was right. Neither of them was acting rationally. Back in the store, she was in full shock, and he wanted to snap necks. That anger wasn't normal. He could blame the war, but he knew it was more.

Her hands were cool as she cradled his face. "I'm sorry I'm doing this to you. I'm trying to make sense of it all…trying to separate my fears of the world from my desire to be with you. The truth is, I do love you. And when I'm with you, I feel safe, like nothing ugly can touch me. And I'm happy. Then when you're not with me, I'm nearly petrified you'll leave me or I'll drive you away. And it hurts."

"Oh, Josie," he said, closing his eyes against the sting. "I'd never hurt you."

She kissed him. Slow, soft hands circled his neck, caressing the taut muscle. Wrapping his hands in her hair, he pressed her closer to him, kissed her deeper. But still it wasn't enough. Tucking his hands under her butt, he lifted her with him as he rose from the chair. Her legs locked around his waist, she clung to him.

Holding her tight, he kissed her as he carried her to his bed and laid her down. Snuggling close to her, burying his face in her neck, he nibbled on the tender skin. Her hands gripped his shoulders. Propping himself up on an arm, he looked down at her. "I love you, Josie. There's nothing you could ever tell me that would change that. If it would help, tell me. If you can't talk about it, I don't need to know anything. But no matter what, don't you dare leave me. When I got here, my head was all screwed up. You made me feel at ease. Take that from me, and I'm nothing but broken."

Skimming her hands down his shoulders to the waist of his shirt, she slid her hands under the worn tee to the solid flesh under it.

"Stop Josie. Just let me hold you."

"No, it's okay. You were meant for me."

He pushed her hands into more neutral territory. "We're not doing this. Give it time. Wait until you trust me."

She broke down in tears and buried her face in his chest. Her body trembled, and he held her close, sheltering her as she let it all out. In combat, they called it decompressing. Some guys drank, some fought, some had sex. Those were the stress outlets they talked about. But Tucker knew they also found quiet places to unwind as Josie was doing, and he did what he always did—said nothing and waited until it was all poured out.

"I'm sorry," she said, hiccoughing.

Kissing her temple, he whispered, "It's fine."

He handed her a clean shirt from his drawer to blow her nose.

"I'll wash it for you," she promised.

"Don't worry about it," he said, smiling. Brushing damp hair away from tear-stained cheeks. "I'll let you blow snot on everything I own."

A chuckle escaped her. "I'm sorry. I'm such a baby."

"It's all right. You're my baby."

Smiling up at him, she touched his cheek. "I really am lucky you're so patient."

"I'd wait for you for a lifetime. You're pretty special, you know that?"

Shaking her head, her eyes glassed over again. "That's the thing. I'm not."

"Shush," he said, kissing her. "I'm not an idiot. I know what I'm talking about."

"You are the most special man ever, and I do trust you. I'd trust you with my life." She kissed him again, rolling toward him. Her hand snaked under his tee shirt. He didn't stop her.

"Mmm," he said, nuzzling her, placing feathery kisses along her collar bone to the hollow of her throat.

"I want you, Tucker," she whispered, her cheeks burning, her words breathless and nervous. "I want to belong to you. I want to close my eyes when you're not with me and feel you."

Tucker brushed loose hairs back. Her eyes were closed tight, but a tear slid down her cheek. He closed his eyes against her pain and leaned his forehead against her temple. "What happened, Josie? Who hurt you?"

"Shhh," she said. "Don't talk." She looked up at him and smiled. Her eyes were glassy, but the happiness seemed genuine. "It doesn't matter. No one can hurt me anymore."

Leaning in, she kissed him. Her hand ran up his naked back. Her soft hand on his warm flesh nearly took his breath away. Rolling her onto her back and pressing her under him, he kissed her until she was pink-cheeked and breathless. He wanted her so much his body ached.

"Josie, Josie," he whispered against her lips. "We aren't going to rush this."

"I want to rush it. I want to do this."

"I know, but I don't."

"You don't want me anymore?"

"Oh hell, of course I do. I just don't want to go back to where we were."

"We won't. I need this. I need you. I swear."

"This is a cruel game."

"No, it's different now. I know it's not bodies out of control. It's you loving me, right? You love me?"

"Of course, I love you."

"Then trust me."

He closed his eyes and shook his head.

Kissing him, she pulled his shirt over his head. Her fingers traced the outline of his tattoo lightly before she kissed the area above his breast. "You're not here by accident. It was fate."

"I have no idea. For all I know, you could be some crazy witch stealing my heart and making it do flip flops."

"I'm sorry," she said, pulling away.

Drawing her back, grabbing one of her legs and pulling it over his waist, he kissed her. "Don't be sorry. Don't ever be sorry. I don't care if you're a damned succubus; I surrender."

As his fingers loosened her buttons, his lips followed the trail of exposed flesh. Her hands gripped his shoulders. He lifted her hips off the bed as he undid her jeans and slid them off. Taking a moment, he gazed down at her. Part of him was amazed she was here, bared and waiting on him. But there was another part of him that hated himself for not walking away.

Chapter Eighteen

Rolling onto his back, he pulled her with him. She nestled against his chest and sighed. Smoothing her hair over silky shoulders, he finally felt peace. He did love her—more than anything or anyone in his life. Her fingertips traced the muscles in his chest as her breathing slowed. "You going to sleep?" he asked.

He could feel her smile against his skin. "I could," she said.

"You all right?"

She smiled up at him. "Perfect. Just keep telling me you love me. Tell me I'm not crazy. We're soul mates. We're meant to be together."

"We were meant to be together. You've made me happy. Happier than I've ever been in my life."

"Mmm, it feels so good. Loving you."

"I'm not letting you go home tonight."

"Why not?"

"Because last time I left you this happy, you hated me the next day."

"I didn't hate you. I was worried you thought…" her words drifted to silence as her lips folded in and pressed together.

"We're past that. I followed a ghost here, and I found you. If that's not fate, I don't know what is."

She rested her cheek against his bicep. "A ghost?"

"Long story. And I'm starved. You want some food?"

"I do. You should make me something. I earned dinner in bed."

"That you did."

Josie rolled onto her stomach and nestled herself into his bed while he threw on boxers and headed to the kitchen. He threw a plate of pizza pockets into the microwave and yelled over his shoulder, "Don't you go to sleep on me. Not after I've slaved over this microwave."

Josie's giggles were muffled by the pillow.

Tucker carried in two plates of food. Josie sat up, tucking her legs under her. "What are these gourmet treats?"

"Pizza pockets. All the goodness of Italy rolled into a tiny crust."

Josie popped one in her mouth. "Oh my, an international treat? You are full of surprises."

"I am."

Wiping her lips with her napkin, she asked, "You mind if I ask you a question? You don't have to answer."

He set his empty plate on the nightstand next to his bed and stretched out beside her. "Ask anything you want."

"Would you tell me about Holly? Did you love her?"

Heat ran up his neck to his cheeks. These sorts of talks were never good. And his story was worse than most. He rubbed his chin.

"Never mind," she said. "I shouldn't have asked that. We barely made it through the last two days, and I'm digging up more trouble. It's none of my business."

"No, it's your business. It's just tough to talk about. I'm the bad guy in the story."

She handed him her plate and took his hand. "I find that hard to believe."

He gave her hand a squeeze. Maybe if he was honest with her, she'd be comfortable telling him what she was hiding. Or maybe she'd think he was a prick and hate him. "What do you want to know?" Tucker asked.

"How did you meet?"

"We went to high school together. For the most part, we were just friends. We dated occasionally, went to a few dances and prom together, but we were never very serious." Unless they were drunk and horny, but he didn't add that. "Sounds normal," Josie said with a shrug.

"Well, when I decided to go to the Marines, my mom was furious. Totally out of her mind. She wouldn't talk to me, hell she barely looked at me. She wouldn't even give me a ride to the processing station; I had to take a bus."

"Was she mad, or was she afraid?"

Tucker sighed and looked across at Josie. He hadn't considered his mom had been afraid. He assumed she was being her usual controlling self. "Yeah, she probably was afraid. No matter the reason, it still sucked to be going through boot camp and get the cold shoulder from your mom."

"Your mom wouldn't write or call?" Josie's head tipped sympathetically.

"I never sent her the address or phone number." Tucker suddenly realized he may have been as stubborn and childish as his mother. "Anyhow," he continued, "I did have Holly. She'd write and call. And when I graduated boot camp, she surprised me by showing up. After graduation, she sort of stuck around."

Josie shifted, tucking a pillow behind her back. Tucker paused his story, watching her get situated. Josie patted him on the cheek and said, "And then?"

He rested his head on her thigh. "We got an apartment together."

"You lived with her?"

"I uh…"

"It's okay. I was surprised is all. So what? You lived with her? You don't now, right?"

Tucker wiped sweat off his brow. "No, definitely not."

"Did you love her?"

"I thought I did. I realize now that I didn't. We had fun together. And since her parents weren't too excited about her living with me, we got engaged."

Josie's brow rose for the briefest of moments. Tucker sat up so he could see her face, be ready to grab her if she tried to run away.

"Go on. I swear, Tucker, you're not in trouble. You're sweating."

He wiped the sweat away. "Well, the engagement didn't last long. I got my orders to deploy to Iraq. Holly went home to her parents and within a month, she was bored. I suggested she take some classes…even sent her the money to pay for them."

"That was sweet. See? Not a bad guy." Josie rubbed his hand with her thumb.

"Yeah, well, you remember that at the end."

"I will," she said with a light laugh.

"She started school, and evidently being a college student with a boyfriend overseas was more stressful than being in a warzone, so she broke up with me."

"Dang, Tucker. She's a bitch. Seriously? I get these strong feelings of guilt from you over her, and I don't at all understand why."

"I didn't feel guilty about that. To be completely honest, I was happy to be free of the relationship. I was having more damned fun dodging bullets in Iraq than dealing with her at home." He grinned.

"When do you become the bad guy?"

"When I came home after my first tour, I was out with friends—of course we had the same friends—so we bumped into each other first night out. One thing led to another, and before I realized, I was back at her place."

A nod was all Josie offered.

Tucker licked dry lips and explained, "It seems really stupid now, but when you're half drunk and home on leave, bullshit is easier to swallow. She swore she never cheated. That even after she broke it off, there was no one for her but me."

"So, then what happened?"

"The next morning, I was eating a bowl of cereal when her roommate joins me and starts telling me what a lying tramp Holly is. How she cheated on me repeatedly, and I bought her lies hook, line, and sinker."

"Wow, what a crappy roommate. Were you upset?"

"No, it was perfect. I was free. As soon as I woke up that morning, I wondered how the hell I was going to get out of the situation. I mean out of all the women I could've hooked up with, it had to be her? I knew I didn't love her, but I owed her something more than a booty call."

"By having proof she cheated and lied, you didn't owe her anything?"

"Nope. Nothing. With that proof, I was done. When she got back from her morning jog, it was easy to break it off." Tucker didn't mention all the curses and shit Holly threw at him. For the record, he knew to never dump a woman in a kitchen ever again. Cabinets were filled with weapons and projectiles.

"Personally, I think you did the right thing to break up."

"I know I did."

"Then why feel guilty? Why are you the bad guy?"

Tucker rubbed his chin. "Holly was always a bit insecure. She was beautiful, but she needed attention constantly. And she had so many self-destructive tendencies. Total drama, twenty-four seven."

"That's hardly your fault."

"But I knew her, Josie. I knew my walking away would send her into a spiral, but I didn't care."

"Did she? Spiral, I mean?"

"Oh yeah, she went nuts. Drank too much, way too often. I wouldn't be surprised at all if drugs weren't involved. Then she got mixed up in a sex tape. I heard it was pretty nasty. I could never bring myself to watch it, although at least ten people sent it to me. It was everywhere. I knew she had to be humiliated. I thought I should call her then…"

"And what? What were you going to call her and say? That you saw her tape? Me, personally? I'd rather the people I care about not know the things that humiliate me. And what were you going to say, *Hey, saw your sex tape…looking good?*"

Tucker chuckled. Ash had said the same thing. "I don't know. I could have assured her it would blow over. People would forget."

With a shrug, Josie said, "That might have helped, but I doubt it. She seems like the type who does what she wants without regret—until she gets caught."

"Maybe. But this was publicly humiliating for her."

Josie pulled her hand back. Twisting her hair into a knot at the back of her head, then letting it fall over her shoulders, she exhaled hard "Look, I don't mean to sound heartless, but I…" Her cheeks couldn't have blazed redder if she'd been burned. "I had a friend who was raped. Held by force and…well, you understand, right?"

Tucker nodded.

"Well, when she told people, trying to get someone—anyone—to help her, they called her a liar. So, I'm sympathetic to the effects of trauma paired with public humiliation. I feel bad for Holly, truly I do. People have no right to tape things and send them all over, but still—she made the choice. My friend had no choice. She had no one to rescue her. I'm sorry, but none of that is your fault. It isn't your mess to clean up."

"I'm sorry…about your friend. Men like that…they don't deserve to live. Did the guy—"

"Yes, he finally went to jail, and in time, she got over it." Josie waved off the conversation, asking quickly, "Did Holly ever get over it?"

"No. She, uh…she drove her car off a bridge."

Josie's eyes widened and her jaw dropped. "She didn't do it on purpose, did she?"

With a heavy shrug, he said, "I don't know. I want to think it was an accident, but in the last message she sent me, earlier that night, she said I didn't have to worry about being embarrassed or bothered by her ever again."

A silence settled over them.

"That's why I feel guilty. I didn't hate her. I certainly didn't want her to die. She sent me message after message begging me for help, and I ignored her."

Wordlessly, she pulled him to her resting his cheek against her breast.

"I could have changed that, Josie."

She kissed his temple. "No. It's still not your fault. She was an adult, and those choices, as horrible as they were, were hers. What were you supposed to do? Let your whole life be a train wreck to save hers? You're a good man, Tucker. Don't you ever, ever doubt that." Leaning over, she kissed him.

They lay there quietly, holding each other until the shadows lengthened to darkness. Her words broke the silence. "The only way you'd have made her happy was to take her back. Then your whole life would have been one drama after another, and you deserve better than that."

He nodded. Logically, he knew she was right, but his heart didn't agree.

***

A storm blew in—a real powerhouse that bent the trees so low to the ground they looked like they were rubber. Metal business signs flapped like flags, banging against buildings. One sign kept clanging and clanging until it flew off, and Tucker barely ducked in time to miss it. The sign lay at his feet, *Forget Me Not Gifts*. It was then he heard her scream. "Josie," he called. He moved through the stinging rain, calling for her. Then she was beside him. When he turned to grab her, she screamed, her mouth opening wide like it was unhinged and twisted. Her eyes flashed black, and she hissed, "You promised to help me."

Then he woke. His body was soaked in sweat, even though the window unit was constantly pumping out cold air. He tossed the blankets off and rubbed his eyes. Trying to slow his breathing, he looked around the room. Josie was gone. He jumped out of bed, dressed, and headed out into the night. The clouds were thick, blocking the moon and every single star in the sky. Using his phone as a light, he made his way to the little graveyard.

"Josie," he whispered.

Twigs snapped, and he heard her moving. It wasn't until she was a few feet away that he could see her.

"Did I wake you?" she asked.

"No, I…I just woke up. Why are you out here? What the hell is it with you and the graveyard?"

"I already told you. It's peaceful. I come here to pray."

He took her hand and started leading her back to the cottage. "You know they make churches for that. Murray said he told you to stop."

She shrugged. "What Murray doesn't know won't hurt him."

"Well, it's creepy. I wish you'd stop, too."

Josie laughed. "It's only because you don't understand."

He stopped, pulling on her hand to bring her back to face him. "So, explain to me."

"You'll think I'm crazy."

"Probably, but I think after tonight, this is the sort of thing we should talk about."

"Hmm," she said, rubbing her hands up his arms. "I suppose you did earn some explanations."

He kissed her forehead. "I worked hard. I may have pulled my quadriceps."

Josie laughed as she moved to his side and wrapped her arm around his. Leaning into him, she agreed, "That you did, and I am very grateful." She brushed her cheek against his arm. "Come on, let's go back. I'll make us some cocoa and we'll talk."

Once they were back in the cottage and settled on the couch with their mugs of hot chocolate, Josie slowly sipped hers. Tucker chugged his and set his mug on the table. Josie took one last sip, then set hers on the table next to his. She leaned against the arm of the couch with her feet propped in front of her, facing him. Taking her legs and pulling them across his lap, he asked, "What's in the graveyard?"

"It's a cemetery. Graveyards are by churches."

"Tomato, tomahto. What's the attraction?"

"It's peaceful."

"Why go at night?"

"Again, it's peaceful."

Tucker shook his head as he rubbed the smooth flesh of her knee with his thumb. "Come on, Josie. Enough of the peaceful crap. It's weird. You can't tell me going to a grave—cemetery in the middle of the night isn't strange."

"Fine. I'll tell you, but I warn you, it's going to sound like I'm off my rocker."

"It can't be much crazier, unless you're sacrificing little animals. You're not—"

"Of course not." Josie slapped his arm and laughed at him. "Okay, so there may be crazier things than the truth."

"Which is…."

"I...I have a guardian, and I hear her best in the cemetery. And I went tonight because I wanted to pray for your protection and for Holly—that her soul has found peace. I believe, for you to have peace, she must move on and find her place in the afterlife."

Tucker closed his eyes. That was the sweetest, most bizarre explanation for insane behavior she could have given. He supposed he shouldn't be shocked. Murray and Hetty warned him. And really, was it that odd? He had a buddy in Iraq who had a St. Christopher's medallion he swore channeled his prayers to Heaven. And Ash kissed his cross before every mission. So what if his girlfriend had a guardian angel? That was normal-ish, right? But it talks? Tucker looked at her. "Talks? It speaks to you?"

"Not in words to my ears. In understanding...to my heart."

"What does she tell you?"

"It's not like a conversation. I go with what is troubling me, and it's like understanding flows through me. Sort of like an epiphany, only I know it's my guardian who helps me understand. I know she's watching out for me."

"So, she's a she. Does she have a name?"

"It's Maggie."

"Don't tell me you're seeing Mad Mags?"

"You've heard of her? Though, to call her mad is a little rude."

"It's not rude, she's not—" He stopped himself before he denied she was real. He'd pushed Josie to be honest with him. What kind of ass would he be if he didn't at least pretend to be taking her seriously? She was obviously a believer. What he thought didn't matter, though the irony of him following Mags's ghost to the island and finding a girl who seemed to be obsessed with her spirit didn't escape him.

"You think I'm nuts," Josie said, crossing her arms over her chest.

"No, I don't."

"Do you believe Mags talks to me?"

"Uh, yeah."

"You do not." Josie gave him a stern look. "You think I'm a flake."

"Don't be ridiculous. I said I believe you."

"You're lying."

Grabbing her by the arm, he pulled her against him, holding her tight. "Just because I'm a skeptical asshole doesn't mean I don't believe you believe. And I certainly don't think you're crazy, or flaky."

Josie chewed her lip as she studied him. "I suppose you're right. You don't believe in anything, much less have faith in things you can't control."

"Touché."

"I'm not trying to spar with you."

Running his hands into her hair, he snuggled her close to him. "It was just a figure of speech. But listen," he said as his hands combed through her silky strands, relaxing her body against his. "I don't like you out wandering in the dark, no matter how good the cause. Stay here or wake me up to go with you."

"I've been doing it—"

"Shh. Please?"

"You think you're jinxed."

"I never said—"

"You're not going to lose me, Tucker. We were meant to be together. You may not have faith, but I do."

He kissed her forehead, allowing his lips to linger against the warmth of her skin. "Look, you mean more to me than I can understand, much less explain. I don't care if you have a whole flock of guardian angels, I don't want you out there alone."

"She's not an angel. Angels are a different species than humans. Humans can't be angels and angels can't be guardians."

"Okay, so what exactly is a guardian?"

"It's a human who has crossed over, but while they were still on this plane, they not only faced evil, but beat it."

"What evil did Maggie beat?" Tucker asked, genuine curiosity grabbing him. He hoped she stabbed her pedophile husband through his black heart.

"She saved countless women from suffering a fate like her own. She was kidnapped as a little girl, you know?"

"I heard that. He kept her as his wife until she went crazy?"

"She only played crazy. If he thought she was touched in the head, he feared her. She cooked his cat, but she didn't kill it. The poor thing must have gotten into some poison. But Mags saw her chance to make him seriously fear her. I mean branding her own forehead and chopping off her toe didn't stop him from putting his disgusting hands on her. But that cat on a platter? That freaked him out good. He built her the little house in the woods after that. He couldn't sleep with her in the house anymore."

"You mean the woods you showed me, where we…" His grin was ornery and full of suggestion.

"Yes, that one. That was Maggie's secret home. Maggie would hang shells on the trees, and women in trouble would just know to follow them. She'd help them hide until a friendly captain would help shuttle them to safety."

"Good lord, how many troubled women were on this island?"

"It was a pirate haven. Kidnapping women was no different than stealing cargo. It was common."

"And Mags saved them?"

Josie nodded. "She did. She could have saved herself, but instead, she saved others."

"Thus making her a guardian."

"Exactly."

"Well, I'm glad she's looking out for you."

"She's looking out for us. She led you to me that night by the pond. We are meant for each other. That night bound us together."

Tucker nodded. If she believed, he'd not argue.

She snuggled against him, her breath warm against his neck. "You're a sweet man to humor me."

"I'm not. I'm just listening."

"You're a horrible liar. A sweet, horrible liar."

Tucker chuckled. "Okay, so I have a hard time believing a guardian angel was in on the premarital sex plan."

Josie looked up at him, one brow lifted high, a smirk on her face. "Man invented marriage. You're stuck with me, Tucker Boone. For better or worse."

Chapter Nineteen

Tucker and Josie's life took on a comfortable rhythm. Days and weeks passed with the same comfortable pattern. Work, play, and love. Tucker couldn't remember a time when his life was so uneventful, yet so perfect. For once in his life, he felt content. Happy.

They were hanging out on her couch, watching a *Die Hard* movie Josie bought him—for his toleration of all her old movies. Dressed in yoga pants and a cotton t-shirt so soft it felt like silk, Josie snuggled into the crook of Tucker's arm holding a bowl of popcorn in her lap. "Can you believe I've never seen this movie? Mother abhorred violence. Hah."

"That's funny, why?"

Josie bit the side of her jaw; her hands pressed into the sides of the popcorn bowl. She shrugged.

Tucker's hands moved over her shoulders, down her back. "Maybe you shouldn't watch it then. I mean it's a good movie, but I can think of better ways to reward me for all the black and white movies."

Josie's eyebrow popped up. "There is?"

"Besides," he said as he took the popcorn from her and set it on the floor. "You know what this outfit does to me."

"You said that about the sundress, and the jeans….oh, and the paint splattered cut-offs."

Nibbling on the hollow of her neck, he gently pushed her back onto the couch. "So, you're starting to see the pattern."

Josie laughed, exposing more of her throat as she tilted her head against the couch. "What pattern?" she asked.

"If it's on your body, it's teasing me."

Framing his face with her hands, she forced him to look at her. "You're something else, you know?"

Looking down at her, he tried to think of the right words. The kind of words poets would use to describe perfection, but all he could come up with was how damned lucky he was.

Outside, a sudden gust of wind made the little house sway on its raised foundation.

Lightning flashed and rain beat against the tin roof and echoed off the glass panes. Josie glanced over her shoulder out the window. Her jaw clenched and her body went rigid.

"It's just a storm. It'll pass."

Josie nodded, her face flush, her hands turning cool against his skin. She nodded and licked dry lips.

Kissing her, he tried his best to distract her from the whistling wind and sudden pounding rain. Her body was taut under him as she wriggled away from his kisses. Brushing his lips across the soft skin under her ear, he whispered, "Relax, Josie. It's just a storm..."

"Please don't," she said as large tears rolled down her cheek.

He wiped the tear away. "It's all right. It's just rain." Before he could say another word, lightning clapped outside. The tiny cottage shook with the force of the strike and the wind whistled through every crack and window. Josie's body trembled beneath him, so he held her closer. Tucking her body into his, he tried to kiss her, but she screamed. Pushing against his chest, she cried, "Don't touch me. Please, don't touch me."

Confused, he let her go and she rolled off the couch, running for the door. When he caught her by the arm, she turned on him with wild strikes, beating on him with her free hand. He didn't want to hurt her, but couldn't let her leave. He'd seen this sort of panic before plenty of times. He once knew a Vietnam vet who went bat-shit crazy when there were fireworks.

As he moved to hold the door closed, she struck him in the face, her nails digging into his cheek and leaving a trail of blood. Shoving at him, she grabbed for the door handle again, screaming for him to let her go.

Fear coursed through every vein. Grabbing her in a bear hug that trapped her arms against her sides, he held her. Her head whipped, and she kicked at him, but he was far too powerful for her to fight for long. He held

her until her wails turned to a calmer sob. Scooping her into his arms, he carried her to the couch, cradling her like one would a child. As he smoothed the hair that came loose during the struggle, his hands shook. Someone, or something hurt her. More than a broken heart or hurt feelings. Tears stung his eyes as he asked quietly, "Who hurt you, Josie?"

She shook her head. As her tears gave way to exhausted sleep, he lifted her, carried her to bed and tucked her in. He kissed her forehead and switched off the light.

Kneeling by the bed, he asked, "What is it, Josie?"

Sniffling and burying her head into her pillow, she said quietly, "Toby."

His heart stopped. "Who's Toby?"

Josie sighed in her sleep. He shook her gently. "Josie? Why did you say Toby?"

"Mmm," she said as she curled under the blanket. "I couldn't save Toby."

"Save Toby from what? Who's Toby?"

She never answered, and as much as he wanted to know exactly what she was talking about, he couldn't risk waking her now and causing another breakdown.

Sitting beside her bed, he ran a hand through his hair and thought of a dog. His sister's dog. "Oh Jesus, please don't let her be Maddy." He sat there a long time, listening to her breathe.

He loved her. More than anything he'd ever loved in his life. If she was Maddy, could he walk away? Give up loving her to be her brother? The thought made him sick to his stomach.

But she couldn't be. It was ridiculous. Josie was right—he had no faith in anything. She was Josie, just like she said...just like Murray said. Paranoia was getting the best of him. There were plenty of people named Toby. Just because Maddy had a dog named Toby didn't mean there was a connection. It was the dream that was freaking him out. Night after night, Maddy haunted him, prodding him to help her. He'd tried. He'd done all he could. All but check out the obvious lead. His stomach felt queasy as he pulled his phone out of his pocket. The picture of him and Josie on the beach. They were perfect together. Before he lost his nerve, he hit send forwarding the picture to his mother asking her to take the picture to Gloria to see if this woman was Maddy.

His phone buzzed immediately. Walking to the kitchen, he answered.

His mother pounced. "You seem awfully cozy in that picture. Please, God, don't tell me you're having sex with this girl."

He didn't answer. Images of Josie under him filled his head.

"Oh, Tucker. What have you done?"

"She can't be Maddy. I'm just ruling out the possibility."

"And what if she is?"

Tucker closed his eyes and rubbed his forehead. "She's not. I'm just ruling it out."

His mom let out a long sigh. "Let me check with Gloria. Until then? Keep your damned pants on."

Tucker hung up the phone and tossed it on the table. Walking softly to her room, he leaned against the doorframe. With the clouds moving west, the moon shined through the window, casting a shadowy glow across her face. As he stood there, certain she was the most perfect, wonderful thing he'd ever find in his life, he suddenly wished he'd never mentioned her to his mother.

Chapter Twenty

"Wake up, sleepy head," she said, kissing him as he slept.

Tucker stretched out on the small couch, his neck stiff from using the armrest as a pillow.

"You should go lay in my bed. I can't believe you slept on the couch."

"You were beat. I didn't want to disturb you."

Josie blushed; her gaze dropped. "I freaked out on you, didn't I?"

Wrapping a hand around her slender neck, he gave it a gentle squeeze. "You were scared. I understand."

Biting her lip, she touched the welts on his cheek. "I did that?"

He took her hand and kissed it. "It's nothing."

"It's just...storms scare me."

He nodded slowly, pulling her toward him until her forehead rested on his. "It was more than the storm, Josie. You can trust me, you know that. Whatever happened...it might help to talk about it."

Her eyes were glassy, but she smiled. "No, it doesn't. Trust me on that."

Brushing his thumb across her cheek, he shook his head. "I want to help."

Her hands gripped his shoulders. She took a deep breath before saying, "You are. I swear. I just have a fear of storms."

"Josie..."

"Shhh," she said crawling onto the couch beside him, pressing her body into his. "Right now, I just need you to love me."

"Of course I love you."

"Then shut up and hold me...and just...let me be perfect a while longer." Her words were quiet, her eyes shining with the tears that were poised to fall.

"You're always perfect to me. No matter what. Trust me. You can tell me anything. Nothing will change how I feel about you." *What if she's Maddy?*

Can I love her then? The thoughts seeped into his head uninvited. Crazy thoughts based on nothing more than a coincidence. Or two.

Wrapping her leg around his hip, she drew her body tighter to his. "I'll tell you everything. One day. But not today. Today, I need you to stop asking questions, stop thinking about what's wrong with me, and just take your damn pants off. Damn it, soldier, can't you take a hint?" her question was asked with a small laugh, but her fingers digging into his flesh belied the humor.

He pulled her closer to him, relishing the feel of her warm body molded to his.

Nibbling from his throat up to his lips, Josie teased him. Her hands made their way under his shirt, shoving the fabric up. Tanned skin exposed, she moved from his neck toward his abdomen. His breath was sharp. He wanted her more than ever. Wanted to strip her naked and bury himself so deep they could never be torn apart, but once again, Maddy was in his head.

"Josie, last night, you said a name—Toby."

Her cheeks flushed red. "I did?" She closed her eyes a moment, then opened them and said, "Can we please not talk about this?"

"Josie—"

"You promised. You said you didn't need to know anything to love me. You said that."

She was right, he did make that promise. But that was before…

"You're scaring me, Tucker." Her hands dug into his shoulders where she clung to him. He'd begged her to trust him. Assured her she was safe with him. What were his choices? In his mind, he only had one--he would keep his promises. Even if it meant taking the wide road to hell.

He rolled her over, pressing her body against the couch. They tugged and pulled at clothes, stripping them off and tossing them. With her arms wrapped over his shoulders, her nails dug into his flesh. Her legs tightened across his hips as her body arched into his, begging him to hurry. Burying his face in the hollow of her throat, he joined her. Her body matched his in such perfect rhythm, he wasn't certain he was even breathing until her body tightened against his, and she called his name in surrender.

Spent and gasping for air, she snuggled closer, settling her cheek against his chest where his heart pounded. Planting a kiss on top of her head, he held her close.

A sharp knock on her door made them both jump. "Josie? You up?"

"It's Murray," she whispered.

Tucker almost knocked over the coffee table getting up and dressing so fast. He handed Josie her underwear and pants, and she did her best to untwist the fabric as she hopped toward the door. "Just a minute. I'm, I...just got up."

Tucker slipped from the living room into the bedroom and hid behind the curtain.

He heard her open the door. Murray said, "I need to go out of town for a bit. I wanted to know if you'd keep an eye on Hetty for me."

Josie sounded winded. "Of course. Why do you need to leave?"

"Nothing for you to worry yourself over. Just need to go to the mainland for a few classes on repairing newfangled motors. Computer chips in them and what not that I can't learn online. Forgot I'd even signed up for the damned thing. Good thing I hired Tucker for the season. Speaking of that devil, have you seen him?"

Josie paused. When she finally spoke, her sputters failed to make a coherent sentence. Murray sighed. "Come on out, Tucker. I need to talk to you."

Tucker came out from the bedroom. He expected Murray to attack him. Instead, Murray motioned him outside.

The morning sun and humidity were oppressive. After last night's storm, the air was so thick, it was almost tough to breathe.

On the porch, Murray reached around him and closed Josie's door. Turning his back to her window, he said quietly, "I have to leave town for a bit. Something's come up I need to deal with."

"Okay. Do you have a list of work for me?"

"No, I'm not worried about that. I should only be gone a week. Go ahead and deliver what's done, keep one eye on the renters, and check in on Hetty every now and again. She gets to worrying, and it can't be healthy for her."

"Certainly."

"And I was going to suggest you stick close to Josie, but seems you got that covered."

"Sir, I—"

"I don't have time for bullshit, boy. I'm not blind. We'll talk when I get back. For now, I don't want her here alone or running about town. Keep her here. Keep her safe. And don't rent out any more of the cottages. Anyone calls, they're all booked. Can you do that?"

"What the hell's going on?"

"I'll explain it all later. Can you do what I asked?"

"Of course. Did something happen? You seem awfully uptight for a guy going to engine classes."

Murray sighed. "I can't get into it now. I have to go. Let's just say, Josie made enemies, and they may be looking for her. I need to find out what they know. I don't think they know where she is, but if they do, she's not safe."

"Holy shit." Tucker took a breath. His heart pounded.

"You know how to use a gun, right?"

"Yeah."

"I put one in your cottage. I stopped by your place first. Don't let Josie know about the gun. I don't want her upset. She lives with trouble; she doesn't need more."

"What the—"

"Save it. I've got to go. Do what I asked, you hear?"

Tucker nodded. Murray gave him a solemn look, glanced at Josie's window, then turned and left. Tucker returned to a nervous Josie. She was shaky, chewing on her lip. "Why did he take you outside and close the door?"

Tucker grinned as he pulled her into him. "I obviously ravished his niece. A *what are my intentions* talk was in order."

Josie let out a sigh, her shoulders relaxing with relief as she wrapped her

arms around his neck. "What are your intentions?"

"I told Murray they were all noble and good. But I lied."

Chapter Twenty One

Tucker delivered the finished appliances and motors. When he asked Josie to forget her work and tag along, she happily agreed. When they returned, he helped her clean up the cottages, and then they went to check on Hetty.

"I'm fine," Hetty grumbled. "I don't know why the old fool thinks I need to be checked up on."

"It's not a check-up, Ms. Hetty. It's a check in. I wanted to let you know I got everything delivered. Here's the stack of invoices." He handed her the papers. "I also picked up three more jobs from people who stopped us while we were delivering. I explained to them Murray was out of town for a bit, but they said they were in no hurry."

"That's fine. What'd you get? I'll log it in."

"A lawn mower, a microwave, and a clock. I wasn't sure if Murray did clocks, but Mrs. Jones was so adamant; I took her word for it."

Hetty shook her head, and the fat waddle under her neck jiggled. "Clarisse and that old clock. Yes, Murray can fix it. It was her grandfather's, so it means a lot to her, but she over winds the damn thing. Murray tells her every time. She never listens." Hetty shifted on her cane. "I suppose you two ought to be getting on to the beach. You can come by later for dinner."

Tucker looked to Josie. She nodded. "Yes, ma'am," he said.

The metal screen door banged as Hetty disappeared into her house.

Tucker turned to Josie and said, "Come on, I'll make you lunch, and then we'll hit the beach." He offered her his hand and led her to his cottage. Murray's words of caution on top of last night's panic attack made him feel like he had a boulder in his gut. No matter how hard he tried to shake off the heavy feeling, it stuck with him. He squeezed her hand a bit tighter, pulling her a bit closer. She responded by bumping her shoulder into him and flashing him a smile that made him want to cry. Or kill whoever would hurt her. "So, what's for lunch?"

"It's a surprise," he said leading her up the steps and into his cabin.

Putting the frying pan on the burner, he turned up the heat and then opened the bologna package. Josie leaned against the counter. "What are you doing?" she asked.

"Frying some bologna," he said, laughing at her look of curiosity. "I told you you'd be surprised." He grinned. "I take it you've never had fried bologna?"

Josie shook her head. "My mother never allowed bologna in the house."

"No bologna? No alcohol? No violent movies. Damn, you were sheltered."

Josie stuffed her hands in her pockets as she shrugged. "No. Just a lot of rules."

"I have very few rules," he said with a wink. "So, you're in for a real treat."

Josie's grin was barely a grimace. The smell of cooked lunchmeat filled the tiny space. Tucker was about to ask her about the rules when she covered her mouth with the back of her hand and ran outside.

Tucker turned off the skillet and followed her. "You all right?"

She plopped herself down on the steps, her head in her hands. "I'm fine. The smell got to me. Made me feel a bit nauseated."

Tucker sat beside her, taking her hand in his. "I'm sorry."

Josie laughed weakly. "It's hardly your fault."

He kissed her cheek. "You relax here a second; I'll find you something less revolting."

She laughed. "No, I'm fine."

"Sit. No arguments," he said as he headed into the cottage.

He returned with his fried sandwich, a cold turkey sandwich for her, chips, and colas. Josie took the food with a smile. They ate and then headed for the shore.

They spent the afternoon at the beach. The surf was mild to the point of boring. Sprawled in the sun, Tucker's thoughts turned to the many, many ways a girl like Josie could be scarred. Rape was the obvious answer. Then he thought of Murray's warning. He'd said *people* were after her. Not a guy. Not an ex. People. There were people after her.

Rolling onto his side, he opened his eyes. He couldn't allow his imagination to wander—there were too many scenarios running through his head, and none of them were good. Instead, he concentrated on right now. She was here, safe and happy, lying so close he could feel the heat from her skin. Smell her honeysuckle scent as the sun bore down on her. It was that same intimate scent that filled the room when her body was warmed and ready for him.

Reaching out, he swept tendrils of hair off her neck. She rolled her face toward him. Her eyes were closed against the sun, long lashes brushing against the faint freckles on her cheeks. The wind blew in soft gusts. Leaning over, he nipped her ear lobe.

"Mmm, Tucker."

Sliding her hair to the side, he kissed her neck, moving slowly down to her back.

A satisfied moan escaped her. Tucker smiled. Running a hand down the curve of her hips, he said, "Come on."

She shook her head lazily. "I was enjoying that."

"A little too much."

Supporting herself on her elbows, she looked up at him as he stood. "You're a tease, Tucker Boone."

"I have to keep you dangling on the hook a little bit. I don't want you to take me for granted. Now, come on, let's hit the water."

Standing, she stretched, yawning and groaning. Grabbing her hand, he pulled her along, though she was slow, stopping at the breaker line claiming she needed a minute to adjust to the water.

Tucker didn't. He dove in and swam out farther than he normally would. Josie waded hip deep into the placid water close to shore. She yelled to him. "Where are you going?"

Swimming back to her, he said, "Just burning off some energy."

"That's too far. You'll get eaten by a shark." Josie lectured as she slowly ran her hands over water so smooth it mirrored the sun's rays, making her look like she was glowing. Drops of water clung to her breasts and shimmered in the sun. Her breasts looked fuller. Much suppler now than that first day on the beach.

A memory from Iraq flashed in his head. One of the Army MP's had sat with them during mess. She was in a seriously pissy mood. When they asked her why, she admitted she was afraid she was pregnant. She'd said her tits were bigger. Ash had told her that was a double win, bigger tits and a ticket home. She almost bit Ash's head off. She hadn't wanted a ticket home. Especially not to a husband she hadn't seen in four months.

There was a collective, "oh" among the group, then Ash, being the dumb ass bastard he was, asked her if she knew any Haji's that did abortions. When she seemed to consider his suggestion, Ash dug himself in deeper by offering her a spiritual lesson in the evils of abortion. The more Tucker thought about it, he was surprised Ash lived long enough to take an enemy bullet.

Cold water to the face brought Tucker back to reality. Shocked he looked to Josie, and she laughed and splashed him again. "You're ignoring me," she said. "I'm trying to keep you from being shark bait, and you're a hundred miles away. Is something wrong?"

"Of course not. Come on, let's head back," he said. Keeping a hand at the small of her back, he walked her silently back to their towels. He was trying to think of the best way to approach this new worry in light of all the changes of the last twenty-four hours. It felt like things were unraveling. He had to make wise choices, like he was playing an extremely tricky, high-stakes hand of cards. Sending his mother her picture was a mistake. He felt it in his gut. He should have trusted they were meant to be together. No matter what. Even if she wasn't really Josie McCoy.

"You okay?" she asked slowly as she moved toward the shore.

On the beach, she dried without looking at him. Tucker didn't look at her either. He stared out across the waveless sea, planning his best approach.

"I thought you wanted to leave?" she asked.

"Sit a minute."

She sat, hugging the towel to her chest like a child would grip a teddy bear. He hated himself for worrying her. Taking her hand, he gave it a squeeze and pulled her closer to him. "I was wondering, when was your last period?"

Josie gave him a weird look. "You don't seriously think? But we used—"

"I know, but things happen. Things fail."

Her eyes were wide. "Are you mad at me? Is that why you've been acting so weird?"

Tucker scowled. "I haven't been acting weird."

"If you say so," Josie mumbled. Sucking in her lower lip, she chewed on it. "I don't remember when my last one was. I don't keep track."

Scooting closer, he lifted her hand and pressed it to his lips. "Have you had one since I got here?"

Josie looked at him wide eyed. "No, but do you really think it's possible? I mean, I can't be. I would know."

"I've been here almost two months."

"Really? Are you mad at me?"

Kissing her forehead, he asked, "Why would I be mad?"

She shrugged. "Isn't that what guys are supposed to do in this situation?"

"If we're in a *situation*, it's *our situation*, and no, it doesn't worry me. As long as you're all right."

"I'm fine. Though, I won't lie. I'm stunned. I never even considered it. Shouldn't I have guessed before you? It's my body."

"And a sweet body it is."

His comment got him an eye roll from Josie, who now seemed more obsessed with pregnancy than flirting. "We need to get a test," she said as she started packing up her stuff.

Tucker helped her pack. "Is there a drugstore on the island?"

"On Ocracoke, we have Ella's."

"No, we'll look farther north. There has to be one on one of these

islands."

She nodded. Her hands shook as she packed their things in her bag.

"You okay?"

"I'm afraid you're going to hate me."

Tucker took the bag she was haphazardly stuffing and dropped it on the ground. He pulled her to him. "Why in the hell would I hate you? That's the stupidest thing I've ever heard."

She nodded, her eyes bright with unshed tears. He kissed her. Cradling her face in his hands, he said, "I love you. Nothing will ever change that."

She tried to smile, but the effort seemed to be exhausting. Her movements were slow and distracted. Tucker helped her pack the bag, and then they headed back.

Tucker checked his phone. The closest pharmacy was a ferry ride away. Not bothering to change, they drove up the island. There was a short line for the ferry, so they waited with the engine running. Tucker took her hand and held it. "It's going to be all right."

She nodded, though she didn't look at all convinced. Tucker wanted to hug her, but a car behind him honked alerting him that his line was moving, and it was their turn to load onto the boat.

As the ferry attendants chocked the tires, Tucker and Josie got out and made their way to the side of the boat. Wrapping an arm over her shoulder, he held her. She rested her head on his chest. Neither spoke. They sat and watched the sea gulls dive and dip into the water. The ferry gave a blast to its horn and a puff of diesel sent the boat on its way.

A few minutes on the rocking boat with the thick smell of diesel clinging to the air was all it took for Josie to shove past Tucker and bolt to the single-stall bathroom. She didn't get the heavy iron door latched. Tucker opened it a crack. "You okay?"

He could hear her heaving. Just saying the word pregnancy used to be enough to make him quake in his combat boots. He might have completely lost his mind, but as he considered all the nausea, the swollen breasts, and now, the motion sickness—all signs she was pregnant. That gave him hope.

They would have a baby. Be a family. He should be scared to death, but he wasn't. The more he considered the scenario, the better he liked the idea. Sure, they were young, but it wasn't like they were teenagers. And no, he hadn't known her long, but he could no longer imagine life without her. This could be a good thing. As long as Josie was all right with it.

She stood. Her legs were shaky, and she grabbed at the walls of the bathroom. Tucker wrapped an arm around her waist and escorted her out, leading her up a flight of narrow metal steps to a seat in the air-conditioned viewing cabin. He bought her a soda and sat beside her. She took it with an embarrassed smile. His return smile was the easiest, most genuine facial movement he'd made in years.

"This makes you happy?" she asked.

"The more I think about it, yeah, it makes me happy."

Leaning against him, she closed her eyes. He kissed the top of her head and made them comfortable for the rest of the trip.

When they arrived at Hatteras, they found the first drug store, and she suggested he make the purchase, since he didn't seem to be suffering any embarrassment. Tucker agreed. There was zero shame on his part. He pushed through the glass door head held high and bought a double pack. When he returned to the car, he handed the bag to Josie. She looked inside and said, "I'm scared."

Brushing fingers across her cheek, he said, "Don't be scared. We'll work it out. No matter what."

She nodded.

As they drove back to the ferry, Josie said, "I don't have insurance. And you know, Murray will probably kill us."

"I'll marry you, so that should please Murray. And don't worry about the costs."

"What if I can't marry you?"

The worries he left on shore returned. He gave her a quizzical look, and she avoided his eyes, looking out the window. Attempting to sound light-hearted, he said, "Don't tell me you're already married."

"Married?" she repeated the question with a shake of her head. "Oh, no. It's not that."

"Then what?" He asked, though he wasn't at all sure he wanted to know. The steering wheel suddenly felt slick with sweat.

She took a deep breath. "What if I told you I'm not who I say I am?"

Anxiety punched him in the gut. What if she was Maddy, and she did run away to escape danger? Murray said there were people who wanted to harm her. Oh God, if she was—no, he couldn't think that way. He'd lose everything. He took a slow gulp and reminded himself not to be paranoid. "Listen, no matter what, we'll work it out. I know you—Josie McCoy. She's the one I love. Who you were before doesn't really matter."

"Seriously? What if I'm wanted for murder or something?"

Shaking his head, he said, "No, you're not."

"You're right. I'm not. But still, I tell you I'm not who I say I am, and you don't care?"

He gripped the wheel as a wave of nausea washed over him. She could not be Maddy.

Could she?

He tried to shake off the thought, but it lingered. Slowly, a new thought took hold. It didn't matter, especially if he was right about the baby. Looking across at her worried, pinched face, he knew this couldn't be her burden. Murray was right, she had enough worries in her life. "Listen, whatever it is you're running from, is exactly that—something *you* are running *from*. I don't know what happened, and frankly, I don't give a damn what it was. You've told me it hurts you to talk about it, so we won't."

She bit her lower lip as tears rolled down her cheeks.

Reaching for her hand, he held it. "Don't cry, Josie."

"I need to be honest..."

He didn't want to hear any confessions. As far as he was concerned, she was Josie. Always would be unless she told him differently, and he wasn't planning to encourage that. "You need to stop worrying. Hell, I don't give a shit if we have to skip the country, we're in this together. And enough with the guilt. You don't have to tell me a damn thing. We might have a baby to think about. That's what matters."

Nodding slowly, a smile twitched at the corners of her mouth. She let out a long, relieved sigh and squeezed his hand tighter. "I love you," she said.

"And I'm crazy as hell over you."

Once they were back on the ferry, they headed straight for the air-conditioned cabin. Tucker tried to talk her into using the test in the ferry bathroom, but she refused. So they waited. When they got back to the cottage, Josie grabbed the bag and headed straight to the bathroom.

Tucker hovered by the door.

Josie emerged wide-eyed and shaky as she handed Tucker the stick.

Chapter Twenty Two

Tucker's heart raced. Suddenly all hope for a happy future relied on this little piece of plastic. Staring into the window, one pink line appeared quickly, then another slowly. "Two lines mean what?"

"Positive," Josie said. Moving closer, she tried to look over his arm. "Is it positive?"

He passed her the stick. Her hands shook as she stared at the two pink lines.

"You're pregnant, Josie."

"Oh my." Josie walked to the couch then sat there, staring at the stick. Tucker kneeled in front of her. "This is a good thing. We'll make this work, I swear."

"I can't even go to the doctor. They'll want ID, won't they? I don't have any—and no way to get one. When I left home, I took nothing. And I can't go back."

Tucker swallowed. His heart raced as his curiosity battled rational thought. Ask her no questions, she'll need not tell you lies. Taking a calming breath, he caressed the sides of her knees. "I have a friend, Santos, you know the guy dating Ash's widow?"

Josie nodded.

"He's a police officer. He has to know how to get ID. I'll call him."

"Even if I can get an ID— me? A mom? I don't know how to be mom."

"You'll be a great mom. You're thoughtful and gentle."

"My mother was horrible."

"You're not her. You'll be the best."

Leaning forward, she gave him a look, like she was studying him. "You're honestly excited about this?"

Placing a hand behind her head, he kissed her. "Zero regrets. Are you all right with it?"

She nodded. "Yeah, I'm just…it feels unreal. I never dreamed I'd be this happy. I'd accepted life sort of sucked, and I've made the best of it. And now? A baby. A tiny Tucker baby."

"We'll call a doctor and get you in. If we pay cash, there should be no questions."

Nodding, she placed her hand over his. "I never thought I'd have a normal life. A baby…"

He planted kisses on her bare shoulder. "I'm going to marry you."

"Are you proposing?" She laughed.

"No, I'm telling you."

"Neanderthal."

He laughed as he tugged loose the string that held her bikini top around her neck. She grabbed at the pink material. "No time, Mr. Boone. We're expected at Hetty's for dinner."

"Fine, I suppose I'll call Santos after we get back from Hetty's."

Josie looked at him. "If I go over and stall dinner, could you call him now?"

Tucker ran a lazy finger down her arm. "If you can stall…"

"She'll expect one of us to be on time. And I have just enough time for a quick shower. That's it."

"Hmm, you could stay dirty. I like you dirty."

Laughing, she stood. "You're so bad. Go. Make your call and meet me at Hetty's."

"I'll wait here until you're done showering. Then I'll walk you over."

She shook her head, looking at him like he had totally lost his mind. "That's the most ridiculous thing I've heard. Why in the world?"

"Humor me. Blame PTSD or shell shock, or whatever, but anytime I feel this damn happy, I get nervous."

Her head tipped toward her shoulder. "Ah Tucker, it's going to be all right. I'll be out in a second."

He left her at Hetty's door. She suddenly seemed reluctant to leave him.

He felt bad for putting the idea of tragedy in her head, but how else could he explain sticking to her like Murray asked? Holding her loosely, with his hands on her hips, he kissed her. "Everything is going to be great. We're going to be a family."

Her eyes glistened, but her smile was broad. "We will, won't we?"

Nodding, he kissed her. "Go on in. I'll be back in a minute."

She kissed him one last time before she left.

Once he was halfway across the lawn, he called his mother. He had to stop her from visiting Gloria.

"Hi, honey," she answered, sounding happy.

"Hey, Mom, you haven't gone to PA yet have you?"

"No."

"Good. Forget about it. She's not Maddy."

"How do you know?"

"I just know," he snapped.

"Feeling guilty for sleeping with her?"

"No. I trust she is who she says she is."

"Oh, my God Tucker, what have done? You're still having sex with her?"

"Damn it, Mom. I never said I was having sex with her. Jesus, what's your problem?"

"I'm sorry, I just assumed. You are Robert's child. I just figured if it wore a skirt, you chased it. So, you're not screwing her?"

"Just drop it. I love her and that's all that matters."

"You can't love her. She could be your sister."

"No, she isn't." Tucker's words were clipped.

His mother took a deep breath. "You're making a mistake. Come home. You need to put distance between yourself and this girl."

"I can't."

"You have to. Does she know who you are? Does she know you may be her brother?"

"Would you stop saying that shit? I swear to God there is no evidence of that. Just stupid clues that mean nothing."

His mother's voice dropped to a near whisper. "What have you done?"

"Nothing," he said quietly. "I haven't done anything wrong."

"Tucker?" she asked with that Mom interrogation voice.

"Fine." She wanted to know. He'd tell her. "She's pregnant." His hand was suddenly sweaty on the phone.

"I hope you're joking. Tell me you're joking."

"I can't."

"Seriously, Tucker? How many times is your dick going to get you in trouble?" his mom shouted.

"It's not the way you think. It's a good thing. It will work out; I know it will."

"Does she know?"

"What? That she's pregnant?"

"No, you dumb ass. Does she know your father is Robert Morgan? Do you know her father's name?"

"No, but her dad died years ago. I'm telling you, she's not Maddy."

"I suppose now's a bad time to tell you Gloria thinks she could be Maddy."

"I thought you didn't take her the picture?"

"I didn't. Ed did."

"Damn it, Mom. You and your f—"

"Stop yourself right there. Don't you dare think you can take that tone or language with me. Considering Gloria and my history, I felt it best Ed go talk to her. Gloria is convinced she's Maddy and wants you to bring her home."

"I'm telling you, she's not Maddy."

"So, you say. Good grief, your kid's mother can be its aunt too."

Tucker panicked. His mind raced, looking for any other answer. He thought of the two girls in the picture. Maddy and her friend. They looked alike. "If—and that's a huge if. If she is one of the girls, she's Ariel."

"That's what Ed said, too. Gloria showed him pictures of Maddy, and your super-sleuth of a stepdad decided she had to be the Stone girl. He was so convinced, I had to email the picture to the girl's mom, and I have bad news for you there, playboy, Amanda Stone says she's Maddy too."

"You did what?"

"Well, Ed wouldn't let it go. He wouldn't let me call and tell you she was Maddy until he was convinced. And I suppose Ed had a point that Gloria was just so eager to believe she was her baby, she had zero objectivity. I looked up Amanda Stone's number and called. She asked me to email the picture, so I did. She said it wasn't her daughter. But she was certain the girl looked like Maddy."

Tucker shook his head. It wasn't possible. Destiny wouldn't have drawn him to someone he couldn't ever have.

"So, what the hell are you going to do? Are you sure she's pregnant?"

"I'm not sure of anything. I've got to go."

He hung up the phone. The hell he wasn't sure. He knew he loved her, and he damn sure wasn't giving up his kid.

His next call was to Santos. When he asked about getting a fake ID, his friend laughed. "You racist son of a bitch. You think just because I'm Mexican, I know how to get fake IDs?"

"I'm sorry, man. That was stupid of me. I thought since you were a cop, and I'm just—"

"Oh, I can get them. I'm just giving you a hard time. Should I ask what you did?"

"I need it for a girl. She can't get a legal ID."

"Oooh found yourself a sexy housekeeper, huh?"

"Now, who's being the damned racist?"

Santos laughed. "I'll find out what it'll cost you. I can assure you, it won't be cheap."

"Whatever it costs. I'll pay it."

Hanging up the phone, he had an ominous feeling. He hoped when the costs were tallied up, he was only paying in dollars and cents.

Chapter Twenty Three

Hetty's front door was open, and he could hear her and Josie talking, so he walked on in. Hetty's exasperated voice brought him to a stop. "You don't know if he's trustworthy or not. You'll say nothing until Murray gets back. For all we know, he came here looking for you."

"And his plan was to stay here for a month, make me to fall in love with him, and then kill me? Seriously, that would be a stupid plan. He's sometimes confused and angry, but he would never, ever hurt me, that I know."

"Bring me that stool. My feet are killing me. And chop those onions finer."

Tucker heard a chair scoot across the floor. "You and your feelings."

"You've always trusted them before."

"True, true. But still, I'm still saying there is no way you're telling him who you are until Murray says all right. You owe the man that much."

The knife paused in the chopping. "You're right. I won't say anything."

"Is he pressing? Trying to find out who you are?"

"No. He doesn't seem to care about my past at all."

"That's good."

"Not even after the other night. I panicked during the storm. He says I said Toby."

"Who's Toby?" Hetty asked.

"My dog."

"Why would you saying your dog's name make someone suspicious? Especially a stranger who knows nothing about your past?"

"True. He was probably more suspicious of why the storm freaked me out."

"Probably thinks Toby is an old boyfriend," Hetty said with a nod. "I'd leave it that way. At least until you can talk to Murray."

"I hate lying to him. He's so good to me. He even offered to get me fake ID."

"Why on earth do you need that?"

"We want to get married, and I need to see a doctor."

"Why would you need a doctor? Or get—don't tell me you're pregnant."

The knife resumed its chop chop against the cutting board. "Then I won't tell you," Josie said.

"Oh my God, you are. You're pregnant."

"A little bit."

"A little bit? How in God's name are you a little bit pregnant? You either are or you aren't."

"Then I am."

"Are you crazy? Did you think this through at all?"

The knife slowed again and he could hear Josie start to cry. "Come here, child. For God's sake, don't you dare cry. A baby is always a blessing. And you'll make a wonderful momma."

Josie sniffed. "I hope so."

Tucker cleared his throat. He wasn't going to let Josie carry the weight of this confession by herself. He found her in the kitchen enclosed in a big bear hug from Hetty.

"You'll be the best mom. I had a baby once, did you know that?"

"No," Josie said.

"Yes, I did. Come, I'll show you his picture." Sliding off the stool she was sitting on, she kept hold of Josie's arm. They saw Tucker at the same time.

"I suppose congratulations are in order. Piss poor timing, but congratulations."

"Uh, thanks?" Tucker wished he could grab Josie and leave. Take her away, curl up, and forget all about the world. But he couldn't. All he could do was pretend he heard nothing, suspected nothing, and pretend he was happy to be here.

"Come. I'm showing Josie pictures of my boy."

She led them to the living room. The ceiling was low and the furniture was covered in afghans and quilts. Evidently, Hetty had kept her promise to declutter. The last time Tucker was in this room, he couldn't see the floor. Tucker thought she'd give up after finishing the kitchen, but she hadn't. There were tables visible and chairs to sit on. Hetty sat in a recliner and motioned them toward the couch.

"Murray and I finished the house, Tucker. Mercy, I forgot what a good man I married. Going through the rooms, remembering all the good times and the bad. We got everything sorted out. It feels good." Hetty looked around the room with pride. "I'm thinking when Murray gets back, we should start having Sunday dinner together. We're sort of like family. Gonna have a baby." Hetty sighed. "And speaking of babies. I've never liked to talk about it, but…" Hetty bent over and pulled an album out from under the table by her chair and set down the album.

It was well worn. Hetty handled it with tenderness, opening each page carefully.

"This is Robert Murray Banks. We called him Bobby."

Tucker scooted closer. It was a picture of a thin woman with a dark-haired baby.

"Can you believe I was so damned skinny?" Hetty said with a hoot. "Dear me, I've tripled my size. Poor Murray. Never complains."

Neither Josie nor Tucker said anything. Hetty kept flipping pages. The newborn became a chubby baby, then a smiling toddler. Hetty and Murray looked happy. Tucker put a hand on Josie's waist. He wasn't sure he wanted to hear the end of this story.

"Bobby walked early. Look at those chubby legs. Boy could he run on them." She flipped through more pages. They made it a third of the way through the book and the pictures stopped. Smiling over birthday cake one minute. Blank page the next.

"What happened?" Josie asked, a catch in her throat.

"He was stung by a bee. We never even knew he was allergic. By the time we got him to a doctor, his breathing had stopped, and he was gone. Happy one day, gone the next."

"I'm so sorry." Josie broke into tears. "I can't believe you never told me."

Hetty handed her a tissue. "Oh, don't you cry. Then I'll cry, and I've cried so much I fear if I start, I won't stop. Josie, do you remember when you first moved here, I asked why you spent so damned much time in that cemetery, and you told me you talk to the angel there?"

Josie dried her eyes with the tissue and nodded.

"And do you remember what I asked you?"

Josie folded the tissue in her hand. "You wanted me to ask why children die if God is so wonderful."

"And what did that angel tell you?"

"Death isn't a punishment. It's a crossroad," Josie said.

"Now, I know I threw the BS card on that when I first heard it. But as I let the idea roll around my head, it made sense and was exactly what I needed to hear. Now, when I look over these pictures, I think of him as being on a trip. A wonderful trip. He had a wonderful life. He never got a broken heart. He never had to say good-bye to so much as a pet. And I know I'll see him again, because you know what else you said?"

Josie shook her head.

"When you first told me this crossroad business, I told you to tell the angel it was full of shit. You know what you said the next morning?"

Josie shook her head.

"You told me, Mags says you shouldn't be such a naughty bird; somebody might clip your wings. There is no way anyone, no human at least, knew what that phrase meant to me. You see, my mother used to say that to me, and I hated it. Then when she died when I was a teen, I wished beyond all wishes I could hear those words again." Hetty sighed. "It's funny, the things you miss when someone is gone. You think it will be the really good stuff—like her fig pudding or her rhubarb jelly. But no, it was that little phrase that used to infuriate me. I never tried to explain that to anyone. I mean, what do you say? I miss my mom cleverly telling me I was a rotten turd? It was a grief I kept to myself. So, when you told me the angel gave you that phrase, I was floored. I knew it wasn't a coincidence. I know you think you owe us, but darlin', I owe you. You gave me peace, Josie. Oh sure, it still hurts. I still miss my boy, but I'm ready to be happy in this life. And I assure you—I am excited about this baby. Is it good timing? Not really. Are there gonna be kinks? Most certainly. But we'll work it out, together."

Josie smiled and nodded.

"Well, good then, let's eat." Hetty heaved herself up. She grabbed the photo album and tucked it back into its spot under the table. Josie was at Hetty's side, handing her the cane. Tucker was up and ready to follow, but he spotted a picture that had fallen onto the floor. The two women were on their way to the kitchen and didn't notice him pick it up.

There were two men in the picture. One of the men Tucker recognized immediately. His dad. He was standing arm and arm with another soldier. Tucker looked closer. The nametags proved him correct. The man on the left was Morgan, the one on the right Banks. He turned the picture over. In Hetty's awkward scrawl, it read *Murray and Rob, Italy 1985.*

His heart dropped as he shoved the picture under the table, wishing he could pretend he never saw it.

Chapter Twenty Four

Tucker held Josie in bed. She snuggled close. His hands smoothed her hair over her shoulders as he listened, without really hearing, to her chatter about the baby. Josie could rattle off names quicker than a machine gun spewed bullets. Simple *mmm hmms* and an occasional *sure, sounds good* seemed to keep her satisfied as his mind tortured him.

After finding the picture of his dad in Hetty's living room, he knew there was a connection between his dad and Josie. Reason told him to simply ask her, but he couldn't form the words. And honestly, he feared if she gave the wrong answer, then what? They could never legally marry, even if Josie could look past them sharing a parent. They'd break up for sure; she might even be repulsed by him, and his child would call someone else dad. Being honest wasn't at the top of his options list.

"Are you listening, Tucker?"

"What?" he asked, looking down at her.

"I asked if you ever talked to your friend. The one who can get ID's?"

"Yeah, I did. He said he knows a guy who can help."

She nodded. "I really should explain. It's just…" She grew quiet and her eyes squeezed closed.

"Don't worry about it, Josie. It's not important. Let's just start our lives from right here. There's no sense digging up the past."

Burrowing tighter, she pulled the blanket to her chin. "It doesn't bug you that I'm not being completely honest with you?"

He took a deep breath. "Honesty is overrated. We don't need to pile our shit on a table and sort through it. We've got more important things to worry about right now."

"You're worried? You said you were happy."

"I am happy. And no, I'm not worried, I just mean we have more important things—"

"No, you said we had bigger worries. Those are your words. I knew something was wrong. I tried to convince myself it was nothing, but you've been lying to me. You say you're happy, but—"

"Come on, you're talking crazy. I'm happy. I swear to God, I'm happy."

"Liar. You're distant, and something is wrong. Very wrong. Is reality finally starting to hit you?"

"There is nothing wrong, I swear. This," he ran a hand across her belly, "gives me more clarity than you can imagine. Nothing matters to me more." He pulled her even closer, kissing the top of her head. He admitted to himself that he was a sick bastard not to be the least bit revolted she could be Maddy. No, he wasn't sad or upset about the baby. His only worry was keeping her; his only guilt was never telling Gloria her daughter might be alive.

"We should get some sleep," he said.

"I'm too wired. We should've watched a movie or went for a walk," she said with a yawn. "We've got so many decisions to make. Like where will we live? Neither of our places are big enough, but then babies are small, but they do grow…."

Tucker tried to listen to her. Tried to be as excited as she was, but he couldn't. His thoughts kept wandering back to the same problems as his fingers moved lazily through her hair. In no time, her eyelids grew heavy, and she was out.

Sleep didn't come as easily to Tucker. He lay there a while trying to relax, but his brain kept imagining the worst outcomes – like Josie hating him, or even worse, Josie hating herself for loving him. The girl already had some issues with guilt. A blind man could tell it wasn't her *friend* who was raped. His eyes burned with the thought. His grip on her tightened until she stirred in her sleep.

"Shh," he said, not wanting to wake her. She looked so fragile and innocent in the faint moonlight that poured in the window. What was he doing to her? How could he lie to her? He should just ask her, "Are you Madison Morgan?"

Then she could tell him no, and they could move on with their lives.

Or she could say yes, freak out from the shame of incest, and have nothing more to do with him. Then she'd have the baby without him. Or would she? Suddenly, the possibility that she could abort crossed his mind.

Oh, hell no, he thought. *I can't let that happen.*

He couldn't be honest. There was too much at stake. But then, he couldn't keep fooling her. Josie was a freaking mind reader; he'd never be able to convince her nothing was wrong much longer.

And who else did everyone say could understand things, verging on the paranormal?

Ariel Stone.

Looking down at the sleeping Josie, Tucker brushed the palm of his hand across her smooth cheek.

Everything about her pointed to Ariel, not Maddy. And Santos said they never found Ariel's body. Relief washed over him.

Crawling out of bed, he grabbed his phone and made his way to the living room. Just like a kid with a wound, he needed someone else to assure him he wasn't going to bleed to death.

"Hey, Mom, did I wake you?"

Marlene cleared her groggy voice and said, "Uh, no, of course not. I was reading. Is something wrong?"

"I couldn't sleep. I keep thinking about this Maddy thing…are you sure Gloria didn't see any resemblance between Josie and Ariel?"

"No, but to be honest, Ed's right; she wouldn't want to see any resemblance to anyone but her daughter."

"That's right. She's desperate to have her daughter back." Tucker felt hopeful again.

"But what explains the Stone woman? Wouldn't she be just as desperate for her daughter to be alive?"

"You'd think…but then, maybe she has been through the murder trial and has come to terms with the loss. Maybe she sees it as opening healed wounds."

"Yeah, that's a good point."

Marlene sighed. "You've really gotten yourself in a pickle, haven't you?"

"Yeah, a big one. I love her, Mom. I love her more than I've ever loved anything or anyone."

"I hate to say this Tuck, but the best thing you could do is walk away. Just leave and never look back. That's the only way she'll never find out you're Robert's son."

"No, I can't do that. I told you, I love her."

"Yes, you can. You think I didn't love your father? I loved that man with every fiber of my being, but I couldn't trust him. Before I got pregnant with you, chasing him from bar to bar while he chased anything in a skirt was fine. But once I knew I had a child on the way, it all changed. You needed stability. I didn't love Ed when I married him. I picked him with my head, not my heart. He was thoughtful and caring…the perfect father."

Marlene was silent for a long time. Tucker was glad to have a moment where he didn't need to speak. His chest was tight, and he wasn't sure he could pull enough air in to breathe, much less speak. His voice cracked when he tried to speak. Clearing his throat one more time, he said, "I've thought of every possible scenario. I know, even if we could legally get away with it, if people knew, Josie and the baby would be humiliated. But that could happen whether I'm with her or gone. She knows my name, and if she is Maddy and ever has a change of heart and goes home, Gloria knows all about me. Isn't it better that I'm there if it should ever get out? Honest to God, if I thought I could just walk away from this and only break my own heart, I'd do it."

"To be honest with you, the idea of having a grandchild somewhere on this earth and not knowing them kills me too."

"I can't let that happen. I don't know what I can do or where we can go, but I won't lose my kid."

"Well, I suppose there is France," Marlene said with a sigh into the phone. "Ed and I were looking tonight, and France allows siblings to marry."

"Shit. Why didn't you lead with that? That's a much better solution."

"Well, it doesn't save you from public humiliation or Josie rejecting you

when you tell her."

"I won't tell her. No one ever needs to know. Not even Josie."

"The truth always comes out, Tucker. I did my best to hide you from Robert, and look where it got me."

Tucker gave a half-hearted chuckle. "So, technically, this is your fault."

"You're such an ass." Marlene's laugh was a bit too loud, then she grew very quiet. "I better watch; I'll wake Ed."

"You go. Get back to sleep."

"I was reading."

"Sure, you were. Thanks, Mom."

"Any time. Nothing is more important than your babies, but I think you know that."

Chapter Twenty Five

Tucker felt much better after talking to his mother, but he still couldn't shake the guilt of deceiving Josie. So, he spent his anxious, sleepless night searching through Josie's belongings. In cabinets, under the sink…anywhere she might have something hidden that would prove she was either Josie McCoy or Ariel Stone.

Five hours later, he had nothing. She didn't even have so much as a credit card or a driver's license in her purse. No pictures. No bills. No letters. Even her phone was clean. He wasn't even listed as a contact. She must have every number in her life memorized. He even looked through the bedroom with a flashlight. Nothing. He'd thought he'd found something when he found a jewelry box, but there was nothing in it but sea shells, and the piece of sea weed he'd picked out of her hair that first day on the beach. His eyes stung as he carefully put the box back in its place on the shelf.

Giving up, he decided to take a shower. As the hot water poured over him, he began to relax and plan. France was the best option. He could probably talk Josie into going there by selling her on the idea of adventure. In France, they could live openly and his mom and Ed and Hetty and Murray could visit them, so there was no need to cut ties. All but Gloria. He tried to shove the skinny woman out of his mind as he climbed out of the shower. When he pulled a towel out of a corner hutch, he noticed a round notch cut into the base, like a finger hole. He tapped on the bottom of the shelf. It was hollow. There was a good bit of space between the bottom and the floor. He emptied the cabinet and took a deep breath. Maybe it was nothing more than a hollow base, not a hiding spot.

His heart beat was suddenly erratic and his mouth was dry. His gut told him to put everything back and walk away, but he couldn't. He lifted the board and underneath was a small, hollow space inaccessible by any means but through the false bottom. Sitting back on his heels, surrounded by all the towels and toiletries he'd emptied from the cabinet, he took a deep breath. It was definitely a hiding spot.

Behind him, there was a commotion. Someone was pounding on the front door. Tucker heard Josie's feet hit the floor, so he dropped the piece of wood and hurried to meet her.

Murray banged on the door calling, "Josie!"

Josie's eyes were round. "Do you think Hetty told him?"

"I don't know," Tucker said. "You wait here. I'll go talk to him."

Tucker opened the door. Murray's face was tight, his brow knitted together over his eyes. "I need to talk to Josie. Alone." Looking over Tucker's shoulder, Murray spotted her. "Josie, get on over to the house with Hetty."

"Can I shower and change?"

"No time. We need to talk."

"But, I—"

"No buts, Josie. You're coming with me."

"But I want to stay with Tucker," Josie said wrapping her arm around his waist.

Murray took a deep breath. "Come on, now."

"Did Hetty tell you about…last night?"

"Josie? Please?" Murray was starting to sweat.

Tucker thought of the mess in the bathroom. He just needed a minute alone, so he gave Josie a nudge. "Go on."

Looking up at him like she'd never see him again, she shook her head. Rubbing the small of her back, he assured her. "It's fine. I'll get dressed and be right over."

"Okay," she said, slipping her feet into a pair of flip-flops by the door. Murray grabbed her by the arm and walked her out of the cottage. Tucker watched until he could see them no more, then he made a beeline for the bathroom. Tossing aside his towel for a pair of shorts, he dressed quickly, then turned his attention to the cabinet. Stripping away the loose board, he found a shoebox. He carried it with him to the couch. It was covered in hearts and butterflies, like a little girl's treasure box. Taking a deep breath, he slowly opened the lid. Right on top was a diary with more butterflies. He opened the cover to find written in large girlie handwriting - *Property of Madison Nicole Morgan. Keep out!*

His stomach tightened, and he seriously thought he might vomit. Setting the book aside, he lifted out a picture. Two adolescent girls on the beach, arm in arm. The back said Ariel and Maddy. There were more pictures of the two girls but none said which girl was which. And it was hard to tell them apart. Similar builds, one with brown hair, one blonde. Looking frantically through the other pictures, he tried to find one that was labeled, so he could verify which girl was which. *Damn it,* he thought. *Who are you, Josie?*

The door swung open. "Tucker," Josie said.

He looked up at her as he dropped the pictures in the box.

"I can explain," he said. "I just found it. I never should have opened it."

"Why you say that, boy?" Murray said, stepping past Josie into the room. "There's nothing wrong with looking through a box of pictures...unless you know what you just found." Murray took another step closer and said, "And I can tell by the look on your face that you know damn good and well what you found, so I'm going to ask you just this once, who the hell sent you?"

"No one." Tucker knew the lie didn't roll off his tongue, and he could tell by the set of Murray's jaw that he wasn't buying the denial either. Tucker let out a long sigh and decided to come clean. "Gloria Morgan sent me. She's looking for her daughter, Maddy. I stumbled onto a clue and ended up here. I swear, I thought it was a dead end. I didn't think I'd ever find her."

"You what?" Murray's voice was sharp. He gave Josie a shove toward the door. "Get on back to the house."

"Murray, I– " Josie said.

"Go girl! Don't argue. Get out of here," Murray yelled at her, and she took off.

"Murray, I swear I can explain." Tucker took a step forward.

"No, you don't. You're gonna stop right there." Murray pulled a gun out of his waistband and pointed it at Tucker. "I trusted you. Hell, I let you get close enough to Josie to knock her up. I honestly thought you were good people. I was coming here to get you and tell you everything, but it seems you know. You sick son of a bitch. How can you use a girl like Josie? Who the hell sent you? Did they pay you to hurt her?"

Tucker held up his hands in surrender. "No. And I'm not here to hurt her. I love her. I swear to God. I love her more than anything in this world."

"Yeah, sure. Lying little asshole. You best just get in your car and get the hell out of here."

"I'm not leaving. Josie needs me."

Murray's answer was to cock the gun.

"Can I please talk to Josie first?"

"I'm gonna give you to the count of five. One…"

"If you'll just let me talk to her!"

Murray fired a shot at his feet.

"You'll have to shoot my ass, Murray. I'm not leaving. I'm not leaving Josie. I'm not leaving my baby." He shrugged. "Go ahead. Shoot."

Murray's jaw clenched, but his hand relaxed, and he lowered the gun.

Tucker decided he best come clean rather than risk Murray losing patience with him and getting trigger happy. "I was looking for my father, Robert Morgan. My mother is Marlene Boone."

"Marlene Boone? Short woman, fiery temper?"

"That's her. She told me about Robert when I joined the corps. When I got out of the military, I wanted to meet him, so I went to his house. Gloria said he'd had a stroke and was in a nursing home. Then she insisted I try to find Maddy."

Murray's eyes narrowed. "Gloria doesn't know Robert brought the girl here. So, how the hell did you know?"

"I followed the clue Gloria thought Maddy sent. The note? *I've gone Mad, Mags?*"

"I don't know anything about a note."

"There was a note. I'll show you." Tucker realized he was at Josie's and his papers were in his cabin. "They're not here. I could—"

"You're not going any damn place. You come with me. We've got bigger problems than a god damned letter."

Tucker followed him to the house. Josie was sitting with Hetty in the living room. Her eyes were red, and she had her legs tucked under her, making her look small and vulnerable. She rocked back and forth, her hands positioned on her belly like she was cradling it. "Tucker," she said with a small cry. "You're still here."

"I'll never leave you. I swear."

"Sit." Murray stepped between them. Tucker sat across from Josie. The space between them was a few feet, but it felt like a million miles.

Murray scraped his lips through his teeth before he explained, "Josie, someone's asking questions about you and getting people stirred up. I'm beginning to think it's Tucker here, but I can never be too sure. When Rob dropped you off, he said he'd explain everything later—who we should and shouldn't trust. Who it was who tried to kill you—but he had that stroke and never made it back."

"Someone tried to kill her? Tried to kill Josie?" Tucker directed the question at Murray.

"That's what Rob said," Josie answered. "I don't remember. The night Rob got me is all a blank."

"So, you see why I'm asking you, Tucker, and you better tell me the truth. Why are you here?"

"I told you. I wanted to find my dad. I went to his house, and Gloria gave me a letter that she figured would lead me to her daughter, and she wanted me to try to find her."

"I've gone Mad, Mags?" Josie whispered.

Tucker's heart stopped. "Yes. That letter."

"That letter brought you to me?"

Tucker nodded. "Gloria was certain Maddy sent that letter for Ariel to find her."

"Ohhh. Oh, my goodness, you think I'm Maddy? That's what's been bugging you."

"Hell, yes. You said Toby in your sleep. Gloria told me about the dog. Then I found a picture of my dad while we were looking at the pictures with Hetty. I knew it wasn't a coincidence you were here. Then I found that diary and shit— I know it's wrong, but damn it, I don't care...I love you."

"Oh Tucker," Josie said, coming across the room and settling herself next to him. "You should have asked me. How long has this bugged you?"

"Since the storm."

Running a gentle hand across his neck, she said, "Maddy was my best friend. My only friend, really. I loved her more than I could have ever loved a sister. It's no wonder I felt so close to you so quickly. Your humor, the things you say. You're a lot like her. Even your temper. She had quite the temper, you know."

"So, just to be clear, you're not Maddy?"

"No, I'm not Maddy. I sent that letter just in case Maddy was alive and she'd need to find me. It took me a long time to accept that she was gone."

"What the hell were you thinking, Josie?" Murray asked, shaking his head.

Josie shrugged. "Only Maddy would have figured it out."

"Tucker did," Murray said.

Josie smiled. "Yes, he did." Her arm wrapped around his back. "It was destiny."

"Jesus, Josie. If he found you, anyone can. Do you know why I left town this week?"

"For an engine repair seminar?" Josie answered.

"No, for crying out loud. That was a lie. It was because I got a letter from Jeb Stone's lawyer asking me to sign an affidavit verifying that I have no idea where Ariel Stone is. Now, why would he do that?"

Josie shrugged.

"I'll tell you why. He's heard rumors you're alive, and he thinks I know where you are. I think they wanted to see my reaction, see if I'd flinch and give away something."

"What did you say?" Hetty asked.

Murray stood and paced. "I told him I never met Ariel Stone. He asked why I came and I said it gave me reason to visit my old buddy Rob, and to meet with them and see if there was any news on Maddy. I told him we're always hoping Maddy will contact someone. Thought maybe they knew something since all their letter said was they'd like to discuss new *developments* in the case."

"Did he believe you?" Hetty asked.

"Seemed to. I asked him, 'Is there a chance the Stone girl's alive? Maybe the girls ran away together?' I was hopeful, almost got myself believing the two coulda run away together."

"All of this, just because Tucker asked Gloria a few questions?"

"My mother asked questions too," Tucker said. "My stepdad took a picture of Josie to Gloria, and then to Amanda Stone. Oh, and a friend of mine. Santos got police reports to see if there were any clues about Maddy's whereabouts."

"Holy shit, son. Did you call the FBI too?"

Tucker thought of Santos's connection at Quantico. He shrugged. It seemed like a good idea at the time.

Murray sighed and rubbed his balding head.

"Why didn't you just ask me?" Josie asked.

Tucker squeezed his hands together. "That seems easy now, but I couldn't. I felt so close to you. I knew I loved you—then the baby. I didn't know what to do. Both Gloria and Amanda swore you were Maddy. What was I supposed to do? I was afraid if I told you who I was, you'd leave me. You'd take my baby…I'd lose you both."

"Oh, my poor, sweet guy." Josie kissed his cheek. "Don't worry, I'm not your sister, I swear. Maddy and I did look a lot alike." Josie's smile was broad.

"That still leaves us with a problem," Murray said with a shake of his head. "People may be a bit too curious, and that could spell danger for Josie. Five years ago, someone tried to kill her, or well, Ariel Stone. That's why she's using the name Josie. I don't know that you can stay here. At least not until we know what's going on."

"But I'm supposed to go to the doctor tomorrow. And…and…I don't…I have nowhere else to go."

Tucker patted her leg. "We'll see the doctor, and then we'll go stay with my friend. At least until we know what's going on. He's a cop. We should be safe."

"That's a good idea," Hetty said.

Josie looked pale. Murray squatted in front of her and took her by the hand. "Don't look so scared. It's going to be all right."

"I don't want to leave. I'm happy here."

"It's just for a while, and Tucker will be with you. Think of what they did to Maddy." Murray's tone was gentle. Josie nodded, but she didn't look convinced.

"What happened to Maddy, Josie?" Tucker asked, taking her hand and holding it.

"I saw Jeb strangle her. Then he gave her body to a guy who put her in the trunk of his car, and he drove away."

"He did what? How the hell did he get away with that? I read all the police reports—"

"I didn't actually *see* it. I saw it, in a vision."

Hetty and Murray squirmed in their seats. Tucker nodded slowly.

"I took a bottle of pills the night it happened."

Tucker nodded. He didn't know if he should tell Josie that he knew Ariel Stone's story. How she had swallowed a bottle of sleeping pills the night Maddy disappeared. How she was hospitalized for the suicide attempt and later murdered the night she was released from the hospital. Or so the story went.

"The night I took the pills, Maddy and I were going to run away. I was sneaking out of the house when my mother caught me. She grabbed me by my hair and yanked me into the garage. As she dragged me away, I spotted Maddy and Toby in the bushes. I shook my head at her. I didn't want my mother to know she was there.

The commotion brought Jeb to the garage and he yelled at my mother for hurting me. He slapped her, and I could tell she was furious. The look she gave me. When she let go of me, I lost my footing and fell. Jeb came toward me to help me up and Toby came into the garage, barking like a maniac. I thought for sure he'd wage war on Jeb and lose, so I tried to stop him…tried to grab his collar, but before I could…" Josie covered her mouth with her hand and choked back a sob. "Jeb kicked him. One kick to the head and poor Toby went limp. He was just a little dog."

Josie took a breath. "I was afraid Maddy would come charging out of hiding, so I ran into the house knowing Jeb would follow. He kept apologizing for Toby, promising me a new dog. I hated him. And I hated my mother who was screaming from the bottom of the steps that she was sending me to jail for trying to run away. She kept screaming, 'I'm calling the police now, you little bitch. And your ass is going to jail too, Jeb Stone. You won't hit me and get away with it.' I knew I'd never get away from them. Not in this life."

"So, you took the bottle of pills?"

Tears shined in her eyes. Her voice quivered as she answered, "Yeah. But as soon as I did, I knew it was a mistake. I could hear Maddy yelling at them, threatening them with the police. Maddy was such a fighter." Josie closed her eyes, and her body swayed.

Tucker held her close, whispering in her ear, "It's all right."

Gripping the arms that held her, she shook her head. "No, I want you to know. Maddy wasn't just anyone. She was the best of us. She had the fire and spirit. She would have been anything she wanted to be. And he killed her. He wrapped his hands around her neck so tight, she couldn't even scream. Her feet kicked at the floor…and…"

As much as he hated hearing the details of his sister's last minutes, he hated even more the impact the memory had on Josie. Her breath was shallow and rapid, her skin pale and clammy. "Stop, Josie. It's over."

"He strangled her. I watched—out of my body…like I was hovering on the ceiling. I know it sounds crazy. I wish I could say I was crazy, that it didn't happen. For a time, I had myself convinced I dreamed it. But where is

Maddy? No one has seen her since that night."

A tear rolled down Josie's cheek. Wrapping his hand in her hair, he pressed her cheek to his chest. She offered no resistance, relaxing against him.

"Did the police check out Stone at all?" Tucker asked, looking at Murray and Hetty.

"A little," Murray said. "But they didn't find anything, and Josie's story sounded too crazy, and there was no body, and she'd told the boyfriend she was running away. And the dog was gone, and they assumed she took him with her."

"Shit. Poor Maddy. You're sure she's dead?" Tucker asked.

Josie sat up straight and brushed away the tears. "It's been years and there has been no sign of her. And she wouldn't—couldn't—have stayed in hiding. She wouldn't have accepted it. She'd have surfaced by now, told someone to kiss her ass. She was a fighter. Hiding? That's Ariel Stone's style."

"And you'll keep hiding too. At least until your memory comes back and we know who tried to kill you," Hetty said, her fat waddle shaking with her head.

"It was Stone, wasn't it? He went to prison for it," Tucker said.

"It's a bit more complicated than that. Josie," Murray said, "you should tell Tucker what you remember."

Josie nodded slowly and took a deep breath. "I remember leaving the hospital. My mom picked me up..."

Chapter Twenty Six

Five Years Earlier

"Sign here. And here."

Amanda Stone signed all the spots she needed to sign to get her daughter out of the hospital. Jeb was in the car, probably getting pissier with every minute he was left waiting.

Amanda sighed. He'd be a prick to deal with tonight. Once again, Ariel had turned their lives upside down. She'd brought humiliation to them all by telling the police, yet again, that Jeb touched her. And as if that wasn't bad enough, she had to add the icing to the crazy cake with her *visions* of Jeb murdering her trailer-trash friend. Jeb was embarrassed and hurt by his precious little Ariel, but would he ever punish her for her deceit and disloyalty? *No, he'd take it out on me.*

"Here's the number for Dr. Andre. Her first appointment will be at 1:00 tomorrow. If you have any issues tonight, call the number at the bottom."

"I'm sure everything will be fine. She was just distraught, right Ariel?"

Ariel nodded, chewing on her thumbnail. Her mother slapped her hand. "Stop that. Stop being such a weak-willed little baby. My God. How are you my daughter?"

Ariel stuffed her hands in her pockets and blinked back tears. The nurse cleared her throat and looked at the young girl. The nurse looked like she was about to speak, but Amanda wrapped an arm around her daughter and said, "Let's go sweetie. You've really put my nerves on edge. But we'll get through this."

Ariel nodded and followed her mother through the long white hallway. The only sound was the click of Amanda's heels on the tiled floor. Amanda Stone was a gorgeous woman. Tall, blonde, thin—she worked hard at perfection. She started from nothing, but she made excellent use of her wits and good looks and see where she was today? She had a bank account that registered in the millions. She wanted to reproduce that flawlessness in her daughter. Teach her to survive, no matter what. But it seemed the harder she tried to help, the wider the distance between them grew.

When Ariel was a little girl, she was Mommy's girl. It was just the two of them. They had no other family, no father for Ariel. Well, Amanda had a few suspects, but none she wanted to be saddled with for life. Ariel seemed to enjoy dressing like mommy and coloring her hair like mommy. It wasn't until nature began turning her into a young lady that Ariel's personality pulled her away. Her mother resented Ariel for preferring books to shopping or old movies to parties, and never, ever, could Ariel learn the subtle art of flirting. As a young woman, Ariel had every asset she needed to make men give her anything she wanted, but she was stubborn and refused to listen, much less follow through. "Try anything this dumb again, and I swear I will kill you myself. Taking a bottle of pills—what the hell were you thinking? Use a freaking gun. Show some gumption at least."

"Yes, Mother," Ariel said.

Amanda turned on her, grabbing her cheeks, her long nails digging into the soft flesh. "*Yes, mother,*" she mocked. "If you'd listened to me, you'd have kept your mouth shut about angels and all that bullshit, and Jeb would be in jail right now. But no, you had to sound like a crazy little bitch; now we're stuck with him."

"You could leave him," Ariel whispered.

Her mother let go with so much force, Ariel almost fell backward. "I'm not living in poverty again. Ever. You remember what it was like without money? You remember whose fault it was that we were poor?"

"Mine?"

"Yes, yours. You had to be broken. I had to quit my job, spend all of our savings on doctors."

"I'm sorry."

"Stop being sorry!" she yelled. "Jesus, I am so tired of hearing you say that. God, I need a drink." She pulled her phone out of her purse and called a friend. "Jaynie? I need a girl's night…Yes, this week has been a nightmare…I'm holding up, barely…great, see you at 7:00…"

"You're leaving me?" Ariel clutched her mother's arm, which she jerked away. "How can you leave me? You know…you know." Tears started falling, her body shaking.

"He's not dumb enough to touch you again. You'll be fine."

Ariel stopped. "I'll run away. I'll go to Maddy's. Her mom and dad will help me."

Her mother latched onto her wrist and twisted. "The hell you will. You will get your ass in the car, and you will smile and play nice until I figure something out. Do you hear me? Go home. Lock your damn door if it makes you feel better, but you're going home. Embarrass me here, and I will have your ass locked back up in a place that isn't half as nice. You understand me?"

Ariel nodded. Tears rolled from her eyes, down her cheeks. Her mother frowned, shook her head, and gave Ariel's arm a tug that made her trip over her feet.

Jeb Stone was waiting, leaning against the car, smoking a cigarette. He was a handsome man. Dark wavy hair. Trim, athletic build. Women threw themselves at the wealthy businessman, so no one truly believed he'd need to rape his teenage stepdaughter. The poor girl was just crazy—talked to angels and tried to kill herself. Poor Jeb. And to think he met her mom when he donated thousands of dollars to Ariel's get-well fund. She'd almost died as a young girl when she walked out in front of a car. Girl probably had a death wish, even then.

Jeb tossed the cigarette on the ground and stood as he saw her coming. "Ariel," he said.

Ariel climbed into the car. She hugged herself and leaned against the door. The drive was filled with her mother's chatter about local gossip. When they got home, Ariel said she was tired and went to her room, locking the door.

A storm brewed outside. She hoped the storm would keep her mother at home, but it didn't. She watched her leave from her window. Within seconds, Jeb was at her door, knocking. "You hungry, Ariel? I made dinner."

"No. I'm tired. I'm going to bed."

He turned the knob, but the door was locked. She sighed gratefully as she heard him walk away.

Ariel called Maddy's house. "Gloria?"

"Arie, honey. I'm so happy to hear your voice. How you doing?"

"All right." Ariel looked at her door. "Sort of. Hey, have you heard from Maddy?"

"No," Gloria said, her voice cracking. "Rob thinks you saw something. Then repressed it or some such thing. He tried to get the police to investigate, but ended up getting arrested."

"I hope I'm wrong. At the hospital, they said I was hallucinating."

"I hope you were hallucinating." Gloria's laugh was nervous. "Can you come over sometime? It'd be nice to spend some time with you."

Ariel burst into tears. "I'd...I would like that."

"Oh, sweetheart. Is your mom home? Can I talk to her?"

"She left."

"You're home alone?" Gloria sounded shocked.

"No. He's here."

"You all right?"

Jeb knocked on her door. "Who are you talking to Ariel?" He jiggled the door handle again.

"I've got to go," Ariel whispered into the phone. As she hung up, she scrambled off her bed and ran toward her bathroom. She'd lock herself in there. Her door swung open and banged against her wall.

"What's wrong with you, Ariel? You know you're my special girl."

Chapter Twenty Seven

Tucker closed his eyes. His fingers dug into Josie's leg.

"He grabbed me…and that's all I remember. Until I woke up in Rob's car. He told me he was taking me somewhere safe. That I was to pick a new name and not contact anyone until he told me it was safe. He said they'd kill me. That they'd tried to kill me."

"And someone had," Murray said. "I was a medic in the Air Force. When they got here, Josie had a wound where a bullet grazed her shoulder and a gash in the back of her head. Bruises on her arms and wrists. Someone had tied her up. I stitched up her head, and we watched her for internal bleeding. Her body healed, but she never remembered anything past Jeb coming in the room."

"Did Rob ever say who he suspected?" Tucker asked.

"Nope. I told him to call the police. He said someone promised to tell him where he could find Maddy. That she was alive, but wouldn't be if he talked to the police," Murray said.

"Do you think the police were covering for Stone?"

"That's entirely possible. Stone is loaded. I assume he could buy anyone he wanted. And Rob kept saying they…*they* wanted Josie, er Ariel dead. Not *he*."

"And you've never been able to get anything out of my dad?"

"No. I might have been able to, but Gloria has me banned from seeing him. I tried to reason with her without telling her about Ariel. But all she knew was Rob was gone three days then turned up naked and half-dead with Amanda Stone in a hotel. Amanda said they were comforting each other, because they were both sad about losing their daughters, and both blamed Jeb Stone," Murray said.

"I don't trust her," Hetty said with a frown. "I watched Jeb's trial on the net, before I got to worrying Josie would see what was going on and shut it off. Amanda Stone didn't give a damn her daughter was dead. *Comforting each other*. Bull. I know Rob liked the ladies, but she did something to trick him."

"She probably played on his sympathies. Rob would've felt sorry for a woman who just lost her kid," Murray said. "And I saw the testimony too. She seemed stunned by all of it. You have to give the woman a break, Hetty. Amanda Stone was obviously not a perfect mom, but she did catch Stone with her daughter. She tried to stop him by jumping him from behind and beating on him."

"Yeah, yeah. And when she woke, Ariel was gone. I heard it all too, Murray Banks. You men just can't see past that perfect face and huge rack to see the woman is a liar. No offense, Josie."

"None taken," Josie said with a small smile and a sniff.

"How does a mom accept her child is dead without a body?" Hetty asked.

"Jeb Stone was covered in blood. Ariel's blood. His DNA was found in her bed, and more of her blood was found in his car. Two girls gone and Jeb at the center of it all," Murray told his wife.

"Jeb Stone swears Amanda killed Ariel and set him up," Hetty countered.

"He also says he and Ariel were in love," Murray said.

Josie took a sharp breath.

"I'm sorry, Josie. That was a stupid thing for me to say. I swear, I think my mind sees Josie as a whole different gal than Ariel." Murray turned red and looked physically pained.

"It's all right. I know what he says. Look, I know you guys are worried, but I know it was Jeb. I know he killed Maddy, and I think he snapped that night and tried to kill me. And he's in jail, so I'm safe here. Tucker is getting me an ID, and I'll be able to openly live as Josie McCoy."

Hetty shook her head. "My gut is saying it ain't going to be that easy. What if Stone is telling the truth—"

"That I was in love with him?"

'No, no, of course not. That your mother tried to kill you to set him up.

Rob said *they*, not *he*. And now, your mom knows you're alive. She's seen your picture," Hetty's voice rose as she explained.

"She said it was Maddy," Tucker said.

"What if she's lying?" Hetty countered.

"It can't have been my mom. It had to be Jeb, and Mom hates him. Even if she saw that picture and knew it was me, she wouldn't say anything. She won't want Jeb out of prison. She won't tell anyone I'm alive. Everything is fine. Jeb's in prison. I'll marry Tucker, have our baby, and we'll live happily ever after," Josie said. Tears spilled down her cheeks as she looked at Tucker. "That's just how it has to be. It's what's right, and damn it, I'm owed some things going right for me."

Chapter Twenty Eight

"No midnight walks, understood?" Tucker said to Josie as they brushed their teeth.

"I won't. Why are you worried?" She wrapped her arms around his waist and pressed her cheek into his back. "Murray and Hetty are natural worriers. Don't let them get you rattled. Jeb's in jail, and trust me, my mother won't say anything. She sued Jeb's estate in a wrongful death suit. She got all his money for killing her daughter. Trust me, Mother loves that money way more than me. I wasn't at all surprised she didn't *recognize* me."

He pulled her around to face him. "But you're not dead."

"Don't. You're letting them make you paranoid. My mother was a mean bitch, but she's not a murderer. As long as Ariel Stone stays dead to the world, she will be happy."

"That's horrible."

"Don't feel sorry for me. I'm happy. I have you. I have our baby. That's all I need."

Tucker wrapped her up, kissing the top of her head. "I don't feel sorry for you. I just want to make sure everything is smooth from here on out."

"It will be."

"So, why do I have a bad feeling?"

Taking a step back, she looked up at him. "Bad feeling?"

"Yeah, it's like a nervous feeling in my gut. What if it wasn't Stone who shot you?"

"It had to be him." Josie wrapped her arms around his neck. "My poor, poor Tucker. You've been so worried; you're probably just emotionally exhausted." She gave him an ornery grin and asked, "So, what were you going to do? If I had been Maddy?"

Tucker buried his face in the curve of her neck. "I don't want to talk about it. I'm just happy as hell you're not."

"You were never going to tell me, were you?"

He held her tighter. Emotions he'd bottled for so long threatened to overwhelm him. He had no defense for his plans to deceive her.

Josie relaxed against him. "It's all right… I was worried if you knew about Jeb—"

Tucker took a step back and stared down at her, his hands firm against her cheeks stopping her from looking away from him. "Don't you ever think that, Josie. Don't you ever blame yourself."

"Now that you know—"

"I knew something happened. I didn't know what, but the night of the storm...I knew. I wanted to talk to you about it, but I was stuck between wanting to help you and scared as hell you'd tell me you were Maddy."

"When I was a little girl, he'd touch me and take pictures of me. As I grew older, he'd show me pictures of people having sex…and his touches became more…intimate. But it wasn't until my sixteenth birthday that he…crossed the line. He told me no one cared about me, but him…that I belonged to him. My special birthday gift was him…coming into my room, and…" Her body started to shake.

Tucker pulled her closer, holding her tight against him. "It's okay, Josie. He can't hurt you anymore. He lied; the prick lied to you. You are so lovable. I love you. Any man would. I'm just the lucky son of a bitch to find you first."

Josie nodded against his chest. "Tell me," her words caught in her throat. She gripped his shirt, as she tried again. "Tell me I belong to you. That my body was made for you."

"Oh Josie, sweetness." He smoothed her hair. "When you said we were meant for each other, you were right. Now, listen to me, if a thief breaks into your home and steals something from you…it doesn't mean it belongs to him. It's still yours to take back. Love isn't taken by force; it can only be given."

"That night in the woods, you asked me if I had done it. I didn't know how to answer."

"It was your first."

"But—"

"No buts. I had to bend over and grab my ankles while a doc stuck a finger up my ass in processing—that doesn't mean I'm gay."

Josie laughed, her body relaxing against him. "I cannot believe you just said that. You have such a way with words."

"So, I'm not eloquent. But it's bullshit you blame yourself."

"I don't. But I wanted to make sure you didn't. I saw how people looked at me, questioned whether or not I was telling the truth…or whether or not it was consensual."

"How the hell does a grown man have consensual sex with a kid? He's a sick prick, and anyone who bought his story is an ignorant bastard."

Josie laughed and gave him a squeeze around his middle. "Am I seeing the Morgan temper in you, Mr. Boone?"

"Well, it pisses me off. It's—"

"Would you make me a cup of tea?"

"A cup of what?"

"Tea? There's chamomile by the stove. I feel exhausted, but my brain is still going a mile a minute."

"Of course," he said. He gave her one last kiss before leaving her to finish getting ready for bed. As he heated the water and made the tea, he tried to feel as calm as Josie. She wasn't Maddy; he should be on cloud nine. But he wasn't. His gut still bugged him.

Carrying the mug in, he sat gently next to her so it didn't spill. She sipped it with her eyes closed, her body visibly relaxing against the stack of pillows behind her.

"Thank you. It's perfect."

Tucker settled himself against his pillows, his arm shoved under his head.

"It was Robert who first bought me chamomile tea. I was never a very good sleeper, and when I'd spend the night with Maddy, he'd make it for me before I went to bed. He was the sweetest man."

Tucker snorted. "Sounds like a real peach."

"Is that sarcasm?" Josie asked setting her mug on the night stand.

"Sounds like he couldn't keep his dick in his pants no matter what. He hears about a lead on his daughter and somehow ends up with your mom in a hotel?"

Josie looked up at him and grinned. "You followed a lead on Maddy and ended up with me."

"Touché." He stared at the ceiling. He was quiet several minutes before he said, "The difference is—Maddy was my sister. A sister I never met. Of course I gave up when I hit a couple of walls. But why would he? She was his daughter. Sounds like a scumbag to me."

"But he wasn't. He was a great guy."

"The affair makes no sense."

"My mother is a gorgeous woman. She usually got what she wanted."

Tucker snorted. "Then why the hell would she want Rob Morgan? From what I saw, he had no money, no power."

"But he was pretty hot for an old guy."

"Holy shit, Josie, should I be jealous?"

She laughed. "Of course not. Though if he were twenty years younger…"

"Why you…you're intentionally goading me. Here, I thought you were so sweet, but you're rotten. How did I not notice?"

Her laughter grew. "You were too busy knocking me up."

In a single movement, he pulled her on top of him. His hands brushed through her hair. "Best mistake ever."

She kissed him. Tucker held her cheeks in the palms of his hands. She was nothing more than soft flesh covering breakable bone. He'd seen too many people die to pretend life couldn't fade away in an instant, and until this moment, he never realized how much that scared the hell out of him.

Chapter Twenty Nine

The storm returned with a vengeance. The fierce winds tore at the sand, ripping trees out by their roots as if they were weeds. A scream, a spine-chilling call for help, pierced Tucker's ears.

"Josie," he called. It was dark, too dark to see more than a few feet ahead. There was no rain, just dry winds whipping from every corner. Sand stung his eyes, making them water. Walking blindly through the winds, his foot stepped from pliable sand to something hard. Looking down, he saw the sign: *Forget Me Not Gifts.*

Tucker sat up straight in bed. His heart raced, and his hands felt icy. Reaching out, he felt for Josie. She was gone.

"Damn it." He yanked on his pants and practically ran from the cabin. The air was warm, carrying the sweet smell of gardenias. There was no storm, not a single cloud dotted the sky. Tucker strode to the cemetery, sure she would be there. She wasn't. He checked at the pond, but still no sign of her.

Something wasn't right.

Josie wouldn't break a promise. He called Murray, waking him and Hetty up. They hadn't seen her either. Tucker stood in the middle of the road, unsure of what to do or which way to go. "Come on, Josie. Where the hell are you?" he asked the darkness. Every time he heard a leaf rustle or a cricket chirp, his heart raced. "Come on, think goddammit." His jaw was tight and every muscle in his body was tense.

As he moved past the cemetery, a sound, like a whisper in his ear, flowed through his head: *You can't hear if you're not listening.*

Tucker spun in the road expecting to find someone behind him. He was still alone. Taking a deep breath, his heart rate slowed, and his breathing normalized. He'd question his sanity later, but for now, if all he had to help him were voices in his head, then he'd take them.

He closed his eyes and stilled his mind, trying his best not to think of

Josie. As serenity passed through him, he saw, like a recalled memory, an image. White gardenias planted along a narrow sandy road jutted with roots and cast in shadows.

As quickly as it came, the vision was gone, and he was back in the middle of a gravel road. Looking around, past the white picket fences and clapboard houses, he spotted a thick grove of trees. Tucker headed toward it. The sandy road was uneven and full of water-filled potholes, but was lined with the big white flowers he'd imagined.

The land rolled, dipping into a stagnant-looking stream. Water bugs and mosquitoes flitted on brackish water that glowed with the moonlight. On the other side of the stream, there was a rickety house with rusted out cars on the lawn and an old boat with cracked fiberglass hull. Hanging sideways by a lone grommet was the sign, *Forget Me Nots Gifts*. A dog barked from the porch, making his way to the steps and stopping. The black hair along his spine rippled, his teeth bared with each growl.

A curtain moved in the window as someone peeked out.

Tucker wished he'd thought to bring the gun. What the hell was he thinking?

The curtain closed, and the porch light flipped on. The girl from the thrift store stepped outside.

"Natalie? Do you remember me?" he asked.

"Of course, you're my hero."

"Have you seen Josie? The girl who was with me at the store?"

"Yeah. At least I think it was her. She ran down the road yelling for some girl—Maddy, maybe? It's the road behind the house. It's an old boating road that leads to a shallow cove. I don't know where she'd be going. There's nothing down that way. Not even a dock."

Tucker took off with the heavy smell of gardenia following him. He was on the right path. His steps quickened. The undergrowth thickened as he made his way out of the copse of trees. The road disappeared and the trees thinned, moonlight breaking through the canopy of leaves. The sweet smell of flowers gave way to the smell of saltwater. Small waves lapped against the shore. Tucker saw movement. There were too many shadows to be one woman out walking. He crouched in the tall sea grass wanting to look before he was seen. The wind whipped the sharp edges against his cheeks.

A movement caught his attention. Moving slowly, he got closer. It was a man and a woman.

"What the hell? You trying to wake everyone up?" the man asked.

"It's an ocean, Greg. People expect to hear boat motors."

"I told you we'll use the oars."

"Fine," the woman hissed. "Paddle if you want to."

"I swear to God, if I didn't love you, I'd be dumping two women in the ocean tonight."

The woman's laughter cut through Tucker. He left his grassy hiding spot, following a path that wound to the water. Moving quietly, he cringed with every snapped branch. In a narrow canal was a small skiff with an open top. A man stood in the boat, legs spread wide to keep it balanced as he wrestled with something on the bottom.

"You can't let her thrash. She'll sink the damn boat," the man said.

"Then I guess she'd drown herself," the woman snapped.

"And when they find her bound body, you have a murder investigation. Shit, Amanda, how many times do I have to explain things to you?"

"I don't know, Greg, maybe one more time? Remember, this is my first time disposing of a body. You're the expert, not me."

"You can't dump her in shallow water. The tide will push her body to shore. Out in the deep, properly weighted, she's nothing but fish food."

"Jesus, Greg, do you need to be so graphic? She is my daughter for God's sake."

The man grunted as he shoved the body-sized object to the center of the boat. "You wanted it spelled out, so stop bitching about it."

Whatever was in the boat thrashed, causing the small craft to rock back and forth in the water. It wasn't a thing in the boat, it was a who, and Tucker was certain it was Josie. And the bitch tying her up had to be her worthless mother. Getting as low as he could to the ground, he made his way to the boat. As he got closer, he heard muffled cries. It was Josie.

Amanda stood in the boat and gave Josie's thrashing form a swift kick. "Stop being a pain in the ass, Ariel, or I swear, I'll kick the shit out of you." Then she turned to Greg. "I don't know why we can't just kill her here. This seems pointless to fight her in this friggin' toy you call a boat."

"Too bad you're not half as smart as you are gorgeous—we row out to the boat we have anchored in international waters. We sink this boat with the little bitch in it. She's gone, and so is every bit of evidence that we were ever here."

"You really think I'm gorgeous?" Amanda asked.

"Of course, dear. Can we please just get going?" Josie tried to sit up, but one quick punch from Greg and her body went still.

Tucker wiped at the sweat that beaded on his brow and stung his eyes. Greg started unwinding the rope holding the boat to a tree along the bank. Tucker moved fast. He had no weapon, but surprise was in his favor. Slipping into the water smoother than a croc, he swam to the edge of the boat. With all his might, he half tipped the tiny vessel. Greg fell, splashing into the water. Amanda screamed and grabbed the sides of the boat and held on. Tucker lunged for the man, grabbing him by the shirt and dragging him under. The water was well above his waist, and Greg was huskier, but shorter with a more limited reach. Tucker spun and wrestled him into a choke hold. Greg reached into his waistband. Tucker saw the gun and knocked it from his hand. It fell with a splash into the black water.

Tucker increased the pressure around the man's neck. The man thrashed, feet dug in, stirring up the stale, rotten mud. The water quickly turned into a nasty, mud-thickened soup. The slimy mud made flesh slippery. Holding onto the man was more and more difficult. Tucker felt a red rage as the man dug into his arm with his nails. Tucker wrapped his elbow under Greg's chin and squeezed. More pressure and the man began to calm.

The voice in his head told him to stop. He needed the man alive. The woman jumped out of the boat and waded to the man. "Greg!"

Tucker slowly released his grip. He laid the man against the bank and turned his attention to Josie. She rolled to her side. Tears stained her cheek. When Tucker reached for her, she flinched. "It's okay, Josie. It's me." Her eyes were wide, and her body trembled. Tucker feared she was in a daze like the night of the storm. "Listen to me, Josie. You're going to be all right. I'm going to untape you. I want you to run." She shook her head. "Yes, you have to listen to me," he said taking her hands in his. "You have to run. Get the hell out of here and get help." She allowed him to peel away the tape from her wrists. Hands free, she pulled the tape off her mouth.

"She pretended to be Maddy." Josie's words were quick and breathless.

Tucker started to work on her feet. She looked at him as if she was going to break down into tears. Then her eyes flicked above his shoulder, and she screamed, "Tucker! Behind you!"

Turning a half second too late, he saw the knife as it plunged into his side. The pain was intense, then he felt numb. He dove at the woman. She tried to stab at him again, nicking Tucker's face, but failing to sink deep into the flesh.

"Stop it! Stop it! Don't you hurt him," Josie yelled.

Trying to stay far enough away to keep from getting sliced, he said through gritted teeth, "Run, Josie. Damn it. Run."

He heard her slide out of the boat and splash in the water. He felt a wave of relief that was short-lived. She didn't run. Shoulder down, she rammed into Amanda and knocked her off her feet. Then Josie lunged at her, taking advantage of Amanda's surprise, and shoved her under water. Greg came up behind Josie and hit her in the head with an oar. Her body fell against the muddy bank and slid under the water. Tucker let loose a scream as he plowed through the muck trying to get to Josie as her body disappeared. Greg grabbed his shoulder, stopping Tucker in his path. Furious, Tucker spun around and head butted the man's thick skull. Greg fell backward, toppling Tucker with him.

It wasn't until they hit the ground that Tucker felt the knife jam into his gut one last time. His only thought was Josie, unconscious and underwater. He tried to get to his feet and get to her, but his vision went black.

Chapter Thirty

Tucker was being moved. A dog barked in the distance. No, the dog was nearby. His hearing was foggy; his vision, blurred.

"Stay calm man, we're getting you help."

Tucker tried to sit up. "Josie? Where's Josie?"

"Josie?" his caregiver sounded clueless. A woman's voice said, "The girl, John. He wants to know about the girl."

John paused a moment. "She's fine. She's fine. We got to get you patched up, so I need you to be still, okay? We got a chopper coming. Going to strap you down and have you ready. You just need to stay with us."

"Where's Josie? Better not be lying to me."

"No buddy, I swear. She's fine."

A gentle hand touched his brow, holding him firmly against the back board while John brought a strap over his forehead and secured it. As John tightened him down, the woman said softly, gently, "Billy Fram is working on her. She has a pretty good bruise on her forehead, but she's going to be fine. She's mostly worried about you. You let us get you on that chopper so we can tell her you're gonna be all right, okay?"

He nodded and closed his eyes. Sound faded and the sky went inky black.

A noise like a squealing freight train woke him. John squeezed his arm. "Almost there, buddy. Stay with me."

Tucker nodded.

"This your first chopper ride?"

Tucker tried to say no. He'd been on chopper rides before. Mostly transport choppers. He'd been on plenty of those. He listened closely for the sound of gunfire. Wondered where they were being dropped now. Suddenly, he wasn't lying on his back strapped to a board anymore. He was sitting by

Ash. "Ash," he said. "Holy shit, I thought you were dead."

"I'm here. In the flesh. Damn, you're looking ugly. They plan on dropping you in the sand box to scare the shit out of Ali Baba? Sure will save on bullets. He'll take one look at you and go lalalalala on home."

Tucker laughed, looking over his shoulder for their CO. He never found Ash's humor funny. Always worried the embed journalist would hear. That guy had a major stick up his ass. Ash pulled a cigarette from behind his ear and lit it with a match he struck off his helmet. "For good luck," he said with a wink.

Tucker smiled and relaxed against his seat, enjoying the thrum of the motor and the smell of Ash's cigarette.

Ash sent a puff of smoke rings toward the chopper roof. "I've been meaning to tell you. Sometimes to keep life moving forward, you've got to learn to roll with it. Except when you reach a crossroad, then you make the right choice. Don't be a damn dumbass, you hear?"

Tucker shook his head. This was deathbed kind of talk and he didn't want to hear that shit. Ash was here. Tucker wanted him to stay here.

"Promise me, man. You won't be a dumb ass."

"Yeah, yeah. I heard you the first time."

Tucker reached out his hand. He wanted to make sure this moment was real, but before his hand made contact, Ash yelled, "Time to go. Catch ya later, pretty boy."

Ash stood and turned toward the open door. Tucker grabbed at his shoulder in a panic. "You don't have a chute." But it was too late. Ash was gone, and Tucker was sucked from the chopper with him. He drifted, as if rocking on air. The sky was a relaxing cradle of powder blue, but the green of the earth was fast approaching. Tucker screamed—was about to hit the ground, then his eyes popped open. Two men in navy blue uniforms carried him from the chopper toward bright red double doors. His body swayed back and forth until they set him on a gurney and rolled him across concrete. The black of night gave way to the harsh fluorescents above him.

Tucker assumed he was at the hospital. He called for Josie one more time, and thought he saw her walking away from him. The gurney rolled through more double doors, then stopped. They lifted him on the count of three and set him on a surgical table. Medical staff swarmed, working in unison, unlatching the straps from the board, sticking him with IVs, and attaching monitors to his chest. He was about to tell them they worked as quickly as a pit crew, but someone put a mask over his face and told him to breathe deep.

The pain in his body drifted away. He was free of the chill of the hospital and was suddenly doused in sunlight. And there was Ash again, standing in a field so green, it seemed fake. The lush grass felt like silk against Tucker's hand as he waded through it.

"You're back," Ash said. "Come on, there's someone I want you to meet." As Ash moved through the grass, tiny butterflies took flight and fluttered around him. Ash called, "Maddy, come meet your brother." Turning to Tucker, Ash whispered, "Seriously dude, she got all the looks in the family."

Maddy ran through the grass toward him. She did look like Josie, but Tucker would never be confused by the two of them. Maddy was full of energy, arms flailing, face as animated as a cartoon as she approached. She yelled his name as if chasing a rock star. Her body slammed into his, and she squeezed him in one of the biggest bear hugs he'd ever gotten. Tucker hugged her back. She didn't feel like flesh and bone. She was like hugging pure energy. Warm and invigorating. In her grip, his body felt buoyant, and the pain in his gut eased.

"I knew you'd do it." Stepping back, she laid a hand on each side of his face. "I'm sorry you had to feel so alone, but I needed you to find her. She needed you, and you needed her. I couldn't let my brother and sister—oops that's not funny is it?" Maddy laughed as she took a step back.

"You know about that?"

"I get feelings. You did well." Pointing her thumb toward Ash's back, she said, "Some people thought you'd do the boot scootin' boogie out of there when you thought Arie was me, but I knew you wouldn't ever leave your baby."

"Boy or girl?"

"What do I look like, a fortune teller?" Maddy gave him a look like he was a fool, then said, "Hey, I'd love for you to stay so I could torture you, but you've got to go. One day, brother, you'll find out what it's like to be harassed by a little sister for an eternity."

Tucker smiled. "I think I'd like that."

She punched his shoulder. "You say that now, tough guy. Just you wait."

It finally occurred to Tucker—if Maddy was here with Ash...he had to know. "What happened to you, Maddy?"

She scrunched up her face and shook her head. "You just tell Ariel I'm all right. Tell her I didn't feel any pain. You have to remember to tell her I'm all right. Promise me you will remember...Maddy is all right."

"How could I ever forget this?" he asked looking around at the beauty of the place.

She smiled at him and said, "Because it's only rational to forget. Now, you don't belong here. You have to go back."

She turned him by the shoulders. He wanted to stay a bit longer, but she shoved him hard. As she pushed him through the field, his feet didn't touch the ground. His feet couldn't get a grip, so he couldn't slow down or stop. A cliff approached.

"The cliff," he yelled over his shoulder as he grabbed at thin air.

"Trust me," she said giving him one final push. Then he was falling, falling—through nothingness. He was about to hit when a voice said, "Mr. Boone. Welcome back to the land of the living."

Tucker was in a hospital bed, hooked to monitors and IVs. Sitting up, he looked around the room. "Where's Josie? Is she here?"

The nurse ignored his question. She grabbed his wrist and checked his pulse. "You need to stay calm."

"I need to check on Josie," he said, trying to sit up.

"Calm down, son," Murray said, getting up from the chair in the corner and coming to his bedside. "Hetty's with her. Doc's checking her over as a precaution. You need to be still. You got stabbed, for crying out loud."

"I'm fine. Take me to Josie." Tucker pulled at his IV. The nurse tried to stop him, but he jerked his arm away. She hit the emergency call button as she yelled at him to stay in the bed. He yanked the tubes out of his arm. The pump sirens beeped. Tucker looked around as edgy as an escaped felon hell-bent on leaving. "Where's my damn pants?"

"They cut them off." Murray told him. "If you plan to go running around, you'll be doing it in a dress with your ass hanging out."

"He's not going anywhere. Mr. Boone, get back in this bed this instant." The nurse stomped her foot on the tile floor. Tucker ignored her as he stripped a sheet off his bed and wrapped it around his waist. "Where is she? Or do I have to check the whole hospital?"

"Come on," Murray said.

"Mr. Banks, you're not helping here."

Another nurse met them at the door. "Sir, you can't be out of bed."

"For someone who can't, I sure am."

The skinny little blonde pursed her lips together. "Are we going to play semantics? You've lost a lot of blood, and unless you want to open some stitches and end up having to get a transfusion, I suggest you get back in that bed."

"I'll be fine; don't worry. I'm not the suing type." He turned to Murray. "Which way?"

"Follow me," Murray said.

"Don't make me call security," the skinny nurse said.

Murray shook his head as he led him down the hall to an elevator. Once inside, Murray hit level B. "This is insanity. You know that, right?"

"Would you do it if it were Hetty?"

"Hetty of now, or the sweet gal I married?" Murray laughed.

"Better watch my back, Murray. If I get caught, I may sing like a canary, and what you said might just slip out."

"Oh, now, you know I'm teasin'. I love the missus. And if it makes you feel better, I do understand, but I have to put up a little fight because those women are going to have my ass when I show up with you. I've already been hearing *I told you so* from Hetty about Amanda Stone. I swear, damn woman will probably put how she was right on my tombstone."

The elevator pinged, and the doors slid open. A security guard was waiting on him.

"I'm sorry, sir, but I'm going to have to take you back to your room. Hospital rules."

"Well now," Murray said, wrapping an arm around Tucker's arm. "I can assure you this boy isn't going back to his room without a fuss. He's stubborn and pig-headed, and his pregnant girlfriend is in an ultrasound to check on their baby. Now, I'm doubting you're going to wrestle this here stitched-up boy any more than I plan to wrestle a bear. So, why don't you just make us all happy and fetch a wheelchair, then we can roll him to his lady and then roll him back without all the fuss."

The security guard, a big husky man with hairy knuckles, nodded. "This your first?" he asked Tucker.

Tucker nodded.

"Hold on a sec." The guard left and returned with a chair. Tucker frowned, but sat.

"Josie's going to think I'm a pussy, riding around in a wheelchair."

"Well," Murray said with stroke to his chin. "I suppose you can impress her later with all your stitches. Over a hundred of them inside and out. Damned wonder that SOB didn't hit any organs. Three cuts—none hit anything but muscle."

"That's because I'm all muscle."

"Good to see that he didn't cut out your ego none." Murray laughed.

The guard snickered along with Murray as he rolled Tucker through the hall.

The guard spun the chair around as he bumped the door open with his rear. He wheeled Tucker in backward, and then turned him. The guard patted Tucker on the shoulder before stepping back to lean against the wall to wait. All Tucker could see was Hetty, but she stepped aside and there was Josie.

The light from the ultrasound screen was all that lit the room.

"Tucker," Josie said, lying on her back looking small and pale. "You shouldn't be here. They said you were in surgery."

Grabbing her hand, he brought it to his lips. "I'm fine."

"You sure?"

"Of course, you think I snuck down here?"

Josie smiled at him.

"How's the baby?" he asked.

"Um, I hope okay," she said, her voice shaky.

"It'll just be a minute, sweetie," the tech said. She rubbed the wand over Josie's belly. Trying first the left side, then the right. She added more gel and then tried again.

"Tucker," Josie said, squeezing his hand tighter.

"Probably too early, love," the tech said as she made another swipe. "How far along are you?"

"About a month," Tucker said.

"Give it another week or two and we should be able to get a heartbeat. Everything else looks good."

Josie bit her lip, but a whimper escaped and tears started rolling. Tucker held her. "It'll be all right."

She nodded against his chest, clutching the fabric of his hospital gown. Two sharp raps on the door, then it swung open, washing the darkened room in light. The nurse from his room found them. She turned on the guard. "Officer Cunningham, you were supposed to bring the patient back to his room, not hang out with him."

"Tucker?" Josie said. "You are not all right."

"Yes, I am," he whispered. "She's just a bitch."

She held his face in her hands. "You have to get back. I can't lose you."

"You won't lose me."

"Mr. Boone, you don't want to worry your pretty little wife when you start bleeding again and pass out," the nurse said from the doorway.

Josie's grip on him tightened. Tucker scowled. "I'm fine. Believe me."

"Go back and rest. Please." She kissed his cheek.

He sat back in his wheelchair. It broke his heart to go, but he had no choice but to allow the guard to roll him away. They were halfway down the hall when Murray came running, catching up with him. "Josie doesn't want you left alone."

"Did you tell her I'm fine?" Tucker asked.

"Yeah, I told her. Women just worry."

Tucker nodded. They made it to his room, and he climbed back into bed. The nurse seemed to jab him a few more times than necessary to get the IVs back in. Once she had him hooked up and pressed the buttons on his medication, she tucked the blankets around him with enough force to stretch the rigid cotton. She gave him a stern look and said, "Move out of this bed again, and I'll have you strapped down."

Tucker let his head drop on his pillow. He felt drained. Or drugged.

***

When Tucker woke, Josie was sitting beside him, using his mattress as a pillow.

He stroked her hair, and she looked up. "You're awake," she said.

"Was I asleep long?"

"A few hours."

"Any word on when they'll let me out of here?"

Josie shook her head. "The only person who checks in is the bitchy nurse, and honestly? I'm afraid to ask her."

He scooted over and patted the bed. "Come, lay with me."

"And let bitchy nurse catch me? No way. I'm fine right here."

"You need sleep. The baby needs sleep."

"I'll be fine. I met with an OB, Dr. Simon, and he said the baby's fine. Said they shouldn't even have wasted their time on the ultrasound. He said I can come to his office next week and will probably be able to hear the heartbeat. But everything else looks normal."

He smiled at her. "Good."

Brushing lint from his blanket, she said, "I was worried. The paramedics had you ready to go before I could even say good-bye. I was afraid I'd never see you again."

He gave her a grin and tried not to flinch as he pulled her toward him for a kiss. "It's over. You can relax."

She shook her head. "You tried to warn me—"

"Stop, Josie. Trust me, I never dreamed that psycho bitch would show up with her boyfriend and try to kill us. I swear—I never saw that coming."

Josie pressed her lips together for a moment, then busied herself with smoothing the edges of his pillowcase. "I know I didn't. I was never close to my mother, but I never dreamed she'd hunt me down and try to kill me."

"I suppose as far as future in-law introductions go, it went well, don't you think?"

Josie laughed. "Jokes, Tucker? You're making jokes?"

His grin grew. "My mother always said I didn't have good timing."

"No, your timing is perfect. I'd be lost without you, literally." Her attempt at levity fell flat. As soon as the words left her mouth, she broke down in tears. "I thought I'd lost you forever."

"Come here. Screw the bitch nurse."

Josie scooted her seat closer. Tucker shook his head and patted the bed. "Lay with me. I want to hold you."

Sobs racked her body. He only had to give her a slight tug to get her to curl up next to him. Brushing away her tears, he tried to calm her, even though his own mind was cluttered with the horror of what happened, and worse…what could have happened.

After a few minutes, she rubbed her cheek gently against his shoulder, snuggling as close as she could without hurting him. "She told me it wasn't personal. It was only for the money."

"I suppose she didn't trust you to stay dead on your own."

"Evidently not."

"So, who the hell was the guy helping her?"

"Greg Walker. He's a cop. He shot at Rob the night I ran away. He must have been working with my mother, even then."

He smoothed her hair. "Rob? My dad?"

"Yeah. I'd called Gloria when my mom left me alone the night I got home from the hospital. I was talking to her when Jeb started pounding on the door, so she sent Rob right over. It was my mom who shot me. My mom."

"Shit. I'm sorry. So, you remember?"

Josie nodded. "It hurt so much to remember that. That must be why I blocked it. All night long, I've been remembering little snippets of what happened that night. It was…is terrible."

"Look at me."

She smiled up at him. It was a weak, teary-eyed smile.

"You need to call someone? A professional?"

"It hurts, but I'm fine. Actually, I feel stronger than ever. I fought like hell that night, Tucker. I wasn't a wuss. And tonight, I didn't run."

"I don't know that I'm proud of you for that," he said, holding her a bit tighter.

"I'm not a coward. That night, I fought Jeb with all my might. It wasn't my fault he was three times my size—I fought. And fought. He'd take pictures of me, and use them to make me feel guilty. He threatened to show the pictures to my mom. I was so ashamed. I couldn't even tell Maddy what he was doing. But, I was just a girl. It's not my fault."

"Of course it wasn't. My sweet Josie."

"I tried to tell a teacher once, but she called Mother and Jeb. I got punished for lying."

Tucker swallowed the lump in his throat. If only he could take all her pain, he would.

Josie took a harsh breath. "Oh well, that's the past. Mother will pay now. So will her boyfriend." She sighed. "That night? She walked in while *her husband* was holding me down on my bed, and she yelled at me. Blamed me for all of it. *You friggin' bitch.* That's what I thought that night. I remember that now. I don't remember if Jeb let me loose, or I got away, but I ran across the room, and I punched her in the face."

"You did?"

Josie nodded. "I did. I was done being abused. I no longer cared what she thought of me; what anyone thought of me. I was leaving. I'd go live with Rob and Gloria. I'd tell them everything, and they'd help me. I ran out of the room and was halfway down the hall when she shot me. It was surreal. I heard the bang, and I turned. I expected to see Jeb, but it was my mother. I lost my footing and I fell down the steps. That must have been how I got the gash on my head."

"Christ."

"It's all right. Jeb jumped her. They were wrestling over the gun in the upstairs hall, so I got up and ran to the garage and stole Jeb's car."

"That explains your blood in his car."

Josie nodded. "Rob met me at the bottom of our hill. Greg, the cop, was also turning into our drive. Rob got out and waved to him. Greg pulled his gun and aimed it at Rob. Rob was quick. He flung open the door and told me to get in. Then he drove like hell until we were out of Pennsylvania. I remember him telling me he didn't know how many cops Jeb owned. I never told Rob it was my mother who tried to kill me. That's a hard thing to admit, you know? I guess that's why I blocked it all out."

"I understand." He kissed her hair. "Moms are supposed to protect their children."

"I'm nothing like her," Josie said.

"That's for damn sure."

"I suppose Jeb will now go free. The police know I'm alive."

"Hell with him. As long as he doesn't come near us."

"He killed Maddy. He needs to pay for that."

"It's out of your control, Josie. You have to let it go."

She nodded, but he didn't get the feeling she was going to let it go.

"Tonight, my mother pretended to be Maddy. She had Maddy's necklace. It was hanging on the post on the porch. I heard someone calling my name, so I went outside to see who was there. I saw the necklace, saw a woman in the shadows. I thought it was Maddy, so I called to her, but she ran,

so I followed her."

"You really should've woken me up."

"I know."

"No more, Josie. No leaving…ever again…without telling me."

Her eyes filled with tears. "I won't. I swear." She felt her pocket. "Oh no! I don't have it. I lost the necklace."

"It's all right."

"But Maddy loved that necklace."

"When I get out, we'll look for it. Maybe you dropped it on the road."

Josie nodded. "I asked my mom how she got the necklace, and she said she found it in Jeb's trunk. That's proof that he killed her, right?"

Tucker's mouth formed a hard line as he shook his head. "I doubt they'll consider the word of a lady who tried to drown her daughter as proof."

Josie shook her head. "It's just wrong. Maddy deserves justice."

"There's an ultimate justice no one escapes. You have to trust that."

"True. But it just doesn't seem right that Maddy suffered…."

"Maddy's fine. She's in a good place."

Josie gave him a quizzical look. "How do you know that?"

A flush crept up his neck to his cheeks. "I don't know…I just have a feeling."

Her smile was slow, and her eyes shined. "Even if you're making it up, thank you. You're precious to me, Mr. Boone."

"I know. I'm a rare find. You better hold onto me tight."

Chapter Thirty One

There was a knock on the door. Josie was up and off the bed in the blink of an eye. Tucker chuckled. "It's not the nurse. You're safe."

Josie turned as Murray and Hetty walked into the room. Poor old Hetty looked wiped out. She'd probably walked more today than she had in years. Murray shuffled in and gave Josie a fatherly rub across her shoulders. "You had anything to eat today, Josie?"

Josie thought a second, then shook her head.

"Well, you and Hetty go get a bite to eat. I'll keep Tucker company for a bit."

Josie looked like she was about to argue, but Tucker sat up a bit straighter and said, "Josie, come on. You have to think about the baby."

"Yes, I suppose I should." She placed a hand on her belly. "I'll go eat. You'll take good care of him, Murray?"

"Of course," Murray said, taking a seat and rifling through the newspapers on the table next to him.

"Shooey." Hetty pulled out her hanky and patted her upper lip. "I hope to goodness the cafeteria is close. I swear to God, I need to lose some damned weight."

"Come on, Hetty. Maybe I could find you a chair?" Josie offered.

"The hell you will. Good Lord, a whippersnapper like you could never push me. Even if we could find one I'd fit in. No, I'll walk. Come on, gal. Let's get going."

Once Josie and Hetty left, Murray pulled the door closed, and then he hurried back to Tucker.

"Something up?" Tucker asked, sliding himself against his pillows and clutching his bandaged side with the effort.

"Nothing to worry much about, but I wanted to let you know Josie's mom hung herself in holding."

"That chicken-shit bitch. How'd you find that out?"

Murray scooted himself forward. "Smitty—the deputy is a friend—he said she did it right there in Hyde County. I'd like to think she was feeling an ounce of guilt, but I'd say it was more fear of knowing she was exposed. The queen of the prom was a scumbag, and the world was about to hear about it."

"Why didn't you mention this while Josie was here?"

"I wasn't sure if that would her. She's already been through a lot." Murray leaned his elbows on his knees.

"She's tougher than you think, but I appreciate you told me first."

"Here," Murray handed him a piece of paper. "This is the number of a good lawyer. Ella says she's tops in the state. And Hetty and me rented you kids a place. We don't want Josie going back to the island."

"You don't want her back? What the hell?"

"Oh no, not forever. Just for a while, 'cos of the baby."

"What's with the baby? She said everything was fine."

"Things look good. Hetty pointed out that if she did have any problems, there are no clinics on Ocracoke, no emergency rooms. Hetty had three miscarriages before she had Bobby, and she's always thought if she could have gotten to a doctor in time, she'd have had more kids."

"But they didn't see anything wrong?"

"No, Josie checked out all right. But she was underwater a pretty long time before we pulled her out. She had to be resuscitated."

Tucker rubbed his face, the stubble bristling against his hands. "No, I didn't know. You're right. She needs to go home and rest."

"Good luck with that while you're here."

"Then I need out of here. You need to find my doctor so I can talk to him."

"They're not going to let you out. We'll take care of her. You just rest and get better."

Tucker shook his head. "You just get me some clothes, and I'll get myself out of here."

"Now dammit, I only told you 'cos I want you to trust that I'm honest with you."

"You're right, you're right. But I'm done with this shit." Tucker muttered as he picked at the tape the nurse wisely wrapped round and round his arm to secure the IVs, "She needs to be in bed, not sitting in a chair all night."

"Well, I'm not breaking you out of here again. And I warn ya, I'll march right down the hall and tell Josie you're being mule-headed."

"You wouldn't."

"Try me, son," Murray said, crossing his arms across his chest.

Tucker gave him a dirty look, but settled himself back against his pillow.

In the midst of an awkward silence, Murray cleared his throat and asked, "Have you called your people?"

"My what?" Tucker asked.

"Your folks? Let them know what's happened?"

Tucker shook head. His mother was going to flip.

"At least you can tell her you're fine. You want my cell phone?"

Tucker took a deep breath. "It's late. I'll call her in the morning."

"Might want to call tonight. It may make the morning news."

"You're kidding me." Tucker's head whipped toward Murray to see if he was joking. Unfortunately, he wasn't. Tucker wondered if they'd ever have peace.

"Nope. Hetty and I passed two news trucks on our way off the island, and I don't think they're there for Ocracoke Days."

"Well hell, I suppose I better get it over with."

Murray handed him his phone. Tucker dialed, then rested his arm above his head and closed his eyes. His mother answered. Even in the middle of the night, she sounded wide awake. "Hello?"

"Hey Mom, it's Tucker."

"Tucker? What's this number? Where's your phone? Did something happen?"

"Everything is fine, but I'm in the hospital at Elizabeth City."

"What?"

"I'm in the hospital."

"Why? What for?"

"I got into a fight and needed stitches."

"A fight? Oh, dear Lord, what's gotten into you? Was it over the girl?"

"Yeah, you might say that."

There was a large sigh on the other end, followed by a mumbled, "I knew finding Rob Morgan would cause nothing but bad. It wasn't enough that she's your sister?"

"She's not Maddy. She's Ariel Stone. Listen, Mom, -it's a long story, and I feel like shit. Can I explain later?"

"You swear you're all right?"

"I swear."

"Then get some sleep. Call when you wake up."

He was exhausted when he handed the phone back to Murray. His eyes felt grainy and sore, so he closed them for a second.

Two hours later, the doctor knocked on the door. Murray told him to come in. Tucker woke, shocked he'd fallen asleep.

"Good to see you awake, Mr. Boone. I'm Dr. Morris. I patched you up. You're a lucky man." The doctor, a tall, lanky fellow with dark thinning hair, walked to the foot of his bed and checked over his chart. "Looking pretty good. You've not requested any pain meds?"

Tucker shook his head. "It's not too bad. Only when I twist."

"Well then, Chubby Checker, don't twist."

Murray laughed at the old rocker joke.

Tucker sat up straighter. "I was wondering when I could head home?"

"Let me have a look at you, and we'll see."

Tucker nodded. Dr. Morris checked his breathing, the stitches.

Dr. Morris finished, put his stethoscope in his ears, and placed it along Tucker's back. "Deep breath in…out slow. Everything looks good."

"So, you think I can go?"

"I don't see why we can't let you go in a day or two."

"Day or two? Screw that. I was thinking today."

Dr. Morris chuckled. "You were stabbed three times, son. I need you on

IV antibiotics at least a night."

"Would you change your mind if I told you I didn't have health insurance?"

"No," he said flatly.

"What if I told you my…Josie, my girlfriend is pregnant, and she was beaten and half drowned, and she's going to insist on staying here with me, and I need her at home resting?"

Dr. Morris wrapped his stethoscope around his neck and stared down at Tucker. Feeling the doctor weaken, Tucker plowed forward. "We rented a place nearby, so if there are any troubles, we'd be right back. And I could take pills."

Dr. Morris checked the bag of meds hanging from his IV pole. "Tell you what, finish this round of antibiotics, and then we'll switch you over to an oral regimen. That will get you out by noon."

"Thank you, Doc, I owe you one."

"I'll let them know to start getting your discharge ready. No twisting. No heavy lifting. No sex. Go home and rest. See me in a week, and we'll go from there."

"Not a problem. Murray, can you get me some clothes, or do I need to wear my dress home?"

"I can get you some ER scrubs, but just remember, no playing doctor," Dr. Morris said with a wink.

"It's a deal." Tucker felt energized. He had things to take care of. Jeb Stone would probably be getting out of prison, so Josie would need a restraining order. He didn't want that son of a bitch to so much as call her on the phone. Next thing he wanted to do was marry her. He hated calling her his girlfriend. It seemed like an insult. He wanted her as his wife. And he needed to visit the attorney Ella suggested. He couldn't imagine Josie being in any legal trouble, but after last night, he wasn't taking anything for granted. Everything looked like it was falling into place, but Tucker needed to be sure. Happily ever after came with too many damned caveats lately.

Chapter Thirty Two

Josie tucked the pillows behind Tucker's back. "Did you want anything else to eat? More to drink?"

"Josie, I'm fine. You need to lie down and get some rest."

"I don't need to rest. I'm fine," she said. "I want to clean the bathroom. I mean it looks clean, but it might not be, and we don't want you to catch something. I can't imagine having a cough with all those stitches."

"The bathroom is fine. Come on, come lay with me. We'll watch a movie."

Josie looked around the place as she considered the proposal. The place was in the attic of an old Victorian. It had been converted into a studio apartment, with narrow, angled ceilings and very little natural light. Tucker had questioned Murray's sanity in renting the place after he made the climb up all the steps, but once inside, he decided it was the perfect place to sleep for days. If only he could get Josie to calm down and relax.

"I'll just give it a quick once-over. Then I'll make you something to eat. You need food to elevate your blood count. They said you lost a lot of blood—"

"Josie, come on. You're making me tired listening to you. Are you all right? You seem…agitated."

Josie sighed and sat at the foot of the bed. "It's just…"

"What? Talk to me."

"When I lay down, I think about…things…"

"I'm going to ask one more time. If you ignore me, I'll have to get out of my comfy position and drag you here. Please, will you come lay down with me?"

Josie crawled in from the bottom and sat cross-legged across from him.

"Come over here," he said.

She moved an inch or so.

"Seriously, Josie, get over here. I want to be able to touch you."

She scooted a little closer. He gave her a look. She said, "What? You have like a hundred stitches."

"This shoulder doesn't. Come over here."

She snuggled next to him, easing her head onto his shoulder like it was made of glass. His hand found his way to her hair.

Josie let out a happy sigh. "This does feels good."

"Yes, it does." He kissed the top of her head.

She relaxed against him. His fingers worked to smooth the curls in her hair. He was almost half asleep when Josie spoke.

"My mother killed herself."

Tucker was instantly wide awake. "How do you know that?"

"A police officer came to the hospital to get my statement about what happened. You were asleep. He said they'd contact you later."

"Josie…you shouldn't have talked to them. Not until you have a lawyer."

"It's all right. He was nice."

Tucker took a deep breath, shaking his head.

"I should feel something, but I don't. I don't feel relief. Or sadness. I just feel nothing. My mother is dead, and I feel nothing."

He rubbed her back. "The last few hours have been traumatic. I think feeling numb is completely normal."

She was quiet for a long time.

"You okay?" he asked.

"I'm fine. Just listening to your heart beat."

Tucker's smile was brief and his eyes burned. Clearing his throat, he said, "We live forward, not backward. All that stuff in the past is over and done with. We have a future to think about."

"You're right. We do. I don't think I've ever planned for the future. I suppose we'll need to decide where we'll live. We will be together, right? Or are you going to leave me now that I'm a ruined woman?"

Tucker's laugh was a chesty grumble. "Damn right."

"Damn right I'm ruined, or—"

"Damn right you're sticking with me. I want to marry you, Josie McCoy."

"Hmm. I suppose you're the best I've met while living like a hermit on a tiny island…"

"Whatever happened to us being soul mates, fated to be together and all that?"

"That? Oh, I was just trying to get in your pants."

Tucker laughed. "You were trying to get in my pants? All you had to do was ask."

"So, I'm learning…another reason I may want to keep considering the field of availables a little more," Josie laughed.

"You evil, evil woman. No more choices for you. I'm not asking. I'm telling. You're marrying me, Josie McCoy. You're stuck with me for an eternity."

"Hmm…I suppose the first thing we need to do is make Josie McCoy really exist. I want to get a legal name change. I will never be Ariel Stone again."

Chapter Thirty Three

Tucker's entire body ached as he rolled out of bed. His first thought was that he screwed up leaving the hospital. He went to the kitchen sink and popped a pain pill and his antibiotics.

"You okay?" Josie asked, coming up behind him and touching his back gently.

"I'm fine. Just stiff and sore. Do you remember what the doctor said about showering? Was that good or bad?"

"I don't remember. Let me check the papers." Josie ruffled through her purse. She pulled them out and skimmed over them. "Twenty-four hours before you can shower. No prolonged exposure. Just wash them and dry them completely. We should put the antibiotic ointment on them."

"Now?"

"No time like the present."

As Tucker pulled his shirt off, Josie went to the sink and scrubbed up more thoroughly than a surgeon. Tucker settled himself on a kitchen chair and started pulling off the bandage in the front. It didn't look too bad. Eight stitches closed the spot where he fell on the knife. Josie smeared the ointment on those stitches and then wrapped it in clean bandages. Next she pulled the bandage off his shoulder. "Oh, Tucker."

"What?" He made a half turn toward her.

"No, no. It's fine. I just can't believe this didn't hit anything. A bit to the left and it could have gone through your neck."

"I'm fine. Don't think that way."

"I know, I know." Taking a deep breath, she added the medicine and the clean bandage. Then she moved onto his side. It was the biggest bandage of them all. Pulling it off carefully, she gasped. "Oh, my God." The slash went from his hip to midway up his back. "That prick," Josie said. Grabbing the medicine with shaking hands, she dropped the tube.

"You all right?"

"No. No, I am not all right. Your whole back is sliced open."

He took her by the hand and pulled her toward him. "Listen to me. It's over."

"No," her voice was shrill. "No, it's not over. I hate them all. They tried to kill us. Tried to kill our baby. That bastard Jeb killed my friend. He put vile, loathsome hands on me. He'll walk out of prison. What will he get? Nothing. He'll go home to his millions, free to hurt anyone else he pleases. How did he survive prison? I thought pedophiles got stabbed or shivved or whatever. If I had any sort of spine, I'd kill him myself."

Tucker thought she was joking, but her face looked grim, determined.

"You're not killing Stone. I can see why you want to, but you're not going to do it."

"I know. I'm gutless."

"No. Because, if you get caught, our baby has no mom."

She nodded, letting out a long sigh. "I can't explain how much I hate him. I hate him more than my mom, and she tried to kill me."

Tucker didn't say anything. He didn't know how she felt. He might not have had it perfect, but he was protected his whole life.

"It's over, Josie. We're planning our future, right?"

Josie nodded slowly. "You're right. It's over. I suppose I need to keep reminding myself of that." She took a deep breath and resumed her work, adding the medicine and clean bandages. When she finished, she slid her hands up his back, to his shoulders. Leaning forward, she brushed kisses across the thick muscles on his neck. "You go lie down, and I'll bring you a sandwich, and we'll watch TV."

"Sounds good," Tucker said, slowly standing and moving back to the bed. Josie made them each a plate of food. Once they were both settled, plates on their laps, and pillows comfortably behind them, she flipped on the TV.

It was then they realized, Josie's story did make national news. *...assumed murdered, Ariel Stone, the stepdaughter of millionaire contractor and land developer, Jeb*

Stone, is alive and well. Mr. Stone has spent the last five years in prison for Ariel's murder. So, how does a man go to prison for a murder of someone who is still alive? And should she pay for her deception?

Josie turned away from the TV and stared at Tucker with her jaw dropped. "You hear that? It sounds like they feel sorry for him. Poor innocent man went to prison."

Tucker grabbed the remote and shut the TV off. "Don't listen to the bullshit, Josie. You know the truth."

She wiped at the tears that rolled down her cheeks. "I don't know why I'm shocked. No one ever cared. No one ever believed me."

"Forget them. We've got each other."

"I want to pretend it doesn't matter, but it does. I do care what people think about me."

"The people who know you will know the truth. None of the rest of the world matters. They don't know you, so how the hell can they judge you?" He didn't wait for her answer. His face felt hot. Of all the crap she'd had to deal with, the media making Stone into a saint was nothing more than bitter icing on a poison cake, and he wasn't about to let her take a bite. He answered his question for her, "They can't. They're idiots, and I don't know why you'd let yourself be bothered by idiots. And another thing…this story will be old news in two weeks. They'll drive by, look over the carnage, gasp a little, say the stupid shit that stupid people like to say, and then move on to the next disaster."

Josie wiped at the tears with the back of her hand and giggled. "That has to be the worst, best motivational speech ever. Don't ever leave me, Tucker. I can't do this without you."

"No chance of that," he said, kissing her. "Now, I don't want you to worry, but I think we need to put going to see an attorney on the top of our to-do list."

"How am I going to pay for that?" Josie asked.

"Don't worry about it."

She shook her head. "You're paying for the baby, now an attorney too?"

"The baby is mine, and its mom being taken care of is pretty damned important."

Josie looked pale. Her hands shook as she rubbed the back of her neck. "I have some money. I just didn't think to bring it. I can call Murray and tell him where—"

"Are you seriously planning to dodge marrying me? Is that it?"

Her eyes widened and her mouth dropped open. "Of course not. Why would you even say that?"

"You seem awfully resistant to me helping…like you don't want to be indebted to me or something. Like there won't be a lifetime of opportunities for you to pay me back." She sat there, looking small and way too damn fragile. Tucker knew she had to understand she wasn't in this alone. There was more at risk in the next few weeks than money. A lifetime of hurts and scars were about to be ripped open, and she needed to accept he wasn't just a guy she dated over a summer. He was a guy who was in it, for better or worse, for the long haul.

"Tucker, I am so sorry. I didn't mean—"

"It's all right." He wrapped her in his arms, his hands running down to the small of her back. Her cheek rested on his chest and she breathed a sigh. Kissing her temple, he said, "Why don't you take a nice hot bath, and I'll make some calls."

"Okay," she said, without moving. Letting out a long sigh, she said, "I wish we were back on the island, just the two of us."

"We'll be back there in no time. I promise."

"I felt safer there. It's so humiliating, Tucker. To know it's being rehashed over and over. Everyone will call me a liar and worse."

Tucker made her look at him; his jaw twitched. "You have nothing to be ashamed of, do you hear me? That bastard will burn in hell."

"He'll get away with it. He always does. He has money and can smile his way through anything."

"Take your bath. Stop thinking about it."

She nodded. He walked her to the bathroom. "You need anything?"

"No."

He turned to leave, but she caught his arm and pulled him back. "I guess I do need one more hug."

He smiled as he pulled her in and held her close. Kissing the top of her head, he promised, "It's going to be all right."

She leaned up on tiptoes and kissed him.

He called the attorney Ella recommended. Her name was Shae Harper, and she must have been expecting his call, because she didn't seem surprised to hear from him. She said she'd been following the story on the news. She offered to take Josie's case pro bono and agreed to meet with them as soon as they could get there.

Tucker was about to call a car rental place when there was a knock on the door. He looked through the peephole. Murray and Ella. With a grin, he pulled the door open.

"Hey, soldier," Ella said. "I hear you're quite the hero. Saved the lady fair and all. I was telling Murray on the way up here, I always thought it was suspicious he had such a gorgeous niece."

"I coulda had a niece that pretty."

"Course you could, you old goat." Ella laughed.

"I wanted to get your car to you, and Ella offered to drive over with me so I had a way back. I didn't realize the price would be so high," Murray said with a grin.

"Thank you, Ella. I appreciate it. I called that attorney for Josie. We're going to go meet with her in a little while. I was just getting ready to rent a car."

Murray handed him the keys. "Thought you were supposed to rest?"

"I'll be fine. Josie needs to know what she's up against."

"Lied to the doc. Can't say I'm shocked. Well, here are some clothes and such. There are a few more bags in the trunk, but I think this will hold you until you're feeling better." Murray set the bags on the small dining table. Stepping back, he said, "Hetty made you some casseroles and fresh bread. She sends her love, of course. Misses Josie pretty awful. Oh, and here's your cell phone. I took the case off and dried out the sim card and battery. It seems to be working fine now. And I found this here necklace. Thought it might be important."

Tucker gave him a hug. It was a spontaneous, short-lived awkward sort of embrace. "Thank you, Murray. You've thought of everything."

Murray's head bobbed. "Well, you know your dad was always there for me. He was like a brother."

Tucker shook his head, suddenly feeling like he needed to try a little harder to get to know the man Murray and Josie described. "We'll have to go see him together."

Murray nodded. "We will, son."

Murray checked his watch. "Well, I better get going. Hetty's been bombarded with reporters since we got back."

"Seriously? Son of a bitch."

"It's all right, son. Don't tell her I said this, but I think she's enjoying it. I know she's feeling it's her duty to tell Josie's side of things—how she had to run away because her momma wouldn't help her. Hid her identity for her own safety. Some of them reporters are saying Josie faked her death on purpose. That we were conspiring to keep Stone in jail. Some even want the case turned over to the Attorney General."

Tucker ran a hand across the top of his head. "Seems like this shit will never stop."

"That Stone fella?" Ella said. "He's on TV offering Josie forgiveness, begging her to come home. Makes me want to vomit."

"So, he's out?"

Murray shrugged. "I think the interview was done in prison, but he'll be out soon, if he isn't already. Stone's attorneys are putting heavy pressure on the state legislature. News said they were holding a special meeting of the Board of Pardons. I mean it's obvious the man isn't guilty of murder. At least not of Josie's. Bottom line—there's plenty of people bitching that the man is in prison while the girl he *murdered* is living it up on the beach. And it is election season, ya know. It's just a matter of time before he's free."

They said their good-byes, and Tucker headed to the bathroom to check on Josie. She was resting in the tub with her head propped on a rolled-up towel.

"Josie?"

She opened her eyes slowly. "Mmm, hmm?"

"We need to get dressed and meet with your attorney."

"Oh," Josie said, standing and reaching for a dry towel.

"Good thing we're in a hurry," Tucker said. "Or I'd have to pop a stitch."

Josie laughed as she dried off. "I have more willpower than that. Trust me."

Stepping out of the tub, she wrapped her body in the towel. "Was someone here?"

"Murray and Ella."

"You should have gotten me."

"They were in a hurry. He brought us clothes and my car."

"Ah Murray. They don't make too many like him."

"No, they don't. I need to shave and wash up, and then I'll be ready."

When he finished and opened the bathroom door, Josie was still in her towel sitting on the bed watching the news. "He says I should come home," Josie said as Tucker walked in the room. "Isn't that so nice of him to welcome me back with open arms?"

"Turn it off, Josie. There's no point in it."

"Seems I've also re-opened the death penalty debate. Who knew little old me could create such a national scandal? And they want to put me in jail? Murray and Hetty too?"

Tucker shut off the TV and sat beside her. Taking her hand in his, he gave it a squeeze. "It will all blow over. I swear."

"That one lady on there said I probably had a crush on him—an Electra complex or something. Stupid bimbo. She probably wants to have sex with him. But Hetty is in my corner."

"You saw Hetty on the news?"

"Yeah, God bless her. She said I wandered to their place scared and alone. Kind of like a lost puppy."

Josie flashed him a small smile. He bumped her forehead gently with his own, allowing it to rest there. "I almost forgot. I have something for you. Murray found it." He placed the necklace in her hand.

She gasped. "Thank you." She held it to her heart. "Thank you, thank you. Poor, sweet Maddy. He had to kill her to get this. She'd not have taken it off. She always wore it. Always." She clutched the necklace to her heart. "It hurts, you know… knowing they just…just treated her like a piece of meat."

"She's happy now, I swear. I don't know how the hell I know that, but I do. I have the strongest feeling that she is in a good place. That she wants you to be happy." Tucker had no clue why he felt so sure about a girl he'd never met, but he did. Maybe there was some sort of sibling bond between them. He took the necklace from her and placed it around her neck. "There. You have to remember Maddy as the happy girl she was, and is. The end of her life wasn't the sum of her, you understand? Don't let that moment be all that defines her."

Josie nodded. "You're right. I know you are. Maybe it's because I didn't get to say good-bye; or that I don't honestly know what happened to her…but I can't let her go. Logically, I say she's gone. She's dead. But in my heart, I fully expect to be walking down a street and see her. She feels that close."

"I don't know…" Brushing a curl back, he kissed her forehead. "Maybe one day you'll get your answers."

"I hope. I don't know if it's that I need to know to prove I'm not insane, or so I can stop searching crowds for her face."

"One day we'll look for her again. But right now, we've got to get going. The attorney said she'd meet with us as soon as we could get there."

They dressed and headed out. Mainland North Carolina was more similar to the lakeside community he called home than Ocracoke was. Soft green grass-covered yards, and trees which actually grew to full height, as opposed to their salt and wind stunted island counterparts.

Josie was quiet as they drove. Tucker reached over, took her hand, and held it. She gave him a squeeze.

"You're not nervous, are you?"

She shook her head. "Not really."

"I don't want it to overwhelm you."

"It won't." Placing a hand on her belly, she smiled at him. "You're right. All of this insanity will pass. This is what's real. This is what I have to concentrate on."

He gave her hand a kiss. "Boy or girl?"

"I don't know. Some days I think boy, then I think girl. I simply have no idea. Isn't that crazy? I mean there is a human life inside me. You can't get any closer than that, yet I have no idea. What do you think?"

Shaking his head, he shrugged. "I don't see a boy or a girl. I see a peanut."

"A peanut?" She laughed.

"Yeah, when I imagine a baby in there, I picture a little peanut-looking thing. I mean a really cute, really special little peanut."

"Peanut Boone. That has a ring to it."

"Only if you want it to hate us from the get-go. I always thought my mom was pushing it with Tucker."

"I like Tucker. Maybe a junior Tucker?"

"Veto. No junior. Maybe it will be a girl, and we could name her Madison?"

"Ahh, that's the best idea." She teared up. "You really are the best, you know?"

Tucker laughed as he pulled the car into a lot. "I can't argue with that. Looks like we're here. You ready?"

"I am."

Shae Harper's office was situated in a renovated bungalow on a quiet side street off a busy freeway. Shae met them at the front door. She was a tall, thin woman with thick, dark hair that fell in waves over her shoulders. She looked more like a supermodel than an attorney.

"Hi. Shae Harper," she said, extending a manicured hand to them. "The rest of the attorneys and staff have gone for the day, which is good. Your story is lighting up everyone's imagination, and I'm not going to pretend this office doesn't have its tabloid feeders."

"I watched some of it," Josie admitted. "It's humiliating."

"Shut it off. Don't watch it. Don't read about it. They're out to sell stories, not do good reporting. It's not worth the stress. Ella said you're expecting?"

"Yes," Josie said as they followed Shae to her office, which was a small, windowless room with little decoration.

"Don't mind the lack of ambience. I just joined the firm. My husband, er, ex-husband, and I used to share an office, but that didn't work out any better than the marriage, so my tenure with Philips and Marr is new. Makes me the longest practicing junior attorney. I took this case to secure my associate status, so when I said I'd do it pro-bono, it wasn't completely out of good will. I clerked for my cheating husband for years, ignoring my own career. That's not me bitching, that's me being straight…I've been practicing law for years, but never fought a case as the lead attorney."

"That's fine. It's good to know you're motivated," Josie said.

"So, tell me your story," Shae said once everyone was seated.

Josie told her everything. When she finished, Shae Harper looked up and asked sharply, "Did you intentionally fake your death to get even with your stepfather?"

Josie glanced at Tucker. She had the wide-eyed stare of a frightened animal caught in a trap. Then she turned back to Shae and said, "Not exactly."

"Not exactly?"

"I didn't fake my death. My mother tried to kill me, and I ran away. I didn't ask her to shoot me."

"Good." Shae nodded her head. "Then change your answer to a simple no. You cannot appear to be equivocating, lest it be construed as guilt when asked that question."

"Uh, I'm sorry?" Josie's voice was squeaky.

"Don't be sorry. Be firm. You ran away. You feared he was coming for you. That's why you changed your name."

"That is why I changed it."

"How in this day and age, could you not know he'd been charged with your murder? That's what they'll ask you."

"I did know. I just didn't care. He could rot in jail for the rest of his life, and it'd still be too easy for him for all he did."

Shae paused and looked Josie over. "That's the wrong answer. I looked through your police report from last night, and you told the police officer that you had no access to the internet."

"And that's true. Sort of. I had no internet where I lived."

"Stick with that answer. Never admit you knew he was in jail. It...complicates things."

"So, it's all right for me to lie?"

Shae leaned back in her chair and tented her fingers. "I'm not counseling you to lie. I'm telling you to pick a story and stick with it. The less legally complicated story is that you were ignorant to what was happening with Jeb. Disgusting as it is, he comes across as likable. His sociopathic smile wins hearts. Don't make him more tragic by admitting you knew an innocent man was thrown in jail."

"Do you believe him? That he's innocent?" Josie asked the attorney.

Shae arched an eyebrow and frowned. "Not at all. I have an intimate understanding of charming psychos. I believed one enough to follow him down the aisle. I won't fall for another. Besides, even if you were a willing participant in his sex-capades, you were a child. The son of a bitch gets no sympathy from me."

Josie's lips folded together, and she sat silent. Tucker took her hand.

"Look," Shae said with a sigh. "I don't believe the lying bastard for a second. I'm just saying, it is what it is. Right now, the media is making him their darling. We will prepare ourselves for as many different scenarios as we can imagine."

Josie nodded.

"And we are starting with your reaction to the question: Did you know? And when you answer, you may look pissed, shocked, and even hurt, but never, ever guilty. And the only correct answer is a resounding no- you did not know he was in jail."

"Yes ma'am," Josie said, her hands twisting in her lap.

"'It's not all bad. I'm giving you the rough stuff first. I do have good news. I hear from a friend of mine in the police department that Officer Greg Walker is scared shitless and begging to make a deal. Maybe he knows something useful."

Tucker leaned forward. "On the news, they keep talking about charging Josie with conspiracy. Can she get in trouble for faking her death?"

Shae shook her head. "It's not against the law to fake your death. Where you get in trouble is the fraud that usually goes along with it. Did you collect insurance money?"

Josie shook her head no.

"And I'm assuming since you were sixteen, you hadn't accumulated debt that your *demise* stopped you from paying, right?"

"No, no debt."

"So, the only way you're on shaky ground is if you're accused of faking your murder to get Stone locked up. But even that has no precedent. It's just TV chatter. It may hurt us in the civil suit. But we'll worry about that later."

Josie looked scared. Tucker gave her hand a squeeze. "It'll be all right."

"They hurt me, and I feel like I'm the one being punished."

"I'm sorry. It does feel that way, I'm sure. But we're going to get through this together. Did you ever tell anyone about the abuse?" Shae asked.

Josie crossed her leg over the other. The top leg bounced nervously. "Yes. I told a teacher in my junior high. She called my mom and Jeb in for a meeting. It ended with the school getting a new wing and me getting counseling. At that point, he was only doing weird things. Like saying sexual things: asking me to look at porn, touching me, but always with my clothes on." Josie shook her head. "It doesn't sound like much, but it made my skin crawl."

"And it escalated?"

Josie swallowed and nodded. "I went out on a date with Troy Miller for my sixteenth birthday. When I got home, Jeb was furious. He accused me of having sex. I told him that was crazy, but he insisted…said he could tell." Josie turned red and had to take a deep breath. "That was the first time…he…you know."

"No, I don't know. I have a good guess, but I don't know what he did."

"You're kidding me, right? Do I have to say it?"

"I'm sorry, but yes. Eventually, you will have to say what he did to you. Possibly on a witness stand with strangers staring at you."

Josie started to cry.

Shae lowered her voice to a near whisper. "Listen, he has the right to face his accuser. He's innocent until proven guilty, and the burden of proof is on us. You were a young girl, living under his roof. He was your parent—"

"He was never my parent," Josie said, reaching for a tissue from the box on Shae's desk.

Shae wobbled her head between a nod and a shake. "Let's say he was a caregiver. Someone entrusted to protect you. He violated that trust in the worst way. You have to understand, in your heart and in your soul, this was not your fault. What he did is a shame on him, not you."

Josie looked to Tucker. He gave her a nod. She took a deep breath and said, "I fought with Jeb about Troy. Then Mike, our neighbor stopped by to return a tool or something. While Jeb talked to Mike, I ran to my room and locked the door, but the next thing I know, he's opening it. I think he used a screw driver on the lock, I'm not sure, but it opened. Then he…raped me."

Josie choked on the words, but once they were out of her mouth, her shoulders relaxed and she seemed more at ease. She looked Shae in the eye and said, "When he was done, he made me shower in front of him. He told me he loved me, and then he tucked me into my bed like I was still six. I couldn't sleep, so he got a bottle of sleeping pills and gave me a couple of them."

"Did you tell anyone?"

Josie nodded. "I told my pediatrician when I went for my check-up. I'd had the same doctor since I was four. I thought she'd believe me, but she didn't. She told me I should be ashamed of myself for lying. I knew then that running away was my only option. When that failed, I found the pills and took them all. The whole time I was in the hospital, everyone told me I was making it up to get even. I'd ask them, *to get even for what?* I had everything. Clothes, car, a house with a pool…I had everything. Everything but a goddamned door that I could keep locked." Josie words bounced off the walls of the small room. She took a deep breath as silence fell over them all. Her face was pale, all but two blood-red splotches on her cheeks. Josie squared her shoulders and looked directly at Shae. "Is that all you need to know? Or do you need details?"

Shae picked up her pen and shook her head. "You did great, Josie. You keep reminding yourself who the bastard is. He had no right. You wouldn't feel ashamed to tell the story if he walked up to you and punched you in the face, so do not ever feel like you're to blame for this abuse. Do you understand me?"

Josie dried her eyes and nodded.

"Tell you what," Shae said. "Let's get the paperwork rolling, so I can get to work." Shae rummaged through the file folders in her desk drawer. "Did you have anything you wanted to ask me?"

"Yes. I want to change my name. I don't want to be Ariel Stone."

Shae nodded. "I'll call in a few favors, and you should legally be Josie by the end of the week. Though I wouldn't suggest McCoy. The judge frowns on picking celebrity names."

"We're getting married. It's not like she'll have the name long," Tucker said.

"Ah, what the heck, it's obscure. He may never notice. If he does, I'll suggest Boone. You wouldn't be the first gal to not change last names in her marriage."

"How about Morgan? Eventually, I'd be Josie Morgan Boone. I like that," Josie suggested.

"Sounds good to me." Shae made notes. Then she dropped her pen. "Okay, here's the plan. I'm going to collect all the info. You'll not talk to anyone. Reporters, police—listen, even if the freaking pope himself calls, you send him to me. I'll start today on the name change, and I'm going to file a restraining order against Stone based on the rape and abuse. I wish we could get one against the media, but it's their right. And I warn you, once the media finds you, they will hound you. Do not engage. Don't even make eye contact. You either, Mr. Boone. They're going to ask you things that will make you want to pop them in the nose, but you walk away. I'll nudge the Applewold Prosecutor's office to see if we can get rape charges filed, but I'm not holding my breath.

"And lastly, I'm going to have to put together a legal team we can trust in Pennsylvania. If they do file charges against you—which I don't see happening, but still must prepare for—I need people familiar with Pennsylvania laws.

"And I'll also get the civil suit filed, because we will definitely sue the son of a bitch. I'm not certain at this point where it will land or which court would be in our best interest. Technically, you and Stone are both residents of Pennsylvania, so PA courts would take the case. But if I can make the case that Josie is a North Carolina resident, and since we'll be suing for more than $75,000, then we can bump the civil suit to a federal court. And that may free us of having to deal with cronies of Jeb's. Any questions?"

Chapter Thirty Four

One week later, they drove to the hospital. Josie was quiet. Today was the day. Tucker was getting his stitches out, and the baby was getting his or her— its sex depended on Josie's fluctuating powers of discernment— own check-up.

"When we're done, maybe do some shopping? Grab some lunch?" Tucker asked.

Josie laughed. "Do I look that nervous that you're offering to take me shopping?"

Tucker grinned. Josie smiled and let out a long sigh. The worry lines on her forehead smoothed. "It's going to be fine," he said.

"Do you really think so? Honestly and truly?" Josie looked less convinced.

Tucker took a breath and shrugged. "Yeah, I think things are fine."

Nodding, she looked out the window. "I just need to hear it or see it. Something that proves it's real. It's like, until then, it's too good to be true."

"Well, we're here. Let's go see how things are going."

Walking her through the hospital, he kept a hand at the small of her back. He lied when he said he thought everything was all right. His gut was twisted tighter than a bowstring.

The doctor's office was crowded with pregnant women, all in differing stages of belly bump. He sat with Josie in a corner and held her hand. A guy nurse with brown curly hair came out and called them in immediately. As they walked back to the office, the nurse said, "I'm John. I'm a nurse, and no I am not gay—not that I have anything against anyone who is gay, but I don't want you fixing me up with your single guy cousins. If you have any of the hot female variety, then we can open a discussion." He ended his introduction to show them their room. "Here you go. This will be your room."

Josie stepped into the pink room. There was a table, two regular chairs, and one swivel chair for the doctor.

Nurse John started taking her vitals. As he checked her pulse, he said, "We've had media crawling all over us. They didn't catch you in the lot, did they?"

Josie shook her head.

"Good. Dr. Simon assured everyone if there were any leaks, every single person on staff would get fired. That must have worked."

"Why are they calling here?" Josie asked.

John frowned. "Seems the hospital let it out that you're pregnant, and that you're coming here for your prenatal care. They've been trying to figure out when your next appointment is."

"Why do they care?" Josie asked.

"It's got everything a sensational story needs. A rich man, a beautiful young girl, sex, lies, baby. It's made for TV, sweetheart."

Josie paled, but said nothing.

The doctor came in the room. "Hello, Miss Josie. You're looking pale and skinny. Are you eating?"

Josie nodded.

"Still having morning sickness?"

"No," Josie said with some hesitation.

"Don't worry. Lie back, let's have a listen." The doctor grabbed a wand and turned it on. He offered a quick, "This will be cold", before a dollop of gel dropped on her belly. With a single swipe from her belly button to her hip, there was the woosh, woosh, woosh he was looking for. "There's your baby. Heart beat sounds good."

Josie laughed. Her body shook and a tear slid down her cheek.

"You okay?" Dr. Simon asked.

"I'm great. Thank you."

"Good then. I'll see you in a month. John will give you papers on nutrition, your vitamins—all that exciting stuff." The doctor turned to John. "I also want blood work before she leaves. Any questions?" the doctor asked, turning back to Josie and Tucker.

They both shook their heads. Tucker wanted to ask about sex, but all things considered, he wasn't sure if it was even appropriate to care.

"All right then. Until next time."

They had their meeting with John, Josie offered up her arm for vial after vial of blood, and then they left. Leaving the doctor's office, Josie wrapped her arm around his and squeezed. "We're having a baby. I shouldn't be so excited. We're unmarried, only sort of employed, and I've only known you a summer, but I'm so happy. Are you happy, Tucker?"

Her eyes shined. Her smile was so brilliant it could have illuminated the depths of outer space. If someone would have told him that poor planning in the heat of one magical moment would bring him to this perfect place, he would have said they were smoking something. But here he was, standing in a hospital hallway looking down at his future. The feelings of guilt and futility were replaced with purpose.

He kissed her until she had to grab a fistful of shirt to maintain her balance. Stepping back, he assured her, "I am the happiest man on this planet. Let's go get these stitches out, and then we'll buy Peanut a gift."

"Peanut. That can't stick. The baby is going to kill you for it when he's twelve."

Josie's phone rang, and she answered. Hanging up she squealed. "It's a good day. Meet Josie Morgan. Shae said I can stop and get the documents." Clutching his hand, she started walking along with him. "You know what that means, right?" she asked.

"All new monograms on your towels?"

She slapped him playfully. "Nope. It means you can marry me now."

Tucker pushed the button at the elevator then turned to her. "I can? Who said I wanted to?"

"I'm a fallen woman and you're to blame. You have to marry me."

Tucker's laugh filled the hallway. "Fallen? We've got to get you watching some modern movies."

Stepping onto the elevator, he pulled her into him and kissed her as the doors closed. "I will gladly marry you. Fallen or not. Once I'm stitchless, let's get you a ring."

Josie sat in a chair while they pulled the stitches out of Tucker's back, side, and shoulder. Finished, Dr. Morris popped off his gloves and told Tucker he was free to go.

As they were leaving the office, Tucker handed his phone to Josie. "What do you think? Or is that not romantic enough?"

It was an all-inclusive wedding package in Vegas. Josie smiled. "I think that sounds awesome. Can we leave tonight?"

"I don't see why not. Let's go pack a bag and buy a couple of plane tickets. We could be Mr. and Mrs. by midnight."

Chapter Thirty Five

Tucker and Josie never made it to Vegas. When they pulled into the gravel parking lot of their apartment, there were three police cars waiting for them. Two sheriff deputies stood in front of them, holding up their hands for them to stop. Their guns were still holstered, but Tucker could see they had their snaps undone for a quicker draw. There were two other deputies squatted behind their squad cars. Tucker assumed they did have their weapons drawn.

"What's going on?" Josie asked.

"I don't know."

"You think Greg escaped?"

Tucker rolled his window down. "Something wrong, officer?"

Deputy Woodruff, or so his name tag said, approached the open window. "Sir, I need you both to step out of the car and put your hands on the hood."

"Is something wrong? Did Meyers escape?"

"Sir, please just get out of the car. Miss Stone…"

Josie opened the door and got out, clutching the teddy bear they'd bought the peanut. Tucker followed behind her, his eyes glued to her form the entire time. The other officer approached.

"Miss Stone, I have a warrant for your arrest," the deputy said.

"You what?" Josie's voice was small as she squeezed the bear tighter.

The two deputies behind the car approached, circling them. The first deputy said, "A warrant, ma'am." He held out a piece of paper. Josie didn't move, didn't even bother to reach for it.

"What the hell? What do you mean she's under arrest?" Tucker's question wasn't answered. In a blink of his eye, he was slammed against the hood of his car and handcuffed. "Settle down," Woodruff said. "We're only doing our job."

The arresting deputy said, "Ariel Stone, you're charged with conspiracy and fraud. You have the right to remain silent…"

"This is bullshit; she gets to call her attorney," Tucker yelled.

Josie's eyes glistened when she turned to Tucker. "It's all right; you call Shae. And take care of this." Setting the white bear on the hood beside him, she held out her hands to the officer. The officer took her by the shoulder and started to spin her. The other officer said, "That's not necessary, Wayne. She isn't going to fight you. Let her be comfortable."

Wayne nodded and clicked the cuffs on her wrists from the front.

"This is insane. What the hell?" Tucker asked. He jerked his arms against the cuffs, but it did no good.

They escorted Josie to the squad car. Tucker tried to rush the officer holding Josie's arm, but the two watching grabbed him by his cuffs and pulled him back. Officer Woodruff shook his head. "Settle down, son. That won't do you or her any good."

Tucker turned to Woodruff. The man pulled off his hat and rubbed his sandy blond hair. His brown eyes were soft and Tucker could see remorse in them.

"We didn't want to arrest the girl. But we didn't have a choice. The warrant came in this morning, and we had to serve it."

Tucker nodded. He couldn't trust himself to speak. His throat felt tight.

Josie was loaded in the back seat. She looked over at Tucker as they closed the door. Through the window, she looked more like a reflection. His heart ached. She looked lost and more than a bit confused. His chest hurt, and his eyes burned. He couldn't do a damn thing other than watch her be taken away.

Once the car was gone, the officer let Tucker loose. Tucker batted the bear off the hood of the car, sending it flying into the parking lot. The damn thing mocked him with its happy little threaded smile.

"I'm sorry, son," the officer said. "She'll be treated right."

"She's pregnant; they know that, right?"

"I'll be sure they know. Call her attorney and then follow me down to the station. She'll be allowed to make bail. And you better fetch that bear.

Seemed to mean a lot to her."

Tucker called Shae. Then he walked over to the bear. Picking it up from the asphalt, he brushed the dirt from its fur before tucking it into the crook of his arm.

Shae beat him to the station. She already had Josie in a room discussing her options.

"Applewold will not consider rape charges against Jeb, but they filed fraud and conspiracy charges against you. It's a joke, but has to be dealt with. They filed a petition for extradition. We could block it, or we could go ahead and face them in court. I think you have a good case to defend your running away. But if you want to slow the process down, we can keep them busy with paperwork."

Josie's hands flitted to her tummy. "I prefer to get it over with."

"Then you're going to be released on a personal recognizance bond, and you will drive yourself to Applewold to turn yourself over to their police."

Josie sighed. "I swear, every time I think I'll be happy, something happens."

Tucker kneeled beside her. "It's a glitch, Josie. We're still on the right path."

Josie nodded. "All right," she said. "Where do I sign?"

A few papers shuffled here and there, and Josie was free to leave. Shae assured her she would meet her in Pennsylvania. They went to the house to get their clothes, and then they drove north. Josie had to report to Applewold Police in two days to be charged.

They drove a few hours before stopping at a drive-thru window. They took their dinner to a hotel and ate while they discussed everything from what was on television to the weather, anything but Josie's looming arrest.

It wasn't until the next morning as Tucker ran his hands over her bare belly that Tucker suggested they run. They should just grab a flight south and never look back.

"I'm tempted," she said. "And I stayed up last night thinking about it, but then I thought of Peanut. We'd be looking over our shoulder all the time. That's no life for our baby. And then, if I was arrested a few years from now, he'd see it. No, this is better. Let's get it over with. Shae says I'll win."

"Shae said you'd never get arrested too."

Josie smacked his arm. "You're supposed to make me feel better!"

Kissing her bare shoulder, he said, "My only intention is keeping you with me."

"Come here, you awesome stud. How about you love me, very gently. No straining the scars or anything. Just love me and know that no matter what, I'm going to be with you."

Chapter Thirty Six

They arrived at the police station with one minute to spare before the police reissued a warrant. The place was crawling with reporters that bombarded their car. Josie flinched and pulled away from the window, clutching his hand. Half the world thought she was a lying slut. The other half thought she was a victim, and the press was eager to keep the debate alive.

A squadron of uniformed officers directed them to the back of the station. The officers formed a human tunnel, funneling her in the back door. Josie reached for Tucker, but got separated in the jostling crowd. Though he could still see her, he couldn't touch her, and that made him feel like he was a million miles away.

Shae was waiting for her. There was another man with her, a handsome guy with blond hair and small wire-rimmed glasses. "Josie, this is Matthew Brandt. He comes highly recommended, so I added him to your team."

Josie nodded, though the look of confusion on her face made Tucker doubt she was listening. The door was closed against the crowd, and the sounds of people yelling her name quieted.

"You okay, Josie?" Shae asked as she led Josie to a small room with a round table and four plastic chairs.

"I'm fine, I guess," she said, scanning the interrogation room with wide eyes.

"Those jackasses leaked that you were coming in on purpose. All of them seem to be buddies with Stone. Josie, they are going to fingerprint you, take your mug shot, and officially arrest you. But then you will be released until your hearing."

Josie chewed on her lip and nodded.

Shae frowned, her perfect pink lips turned down. Rubbing Josie's arm, she said, "I'm really sorry about this. This is such a sham."

"You need to tell her about the deal," Matthew said.

"Oh yes, the deal." Shae sighed as she pulled a stack of papers from her briefcase. "The prosecutor has offered a plea bargain. You will admit to fraud and defamation of character and only get a year's probation."

Tucker stood up straighter. Normally, he'd relish the fight. He wanted nothing more than watch Stone go down, to pay the price for hurting Josie and Maddy. But the temptation for her to sign this paper and walk out of this building with this mess behind them...he felt like an alcoholic being offered an ice-cold, refreshing drink. He knew it was the wrong choice, but his mouth nearly watered for it. Maybe he was so tempted because his gut screamed that they were not on the happily-ever-after course. "Take it, Josie. Take it and we leave for Vegas tonight."

Shae arched an eyebrow at Tucker as she explained further, "You realize, it's basically Josie admitting that she lied about everything. The abuse. Maddy. All of it. She will be legally bound to never tell the truth, and in one fell swoop, she would restore Jeb Stone's tarnished reputation. For the rest of her life, Josie will be called a liar. It's your choice. As your council, it's legally sound and absolves you of a future civil suit."

"Civil suit?" Tucker asked.

Shae grimaced. "Jeb has the right to sue Josie for damages. He lost nearly all his assets to Amanda in the wrongful death suit she filed on Josie's behalf. If the prosecution proves Josie did any of this on purpose, she could be looking at jail time and Jeb could sue her for her assets."

"Little good that would do him," Josie said. "I have nothing."

"It would be up to the judge, but he could order that you pay from future earnings," Shae said.

Tucker felt dirty for trying to talk her into signing, but he couldn't stop himself. Idealistically, he agreed with her. But he no longer gave a damn about ideals. He wanted her free. He wanted their child safe. He sat beside her, turning her toward him. "Take the deal. What does it matter in the long run? We can walk out of here today, be married by midnight. Please, Josie?"

Josie looked crushed. Her brow furrowed and her breathing shallowed. "I see your point," she said quietly. She picked up the plea and read over it, her head slowly shaking back and forth. "What's this?" Josie pointed to a paragraph in the middle of the second page.

"Oh, that," Shae said. "You sign the deal and commit to the confidentiality clause, you will get three million dollars for your troubles."

Josie's laugh was far from pleasant. "Once again, money saves him. If I sign this? I'm no better than a whore. No, I'm worse. At least someone who sells her body for money does it on her terms. Me? I'd be letting him get away with taking something from me that was way more valuable than my virginity. He took my joy, and my trust. To this day, I panic when I'm in crowds. I have nightmares…not because he used me for sex, but because I was powerless to stop him. Do you know how bad it sucks to try to feel powerful when you know damn good and well you can't even stop a man from wrestling your pants off your body? I may have come to terms with that physical weakness, because I've told myself that he can't change who I am inside, but," Josie laid the paper on the table, "if I sign this, then I'm nothing but a pathetic coward, and he wins."

Shae pulled the cashier's check from the pile of papers and ripped it into a hundred pieces. "Matthew, will you come with me to present this to Mr. Stone as our answer?" Matthew nodded as they left.

Josie looked to Tucker. Pulling him closer by the collar of his shirt, she kissed him. "I'm sorry, Tucker. I know you're worried, but he won't get away with this."

"I'm scared, Josie. None of this has gone our way."

"I can't let him get away with it. I could never look at myself in the mirror."

"You're right. I know, you're right." Burying his face in her hair, he couldn't stop the tears. Of all the shit that had gone wrong this year, this was the toughest. He felt like he should be able to do something to stop this, not just kiss her goodbye and send her out there to the wolves.

But that was the only option he had. Taking a deep breath, he put on a smile that was more grimace and said, "You know I'll support anything you need to do."

Her hand was soft against his face. "Thank you. And don't worry. It will be a memory in no time."

But it wasn't. She was fingerprinted, photographed, and taken across the hall to the magistrate to be arraigned and read her charges. The whole time she was wide-eyed and pasty. It was like the Applewold PD snared a rabbit and relished torturing it. Tucker's gut ached, and his body remained tense. When the prosecutor came in and tried to strong-arm her into taking the deal she'd already rejected, Tucker wanted to punch him. He disliked Bill Rogers on sight. His suit was too well-fitted, his cologne too strong. He looked more like a slick, high-end car salesman than someone who was supposed to be upholding the law.

While looming over Josie, Rogers tossed the papers at her. "You might want to give these a second consideration," he said. "Sign them and you walk away today. Don't sign and I swear, I'll do everything in my power to make sure you get to see what it's like to do some jail time. You and everyone who helped you pull off this stunt."

Josie's head whipped with that information. "What do you mean?"

Rogers sat, leaning his body too close to hers. "I don't buy for one second that a sixteen-year-old kid pulled this off on her own. I'm going to turn over every rock and flip every stone until I find out, then every person who helped you hide will go to jail."

Josie's hands shook.

Shae stepped forward. "Stop trying to bully my client."

Rogers stood and looked the petite attorney in the eye. "I'm trying to get her to make the rational choice. A conspiracy to commit fraud is what I see, with a whole lot of people helping to make it happen."

"Speaking of conspiracies, how much is Stone paying you?" Shae asked.

"Excuse me? Lady, you aren't even licensed in this state. I could have you disbarred for trying to practice without a Pennsylvania license."

"You could have her nothing." Matthew stepped between Rogers and Shae. "If anyone should be worried about their career, it's you. You have an election coming up…you better hope to hell you picked the right side. Or

hope that Stone is paying you enough to cover a very early retirement."

"You better be careful what kind of accusations you toss around," Rogers said, leveling a stare at Matthew.

With a shrug and a grin, Matthew said, "Sorry. I didn't mean to hit a nerve."

"You didn't hit a nerve, you feckless little squib. We'll see who's on the right side when this case is taken to the Attorney General. The people of Pennsylvania cannot allow spiteful, spoiled children to fake their own murders as revenge for getting dragged home from a party. Isn't that what you did, Ms. Stone?"

Shae placed a hand on Josie's arm. "My client has nothing to say to you." Shae maneuvered her toward the door. "We're done here. We'll need a police escort out the back, since you guys seem to have let every reporter in the area know she was coming in."

"Who says she gets to go? We'll have to hold her until bail is set."

Shae and Matthew both charged at the man, pointing out the terms of surrender. While they argued, Tucker looked to Josie. Reaching out to her, he took her hands in his and pulled her to him. Her body trembled. He wrapped his arms around her and held her.

"Tucker, I'm scared."

"It's okay. Everything will be all right." His words sounded solid, though his heart was breaking.

Chapter Thirty Seven

Shae and Matthew won the battle. Tucker wrapped an arm over Josie's shoulder and protected her from the press as they made their way to his car. Tucker drove in random turns and circles until he was sure he lost all the reporters trying to follow them.

The couple didn't make it to Tucker's mom's house until after dark. Tucker was never so glad that no one in his family shared a last name. As of yet, the press hadn't tied him to the Morgans, and they hadn't figured out that his mother was an Adkins, so there was no one camping outside the single story ranch he grew up in.

"Ready to meet my mom?" Tucker asked. Linking his fingers in hers, his thumb caressed the smooth skin on her hand.

"I'm not sure. I thought that was supposed to just be a drop-in at the police station and leave. I thought they were going to put me in a cell."

"Thank God for Shae. I could've kissed her."

"Now, let's not go that far." Josie laughed.

Coming closer, his lips found hers. "Figure of speech. My kisses are only yours."

"Good. I'd hate to have to fire the best attorney ever."

"She did go right at him, didn't she?" Tucker asked with a chuckle.

Josie nodded. "She backed him right down. I don't know why I was shocked that they tried to renege on the deal. I figure they are all on Jeb's side."

"You really think he bought off everyone in Applewold?"

"He is the richest guy in town—heck most towns." Pressing her forehead to his chest, she added, "This is going to be harder than I imagined."

"We'll make it." The porch light flipped on. Tucker sighed. "That's my mother. She's not overly patient."

"Yay," Josie said weakly.

She climbed out of the car slowly. Tucker came around to her side and wrapped an arm around her waist. As they approached the porch, his mother stepped out. Josie's brows popped up when she saw her. Tucker was used to the reaction since he looked nothing like his mother.

"Geesh, I was wondering if you remembered how to get in the house," Marlene Adkins said as she waved them in. "What were you doing out there?"

"I was prepping Josie on how to deal with my mother," Tucker said.

"Tucker," Josie scolded, instantly red-faced.

"Probably making out, knowing you," Marlene said with an eye roll.

Josie gave him a look. Tucker shrugged.

They followed Marlene into the living room. Ed Adkins stood as they approached. "Tucker," he said. "Glad to see you home. This must be Josie. Nice to meet you." Ed gave Josie an awkward side hug. "I'm, uh, happy to see Tucker look so...well, happy." Shy, tiny Josie looked like she could be Ed's daughter. They were both short, small-framed, and prone to rosy cheeks.

After introductions and news of their drive, Ed was out of conversation. He mumbled something about it being Shark Week and wandered back to his chair.

Marlene frowned. "I swear to God, I hate cable. He sits in that damned chair and flips between National Geographic and Discover. Good of you to be sociable, Ed. Nice way to get to know Tucker's girlfriend."

"Leave him alone, Mom. Ed is fine."

"Maybe if he'd been more of a dad, you wouldn't have had to go looking for your own and not ended up in this mess."

Tucker pulled Josie closer. "I'm not in a mess. But I am tired, and Josie is worn out. I'm taking her to bed, and we'll talk more about all of this in the morning."

"So soon? Seriously Tucker, you owe me an explanation. I've been through incest, pregnancy, stabbings, legal trouble, and crap all over the media. I deserve to know what the hell is going on."

Tucker didn't want to fight with his mother, not now. Josie had seen enough drama for a lifetime, so he relented. "Let me get Josie settled, and we'll talk."

"I don't need to get settled," Josie said.

Tucker looked down at her, and Josie nodded. "Fine," he said.

"Fine," Marlene echoed. After seating them around the kitchen table, she made them cups of cocoa and set a plate of homemade banana bread in front of them. "So Josie, are you absolutely certain you're pregnant?"

Josie's hands slid from her mug, off the table, to her lap.

"Yes, she's pregnant. We went to the doctor a few days ago and heard the heartbeat," Tucker said.

"Okay. So, what are your plans? I'm not saying you have to get married. I never married Tucker's dad, so not pushing that. Just asking."

"We'd be married now if it weren't for them arresting her," Tucker said.

"Without even talking to your mother?" Marlene asked.

"Things are chaotic right now, if you haven't noticed."

"Oh, I've noticed. It's all over the TV. Seems you're breaking new ground faking your own murder to get someone sent up the river. "

"That isn't why she did it," Tucker snapped, pushing his chair back from the table.

"I only know what I see on the news. It's not like you're giving me information."

"I'm not in the mood for this tonight. I'm going to get Josie settled in, take a hot shower, and then we'll talk."

He held out his hand to Josie and she took it. Turning to Marlene, she said, "It was nice meeting you, Mrs. Adkins. And uh, thanks for the cocoa."

Tucker pulled her along. Flipping on the light to his bedroom, he wished his mom had redecorated. Josie sat on his Pittsburgh Steelers comforter and looked around his room. "Was your obsession with cars or the naked women hanging on them?"

Tucker sat beside her. "It was the cars. Definitely the cars."

"Liar." Josie laughed.

"I got those when I was twelve. Won them throwing basketballs at a fair.

How about tomorrow, you can wash my car in your panties, and I can get some poster replacements?"

Josie leaned into him. "Not going to happen."

He kissed the top of her head. "I didn't figure."

They sat quietly a moment, then Tucker cleared his throat. "Let's get you some sleep."

"I am so tired."

"You go to the bathroom. I'll make sure there are no cooties in the bed," he said.

"Good deal," Josie said, standing. Tucker pointed to a door. Dragging her overnight bag, she disappeared into the bathroom.

Tucker pulled the blankets back and fluffed the pillows. Then he made a quick sweep of his room, hiding or destroying anything that could be humiliating or questionable. In his top desk drawer, he had a stack of half-nudes from Holly. He ripped them into dozens of pieces and shoved them to the bottom of the garbage can. On his bulletin board, there were prom pictures of him and Holly. Seemed cruel to leave them up when Josie didn't ever get to go to a prom. There was also a picture of him and Ash standing arm and arm in front of a Humvee. He moved it from the corner to the center of the board. "I miss you, you dumb son of a bitch."

"Who's a son of a bitch?" Josie asked. She was dressed in her pajamas, looking soft and ready to snuggle. Tucker wished she didn't have dark circles under her eyes, or he'd talk her into delaying sleep for ten, fifteen minutes. But he doubted she'd be awake for five once her head hit the pillow.

"It's Ash." He pointed to the picture. "That's us posing like a couple of tourists. Ash wanted to make a poster that said Bagdad or bust, but we didn't have any paper."

"You guys look like you're having too much fun to be at war."

"Ash was like that. I don't know that he had a bad day. Well, until he got shot in the heart." Tucker sighed, his body feeling as heavy and tired as Josie looked.

Wrapping an arm over her shoulder, he pulled her in for a hug.

"I'm sorry, Tucker. I know how it feels to lose your best friend," Josie said.

"That you do, baby. That you do."

Scooping her off her feet, he carried her to bed, and laid her down. Pulling the blankets up to her chin, he brushed her hair back from her cheeks. "It's all going to be all right. Today was rough, but you made it."

"We did. Thank you for sticking by me."

"Where else would I be? I love you. I love my peanut. Speaking of which, how's he doing?"

"Fine. I guess." Josie's hand moved to her belly.

Tucker kissed her. "You go to sleep now. I'll see you in the morning." He kissed her one last time before backing out of the room. He flipped off the light and closed the door.

He made his way back to the kitchen. His mom was on her laptop. She turned as he came in the room.

"What are you doing?" Tucker asked.

Marlene closed the lid on the laptop, looking guilty. Tucker reached over her shoulder and flipped it open. Jeb Stone's construction page.

"I was only curious. What kind of monster does what he did?"

Tucker sat beside her and scrolled through all his holdings from warehouses to garages. Tucker wondered if the police ever searched these places. Several were isolated from everything but trees and grass. Perfect places to hide something. The last page of the site was an "About Stone Construction" page. There was the *happy* family. Jeb, Amanda, and Ariel. Tucker slammed the laptop closed.

"You'd never guess from that perfect picture, would you? People would hire them to build their house and never know they were hiring a monster." Marlene said with a shake of her head.

"What did you always tell me about perfection?"

"Never trust it," Marlene said with a sigh. She got up and got herself and Tucker a cup of coffee. Carrying it to him, she said, "She's awfully pale. Did they check her iron?"

"I suppose. They took blood. This is just a lot of stress on her."

"Did she really fake her murder?"

"She was scared and ran away. She just wanted to hide from her stepdad."

"On the news, they're saying she's crazy. That she set the whole thing up. The murder. The alleged rape. That Stone guy? He says it was a mutual relationship."

"He's a liar."

Marlene was quiet a minute. Then she scratched under her eye. "Can you imagine what it's like to get screwed by your own stepdad?"

"No Mom, I can't," Tucker said, his brows furrowing together.

"Don't get mad. I'm just sayin'…that's got to be one of the worst. And seriously? If I was her mother, I'd have ripped that jerk's balls off. I still can't believe how her mother acted. Oh my God…do you think me sending Ed to her with that picture of Josie is why she and that guy came and tried to kidnap her? Is that what got you stabbed? I was trying to be nice to a woman I thought was suffering. She wasn't suffering…that greedy, hateful whore. I wish she hadn't killed herself. I'd go back to her house and I'd string her up myself. But I'd punch her in the face first."

"Easy there, tiger. Slow up and calm down. Be nice to Josie. Be a little less out there, all right? This has all been hard on her."

Marlene nodded. "I'll treat her with kid gloves. It's just so bizarre. I mean things like this only happen on TV, not real life. At least not in our lives."

"Thank you," Tucker said, giving her a big hug. "I think I'm going to hit the hay too."

"I made up the spare bed."

"I'll just bunk with Josie."

"Seriously? Not even going to pretend?"

Tucker rolled his eyes. He could always count on his mom to be a moral wild card who played her hand as she fancied. "I'm not planning to have sex with her, Mother. I'm just going to sleep with her. Besides, what are you

worried about? That I'll knock her up?"

Chapter Thirty Eight

Two weeks later, Josie had her preliminary hearing. It was the first time she had to be in a room with Jeb Stone. Her legal team had grown to include three more lawyers. A total of five now shielded her from Jeb's charges. But even a team didn't stop her body from trembling when she made eye contact with Stone.

In a glance, Tucker measured the man. If he'd passed him on the street, he'd never know Jeb was a monster. He appeared on the surface like a typical, middle age man. Thick brown hair, a firm jaw line. He was technically a handsome guy. It wasn't until Tucker made eye contact with him that he understood. Tucker took a seat behind Josie. When he leaned forward and kissed her, he glanced at Stone. The face he turned to Tucker—the narrowed eyes and clenched jaw—was akin to the look a husband would offer his wife's lover. It was far from the paternal look of concern he'd been sporting for reporters.

The bailiff entered the courtroom and called for all to rise. Judge Smith entered the chamber, tripping over the door jam and lurching forward. The man's disheveled hair and mint green bow tie sticking out of his collar didn't inspire confidence. Tucker cracked his knuckles and prayed to God that He'd replaced all the man lacked in coordination and fashion sense with a damn keen mind. Once seated, Judge Smith asked them to take their seats. He adjusted his glasses and looked to Matthew. "Counselor, I see here you have requested a change of venue?"

"Yes, your honor," Matthew said. "Considering the many alliances and friendships Jeb Stone has in this area, it would seem my client would be better served in a neutral district."

The judge perused the paperwork, then turned to Josie. "Ms. Morgan?"

As Shae had advised her to do, Josie stood. She gripped the edge of the table as if she needed the physical support to speak with the judge.

"Ms. Morgan, did you know you were presumed dead?"

Jeb Stone cleared his throat, catching Josie's attention. She glanced his way. He leaned forward, nodded at her. All the color drained from Josie's face, and she said nothing. Tucker sucked in air.

"Ms. Morgan, did you or did you not know the world thought you were dead?" Judge Smith repeated the question.

"I...uh," Josie turned to Shae. The attorney gave her a nod, but her perfectly sculptured brows pulled together with worry.

"It's a simple question. Did you know you were presumed dead?"

Tucker was trying to send her a mental message as a sweat broke out over his body. *Just say no. Please God Josie, just say no.*

Josie mumbled, "I don't think I feel very well." Her knees buckled, and she collapsed. Matthew was quick to step up and grab her before her face smacked the table. The room was instantly abuzz.

Tucker leaped over the railing to get to her, but her attorneys and the bailiff were in the way. Josie woke, red-faced. She wiped at her forehead. "I'm okay. Tucker?"

Tucker shoved his way through. She wrapped her arm around him, nuzzling her face in his neck. "I don't want to see him, Tucker."

"I know, sweetie. I know." Squeezing his eyes closed, he held her tighter, wishing he could make all this stop.

Matthew stood and faced the judge. "Your Honor. Ms. Morgan is expecting, and the last few weeks have been quite traumatic. From the kidnapping, to her own mother's attempt at murder, an arrest, and now the stress of being in the same room as her abuser. It's a lot to absorb."

"Would counsel prefer a postponement?"

"I think it wise. I think my client should see a doctor."

Judge Smith nodded. "You will keep the court apprised of her condition. Court is hereby adjourned until further notice."

"I object, Your Honor. I think Ms. Morgan should have to answer the question. Feeling light-headed shouldn't get her off the hook."

"Excuse me, Mr. Rogers? Are you telling me how to run my court?"

Judge Smith asked.

"Not at all, Your Honor. I'm just suggesting the dizziness could be a ruse."

"You're suggesting I'm so gullible as to be deceived by a swooning female?"

Mr. Rogers turned red, but said nothing else. The Judge stood and left.

It was over for the moment, but Josie was still shaking. Tucker held her icy hands in his. "Come on. Let me take you home."

She nodded and stood. As they made their way out of the courtroom, Jeb stepped in front of them. Josie dropped behind Tucker, holding onto his waist. "Josie," Jeb said, "this is ridiculous. Come home, and we'll forget about this. No more courts, no more fighting."

Tucker was overwhelmed with how good it would feel to smash Stone in the face. It wasn't until he felt Matthew pull on his arm that he realized it was raised in a fist.

"It's not worth it," Matthew assured him.

Tucker took a breath. He wasn't sure it wouldn't be worth it. He looked to Josie; she shook her head. "Please Tucker, no." Taking a deep breath, he wrapped his arm around her shoulder. Only for her would he walk away. He didn't let go until they were in the car. Getting through the press was less stressful each time. They were nothing more than a blathering crowd of nibshits yelling the same questions Josie refused to answer a hundred times already. All Tucker had to do was get to the car and let the lawyers do the talking.

Tucker suggested taking her to a doctor.

"No, I'm fine. We'd probably have to get through the press again, and I just want to go home. I hate this. Why does he still scare me?"

Taking her hand, he squeezed it. "Post-traumatic stress. I've seen a lot of it. Certain things trigger the old feelings, and it's not exactly something you just rationally make yourself get over."

Josie nodded and took a shaky breath.

"I want you go to the doctor. For me. It would make me feel better."

"I'll go. I feel like it's a waste of time, but you're right. I have to think of the baby, and I suppose his dad's peace of mind."

They stopped at the local ER. Her blood pressure was high, but the baby's heartrate was steady. The doctor assumed it was stress and gave her orders to rest.

Once Tucker got her back to his mother's, he made her a comfy spot on the couch. Handing her the remote, he said, "We'll watch a movie. Mom might have something old enough to entice you."

"Tucker," Josie said quietly.

"What, sweetie?"

"What if I can never face Jeb? How will I get justice for Maddy if I can't even open my mouth and speak?" Josie's chin quivered as tears pooled in her eyes and spilled down her cheeks.

Tucker lay down beside her, holding her.

"Right now, the only thing that matters is you. We need to get you through this and then we'll think about Maddy," he said.

She shook her head. "No one cares. You don't even care. You wanted me to let him off, to say I was lying."

He took a slow breath. "It's not that I don't care. It's just that I love you so much. I'd do anything to keep you from having to go through all of this. And I'm worried about the peanut."

She moved in closer, her cheek resting on his chest. "I know you love us. And to you, Maddy is just an idea. You didn't know her like I did."

"Just rest for now, okay? I'll talk to Shae, see if she has a suggestion. Maybe you could meet one on one with the judge. I think I've seen on TV where judges will talk with victims. It's worth asking. If it's possible, I think he'd do it. He seemed nice. And he sure as hell didn't take Rogers' crap."

Josie nodded.

"I'm going to go make you something to eat, and you're going to eat it all." Giving her three quick kisses and one big one, he didn't leave until she flashed him a weak smile.

In the kitchen, he grabbed a leftover casserole, dipped some out on a plate, and popped it in the microwave. He could always count on his mom to have food. As he was putting the lid back on the casserole pan, his mother and Ed came in. "Hey there, movie star," his mom said.

"What?" Tucker asked.

"You're all over the news. Looks like you were about to take a swing at Jeb Stone," his mother said.

"I can understand why you'd want to sock him, but keep your temper. It's what he wants," Ed said quietly.

"You should listen to Ed," Marlene said.

"I didn't realize it was on TV, or looked that bad."

"You looked like your father. All emotion and fury. I doubt there was a rational thought going through your head. Amazing how much you're like him."

"No thanks to his influence though, right?"

"Nice jab," Marlene said. "I've said my piece over it. I've apologized to him. I've apologized to you."

"You apologized to him?"

"Yes. I went to the nursing home and saw him. Ed went with me."

Ed nodded as he took cookies out of a cookie jar.

Tucker figured if his dad was going to throw things at anyone, it would be his mother. "How did it go?"

"Well, he can't really talk, but I think he understood. He sort of nodded."

Tucker got the plate out of the microwave, and grabbed a fork and a napkin.

"Tucker, I'll have dinner ready in an hour," Marlene complained.

"It's not for me; it's for—"

A scream from the living room made him drop the plate. It smashed on the floor.

"Tucker! Tucker!" Josie yelled.

He was across the room in seconds.

"The baby, Tucker, the baby."

She stood, her legs soaked in blood.

"Oh Jesus, oh Josie." He lifted her off her feet and was heading to his car. "It's all right. I'll get you to the doctor."

"I'm losing it. I don't want to lose my baby."

His mother held the door open, and then ran ahead and unlocked the car door. Tucker set Josie in the seat then hurried to the driver's side. His mom handed him his keys with shaking hands. Ed placed a blanket over Josie, then wrapped an arm around his wife as they watched them drive away.

Burrowing into the blanket, she cried. Tucker felt like crying too, but he couldn't. He rubbed her leg. "It will be all right, Josie. It's all going to work out."

"When? It will never end."

"We'll get through it all. Together."

Shielding her face with the blanket, she cried. Her body shook with each fresh wave of tears. Tucker cursed every red light and rolled through every stop sign. He got her to the ER as quickly as he could without tossing her back and forth in a speeding car. He pulled into the ambulance bay and barely had the car in park before leaping from his seat. He ran to her, scooping her up. Hospital staff met him at the door, quickly bringing gurneys, taking her from him, and hustling her away. An orderly offered to park his car so he could go with Josie. Nodding, Tucker followed behind the team working on her. He stood in the corner of the room, watching. Josie lay there, her eyes squeezed closed.

"Call in the OB on call and let's get her to surgery," the doctor said, stepping back. Within seconds, Josie was gone.

An ER doctor, a short man with a shadow of hair around the crown of his head, approached Tucker. "You the dad?"

I was, Tucker thought, instantly regretting giving up hope so easily. "Yes," he said.

"We're calling in an obstetrician, just to be on the safe side. Any precipitating factors? A fall, any sort of impact?"

"She passed out today, but uh…" Tucker tried to remember when she fell in court. He didn't remember her hitting anything. Matthew caught her before she made impact with the table. "I don't think she hit anything. She's under a lot of stress." Tucker took a deep breath.

The doctor nodded. The look on his face said he knew who Josie was. Most people in the area did. Her picture was in every newspaper, every morning. Placing a hand on Tucker's elbow, he said, "We'll take good care of her."

"I heard you say you wanted her in surgery? Is she going to be all right?"

"That's just a precaution. We have a mobile team waiting on her in pre-op. They'll be able to do an ultrasound and other tests the OB will need for a diagnosis and plan of action. If it is surgery, they'll be prepped and ready to go."

Tucker knew the answer in his gut, but had to ask, "And the baby?"

The doctor rubbed his ear as he said, "Let's see what the OB says, okay? Come, I'll show you to the surgical waiting room."

Seated in the small room with low lighting he assumed was meant to reduce stress, he called his mother and Murray to let them know what was going on. His mother assured him she was on her way. He almost told her it wasn't necessary, but it was. He may as well have been six again and afraid of the dark. He wanted someone, anyone to tell him everything would be okay.

"Tucker?"

It was Shae. Dressed in jeans with her hair in a ponytail, she looked less like an attorney and more like a friend.

"Hey." Tucker stood and gave her a hug. Then they sat.

"So, is Josie going to be all right?"

"The ER doctor said she would be. But the baby…" Tucker's words wedged in his throat. He shook his head and looked at the floor.

Shae took his hand and squeezed it.

"How did you know?" Tucker asked.

"I called your mom's to check in on Josie and she told me you were headed to the hospital. And I'll warn you, I got a call from a reporter to verify the story on my way over here."

"What the hell? It's been like fifteen damn minutes." Tucker rubbed his hands across his face.

"All it takes is a single leak. A nurse, a custodian. Or it could have been the earlier ER visit. I don't know."

"Can't they give her some peace?"

"It's their job, Tucker. I know it sucks. I know it's wearing on you, but she's the story of the hour. On the bright side? When it's over, there will be another story, and everyone will forget. Or she could get a million-dollar book deal."

"Screw that." Tucker banged the back of his head against the wall. "Are they pestering Stone like they do her?"

Shae sighed. "I really don't know. He takes every opportunity to do interviews, blathering on and on about his pain and love for Josie. Makes me want to vomit. Such a maniacal, egotistical bastard. He approached me after the hearing today. Gave me this." Shae dug a card out of her purse. "Said he wanted me to give it to Josie. It's his number. Like all that stops her from being with him is her not having his number. He's insane. Why can't the world see it?"

Tucker took the card from her. Shae gave him a look, brow lifted, lips pursed. "Don't do anything stupid. I mean seriously, if you beat him up—like I thought you were going to in the courthouse? That only adds to his victim persona."

"Who says I would beat him?"

Shae shrugged. "I don't know. Maybe it's the look of pure hate on your face when you look at him. Or maybe it's the fact that if Matthew hadn't grabbed your arm, you'd probably have taken a swing at him this morning?"

"That was impulse. I won't let that happen again. No need to be sloppy."

"Oh Tucker, give the number back."

"No," he said, slipping it in his pocket.

"You know I have no license in Pennsylvania. I can't be your defense?" she said it like she was joking, but there was a steely undertone.

"Don't worry, Shae. I'm not stupid."

"Stupid, no. Pushed to the edge..."

He smiled. "I'm fine. Go. Do what you need to do, and I'll keep you posted."

Once Shae left, Tucker looked at the number on the card, wondering what sort of sick freak does what he did and thinks it's justified. He had no remorse because he thought it was his right. People like him didn't deserve the air they breathed.

"Tucker?"

He stood and gave his mom a hug. She patted him on the back. "It'll be okay. It just has to be."

He nodded, but didn't answer. Gripping her tight, burying his face in her shoulder, he cried. After a few minutes, he pulled away. "I'm sorry," he said.

"No need to be sorry." She took his hand and led him to a dark blue love seat. "This is heart breaking. Not to mention scary as hell. And infuriating. And confusing. Dear God, I watch the news and one guy says it should be a case considered by the Attorney General. Then another says it should be in federal court. Honestly? I don't think they know what to do with this case. I heard from a friend who knows a secretary in the circuit clerk's office that Judge Smith doesn't buy Stone's story. That's a good thing, right?"

Tucker nodded. "Yeah, unless it does go to the Attorney General. Or Shae and Matthew get their change of venue."

"Why would they want to do that?"

"I suppose they don't want to risk it. Judge Smith may be neutral, but what if he isn't? What if the entire township is crooked?"

Marlene hugged her purse. "I suppose you should listen to your attorneys. That's why they get paid the big bucks."

Tucker rubbed his eyes. "Nope, they're doing it for free."

"Well shit, Tuck, don't you think you ought to get the best, not the cheapest?"

"Trust me. If we had to pay them, we couldn't afford them."

"Oh, well that's good." Marlene shifted in her seat until she was facing him. She took a deep breath and said, "Tucker, I think we need to sway the public opinion. Stone whines on TV all the time, why doesn't Josie tell her side?"

"She passed out talking in court. How the hell could I ask her to stand in front of cameras? Have you heard the shit they ask her? Was she in love with Stone? Why did she lie?"

"Then we find someone nice, maybe Oprah. Oprah was abused. I bet she'd speak out for Josie."

Tucker took a deep breath. He knew his mother meant well, but how the hell was she planning to get Oprah's phone number? The improbability of the plan made his spine tight, sending tension to his neck and head and making him snap at his mom. "No one is calling Oprah. Josie is not talking to the press. I'll deal with this."

A nurse came to the door. "Mr. Boone?"

Tucker stood. "Yeah?"

"You can see her now."

Tucker followed the nurse through the hall. "How is she?"

"She's fine. Anxious to see you," the nurse said with a smile.

She pushed open a door and waved him on in, then she slipped away.

There she was. Curled up in the bed, she looked too small and delicate for the harsh white walls and beeping monitors in the room. When she spotted him, her face lit up with relief. "Tucker."

"Hey, sweetie," he said, rushing to her.

She bit her lip to still it from shaking and held her arms out to him.

Tucker gathered her in his arms and held her. Kissing her forehead, her cheeks, the curve of her jaw. She nestled her face in the hollow of his throat. "I'm sorry, Tucker."

"Sorry?" he asked. Pulling away a bit, he brushed away her tears. "What do you have to be sorry about?"

"I should've listened to you. I should've taken the deal. It's my fault." She started to cry. Her hands wrapped around him, gripping him. He climbed into bed beside her, holding her against him. He hated himself for telling her to take that damn deal.

"No. Josie, no. You can't think that. This is in no way your fault." He wanted to ask her about the baby, but he couldn't form the words. His heart knew, and he wasn't brave enough to confirm his worst fears.

"The baby's gone, Tucker. And it's my fault. I didn't take care of it. I was selfish, and now I don't have him anymore. I feel hollow. Like a part of me is gone. I wish...I wish I could go back and do it different. I'd think of him first. Instead, I thought of vengeance and—"

"No, Josie. You weren't after vengeance. You wanted justice. It was the right thing to do. This would've happened either way. You have to believe that."

Shaking her head against his chest, she said, "No. It's my fault. You...you...warned me." Josie sobbed. He kissed her, held her tight. "No, sweetie, no. It wouldn't have mattered. Nobody could have taken better care of our baby than you did."

She burrowed closer, and he wrapped her up and rocked her.

"I'm so sorry, Tucker."

"Stop it. You have nothing to be sorry for. I love you, Josie. I love you so much."

Tucker held her as she sobbed. His mind replayed all the abuse. Amanda kicking her in the boat. Greg Myers punching her in the head. Her limp body sliding underwater. Cops cuffing her and taking her away. The reporters harassing her. Jeb Stone staring holes in her. It wasn't fair. She was the most loving person he ever knew. She'd never hurt anyone. Why was it right that she suffered? Why wasn't it Stone who suffered? Why didn't he wrap a rope around his neck and do the right thing like Amanda Stone did?

Chapter Thirty Nine

Josie's cries turned to snuffles and soon her breathing slowed. She was asleep.

He eased himself away, careful not to wake her. The vinyl mattress crackled under him, and he cringed with every sound. Feet on the floor, he tucked the blankets up around her and switched off the light above her head. Gazing down at her, he couldn't help but think all the things he'd come to believe in the last month were nothing but bull. Things don't happen for a reason. The universe doesn't protect the innocent. There was no God, no Heaven, no Hell. Just humans, some good, some wicked. And sometimes the good people needed to keep the wicked in check.

He kissed her hand and headed out into the hall.

His mom was still in the waiting room. She stood as Tucker approached. "Is she all right?"

"No. She's heart broken."

"The baby?"

It wasn't a topic he wanted to discuss. It hurt to lose the baby. Even though his rational mind told him they could try again, they would never have *this* baby. And this baby was special. It was a promise of a happy ending where fate and benevolent universe conspired together to right wrongs and administer justice. No matter how bad things got in this screwed up situation, that baby gave him hope. Now, all he had was an empty space in his gut that grew bigger and darker as he realized all the assurances he made Josie were no better than lies. He couldn't promise her anything. Hell, she could go to jail along with Murray and Hetty— Stone could walk away a hero. It was bullshit. All of it.

He shook his head in answer to his mother's question, but said nothing. He wasn't going to talk about it. Hell, he was done thinking about it.

His mother said, "I'm so sorry."

"I need to get some fresh air. Could you wait with her?"

His mother looked at him with the same skepticism she gave him when he said he was studying at the library on Saturday nights. "What are you doing? Why are you leaving her?"

"They gave her a shot. She'll be out for hours."

"Tucker James Boone, what the hell are you planning to do?"

"Nothing. I need to take a walk, so I can think. Please, just stay with her?"

Tucker turned and walked off. His mom followed him to the emergency exit, grabbing at his arm. "Tucker, please, don't do anything stupid. There will be more babies."

Tucker brushed her off and left. Screw platitudes. When Ash died, he was supposed to accept it as God's will and be happy that he died quickly. When Holly died, he was the bad guy. It didn't matter to anyone that she brought insanity to every portion of her life and crashed her car while she was probably higher than a kite. No, she was vindicated by death, and he was the asshole. There was one good thing left in his life. One. And he promised to protect her. If the system wasn't going to punish Stone, he would. The son of a bitch would never look at Josie again.

He drove back to the house and went to the basement. Opening the gun safe, he looked over the rifles. He knew the one he wanted and hoped Ed hadn't left it at his hunting cabin. There in the back corner he spotted it. His lucky 270. It was with this bad boy he'd gotten his first deer and impressed the hell out of his friends by hitting a buck at 460 yards when he was only fifteen. He pulled it out and wrapped it in a blanket. Then he filled his pocket with ammo, though if he was lucky, he'd only need a single shot.

He drove the hour to Applewold with surprising calm. He knew what he needed to do. If Jeb Stone was dead, the problem would be over. Josie's stress would be gone, and she and Maddy would have their ultimate justice. Tucker pulled over at a dive bar along an old country road. Inside, there was a handful of early evening drinkers already enjoying a beer. Tucker asked the bartender if he could use the phone. The guy handed him an old rotary dial. Tucker thanked him and dialed the number Shae gave him.

When Jeb answered, Tucker said, "Money doesn't buy everyone's silence. Meet me at Cisco's or read about it in the news."

Then he hung up, thanked the owner, and left.

Cisco's was an old warehouse for Stone Construction. The place was out of town, isolated—perfect place for a murder. Tucker parked his car along a gravel road that led up a hill away from the warehouse. From this spot, Tucker could look down on the parking lot. He didn't need to confront Stone; he just needed him to show up.

Tucker left his car and waded into the brush and weeds into the woods along the road. He settled himself in the grass. Rolling the blanket soaked with Josie's blood into a ball, he set it on the ground and propped his rifle against it. Looking through the scope, he lined it up with the No Parking sign.

He only had to wait a few minutes before a red truck rolled into the lot. The evening sun shined off the glass, so Tucker couldn't tell if the person in the vehicle was Jeb Stone. Tucker slid the bolt back, and systemically loaded the brass bullets, locking the last one in the chamber. Wrapping a finger around the trigger, his hand was suddenly sweaty. The tall grass blew in the wind and itched his cheek, but he couldn't move. All he could do was wait and pray, willing God to give Stone the balls to open the door and step away from the truck.

Seriously, dude, have you lost your mind? What are you thinking?

Tucker looked over his shoulder, half expecting to see Ash, or his ghost. But there was nothing but grass and blue sky. Tucker rubbed his forehead with the back of his wrist. The truck door opened a crack. Someone put a foot out.

Tuck, buddy. I warned you about the crossroads. You're here. You have to make the choice. Don't let it be the wrong one, dumbass.

In a flash, his brain absorbed an image. Josie clutching his hand, only letting go when a voice told her to push. She was having his baby. It wasn't their first. He didn't know how he knew, he just did. She smiled at him. Their life was good.

If he walked away.I

If he didn't walk away, he'd be the first person the law would come for. There would be ballistics…forensics. Most of that was TV bullshit, but what if they did trace the bullet to this gun? A gun registered to Ed. Tucker closed his eyes and sighed. Ed would never turn Tucker in.

He heard the door slam shut. Looking through the scope, he could see the lines on Stone's face. It would be so easy to squeeze the trigger, and all of her problems would be gone. He could do it in one bullet. The jackass was staring right at him.

Tucker would have to confess. He couldn't let Ed take the fall. Chances were good he'd only get ten to fifteen years for a crime of passion. Maybe be out in five with parole? That was worth it. Josie would be free. Maddy would be vindicated. He opened his eyes again. Stone scanned the horizon, so calm. He had to think he was back in control of the world around him. Tucker wanted nothing more than prove him dead wrong. He wanted Stone to try his bullshit on St. Peter and see if he bought the mutual love story. No one escaped final justice. Wasn't that the promise the universe used to pacify its inhabitants?

Chapter Forty

Her hospital room was lit with low light. He could hear the hum of the television from the door. When he stepped into the room, his mother looked up. Once she saw him, she was on her feet, jerking him into the room. Closing the door behind him, she hissed, "What in the hell did you do?"

"I told you. I needed to take a walk."

"With a hunting rifle?"

"I didn't—"

"The hell you didn't. Ed said you left the gun cabinet wide open, and your lucky 270 was gone. He was scared to death you were going to...you didn't, did you? Kill Stone? Ed said if you did, you've got to get him the gun, so he can get rid of it."

"I didn't kill anyone. I felt like it, but I didn't."

Marlene patted her chest. "Thank God. Now, are you done with the insanity? She's been worried sick. Damn it, she needs you here."

"She woke up?"

"Hell, yes. About twenty minutes after you left. They gave her more medicine, so she's finally resting. The doctor said the bleeding is under control, and as soon as her blood pressure stabilizes, they'll let her go home." Marlene looked down at Josie. "She'll be happy to see you. When she woke, she asked for you. I told her your walking story, but she didn't buy it either. She tried to call your phone, but you didn't answer."

"I forgot it at the house." He'd ditched the phone. He knew it would ping off cell phone towers.

His mom gave him a knowing look. "Mmm, hmm, I bet. I think she had a gut feeling that you were thinking of doing something stupid. She's a hearty prayer. I'll give her that."

Tucker chuckled. "That she is." Tucker gave his mom a hug. "Go on home. I'll take it from here."

Marlene closed the door gently behind her, but Josie still woke up. Her eyes fluttered open, and she sighed. "You're here. You scared me."

"Nah, not me." He took her hand and kissed it.

"You're such a bad liar. The pain of losing the baby was nothing compared to the thought of losing you. I don't need you to avenge me...I need you with me."

"I won't leave you. I thought it through and put the gun away."

"Gun?" Her eyes were open wide. "Tucker, what did you do?"

"I was going to put a bullet in his skull. I had my gun, an excellent vantage point, and he was right in the middle of my cross hairs, looking right at me."

"No Tucker, no. We have to let go of the anger. We have each other, but we won't if we let our feelings rule our hearts."

"I won't do anything stupid. I promise. I was pissed. I wanted this baby more than I ever thought I could want anything. And it killed me, seriously killed me, that you blamed yourself. It burned a freaking hole through my heart that you would ever think this is your fault."

She reached out and caressed his cheek. "Come, kiss me."

He leaned forward and kissed her. When he pulled back, she smiled at him. "Your mom told me sometimes the flesh can't contain the spirit. Our little peanut must be one big ball of energy if he needs a stronger body. This was God's doing, not mine. Not Jeb's."

Tucker shrugged. Tears clouded his vision. Josie kissed him. "It will happen. We will be a family."

Tucker brushed away a wayward tear. Embarrassed, he got up and walked to the window. "Tonight, while I was laying on that hill waiting on Stone, Ash was in my head. It was like he was right there with me, stopping me."

"Thank God for Ash. Even if it's just you and me. That's all I need."

"There will be other babies," Tucker said. "When I was up there, Ash told me to think it through, then I had this feeling...or a vision...though it wasn't really a vision."

"It was like a memory that hasn't happened yet?"

"Exactly," Tucker said. "It was like an image, but I understood the image. We were having a baby, and it wasn't our first. We were happy." He returned to her side, locking his fingers in hers. "You were holding my hand, and I could feel it. I could hear the doctor tell you to push. I could smell the antiseptic soap from the delivery room. I also knew, without a doubt, if I pulled that trigger, I'd lose that."

She relaxed against him, nestling her head on his shoulder. She smiled. "Seems you have your own guardian. Ash is looking out for you."

"I don't know about that, Josie. He called me a dumbass. Not exactly harp-strumming sweetness."

Her laugh was soft. "He speaks a language you will hear."

He nodded. "We will get through this, won't we?"

"Yes, we will. As long as we have each other," she said.

"Well, I'm not going anywhere, and I'm not letting you go." He brushed his thumb across her cheek.

Her eyes were getting heavy. Crawling in bed with her, he held her. He kissed her brow. "Sleep sweetie. I'll be right here."

"No walks?"

"No walks. I have way too much to lose."

Chapter Forty One

The next day, the hospital discharged Josie. His mom brought her a change of clothes on her way to work. They snuck out via a loading dock to avoid the press. Josie looked paler than usual, and her smile was as weak as morning sunshine that glowed bright, but lacked its full warmth.

Reaching for her hand, Tucker brought it to his lips. "Can I get you some breakfast?"

Josie shook her head. "Your mother force-fed me an omelet while you were getting the car. She said I needed the protein."

"That's my mother."

"Speaking of parents. any chance we could visit your dad? Or is that weird?"

"Why would it be weird? Are you sure you're up to it?"

Josie nodded.

Shifting the car into drive, he headed for the nursing home. The hospital was only a few blocks away, and they arrived in a few minutes. Josie frowned as she looked the building over. Tucker hadn't considered how shabby the nursing home looked on his first visit. He supposed it wasn't the best place, but it wasn't the worst either. Evidently, Josie expected better things for Rob Morgan than his own son did. Tucker sighed as he got out and walked to her side of the car.

She already had her door open, but he gave her his hand and helped her out. His gesture got him a pat on the cheek. "I'm fine, Tucker. Stop worrying."

Her assurances didn't register with Tucker. He still kept an arm around her back like he feared the antiseptic and urine smell of the place could be toxic. The workers manning the front desk didn't pay any attention to them as they passed. No one bothered to question their presence at all, until an old man shuffled out of his room in his slippers and his crookedly buttoned pajamas. "Hey, boy," the man said, "someone stole my teeth. Tell my son, all right?"

"Uh? Okay?" Tucker said. The guy nodded and headed back to his room.

Tucker led Josie farther down the hall to his father's room. His dad looked the same as the first visit…sitting in his wheelchair, in the dark, staring out the window.

"Rob?" Josie practically ran to the elderly man. Tucker was right behind her and tried to pull her back. She shook her head. "I'm fine, Tucker."

Josie was down on one knee in front of Rob hugging him. Rob pulled back a little and grunted, pointing toward the door. Tucker feared the worst was coming. He instantly regretted bringing Josie here. If his dad threw something at her—

"Turn on the light, Tucker. I think he wants to be able to see us."

Rob nodded and smiled. Josie pulled up a chair and sat in front of him, holding his hands. "Oh goodness. I've missed you so much." A tear slid down her cheek. "Tucker said he came to see you a while ago. Do you remember that visit?"

Again, Rob nodded. Josie's smile was broad. "You won't believe this, but he found me."

Rob's eyes were soft as he looked Josie over, but then his shoulders stiffened and he shook his head. He pulled his hand away from Josie and pointed to the door.

"What is it?" Josie asked.

"I think he wants us to leave," Tucker suggested. "I don't think he likes having company."

With a grunt, Rob spun around, using one foot to move the chair. He rolled to a dresser where he knocked the TV remote to the floor. Letting out a growl, he pounded his foot on the floor.

"What is it?" Josie asked. Turning to Tucker she said, "I don't think he wants us to leave. I think he's trying to tell us something."

Rob nodded.

"Paper," Tucker said. "Maybe he could write something on a piece of paper." Tucker moved to the dresser and looked around. He couldn't find a tablet or even a magazine.

Josie grabbed a roll of toilet paper from the bathroom. She ripped the paper wrapper off the roll and handed it to Tucker, then she dug in her purse and pulled out a pen. Tucker set the pen and paper on the table and slid it in front of his dad. Rob tried to write a word, but all he got was a squiggly line. He grunted and threw the pen at the wall.

A discouraged-looking Josie picked up the pen.

"Wait," Tucker said. "My phone." He pulled his phone out of his pocket and put it on notepad. "Here," he said laying it on the table in front of his dad. He showed him how to use it. Rob nodded. Waiting for his dad's twisted fingers to hit the little buttons was frustrating, but Tucker kept his eagerness well hidden. He tried to read over his shoulder, but his dad's head was so close to the phone, Tucker couldn't even see the screen. When Rob finished, he sat up as straight as his crooked body allowed.

Not safe ariel not safe

Tucker read the words and looked at Josie. His heart skipped a beat. The danger had to be over. "Amanda Stone committed suicide, and Greg Meyers is in jail. Is she still in danger?"

Rob's brow furrowed. He looked like a man who was just told the moon fell from the sky. Tucker pulled up a chair and told him the whole story from the time he was last at the nursing home to this morning. Rob listened intently, holding a hand out to Josie when Tucker explained she'd lost the baby. Josie cradled his hand in hers.

Once the tale was told, Tucker asked, "Is she still in danger?"

No, Rob typed as he relaxed in his seat. A grimace that may have been a smile twitched his cheeks. He leaned forward and typed *happy*.

Josie's smile was radiant. It had all the intensity of high noon. "I'm happy too. I've missed you. I've missed Gloria. And I have Tucker. He's perfect for me, Rob. Can you believe it?"

Rob nodded.

Josie patted Rob's leg. "Now, we need to talk to Gloria about getting you out of here. You do want out of this place, don't you?"

Rob nodded.

"I figured as much. You poor man, I don't believe for one second you were having an affair with my mother."

Rob shook his head and frowned.

Josie was quiet a minute. Then she asked, "They tricked you, didn't they? They told you they knew where Maddy was. Then what did they do to you?"

Rob's eyes filled with tears.

Josie moved closer and gave his hand a squeeze. "We'll get to the bottom of this, I swear. But first, I need to talk some sense into Gloria. Today. I don't want you to have to spend another night here. You saved my life, you know?"

The tears spilled over and down the man's wrinkled cheeks. Josie wiped them away.

Tucker approached his father, kneeling in front of him. It finally occurred to him that this man knew what happened. Maybe he knew something that could help Josie. "Dad?" Tucker said.

Rob's gaze fell on Tucker and his face lit up.

"Can you help us? Stone is out of prison and they're charging Josie with conspiracy."

Rob's fingers shook as he typed. *Killed maddy*

"Who killed Maddy?"

Stone

"Can you prove it?" Tucker asked, his body tense. If they could prove Stone killed Maddy, that would surely clear Josie.

Yes

Josie turned to Tucker. "We need to call the police."

"No. We can't call the police. We can't trust them. Look at how they treated you?"

Rob knocked on the table. Tucker turned and saw a new word on the notepad: *King*

"Is King a cop?"

Rob nodded.

"One we can trust?"

He nodded again.

Tucker called Shae and gave her the information and asked her to hunt this man down. There was no way in hell he was calling the Applewold police station and asking for him. For all he knew, the man would end up floating in Lake Erie before the end of the day if the wrong people knew he was contacted by them.

Chapter Forty Two

By dinnertime that evening, Gloria's trailer looked like the operational headquarters for a joint task force. Detective King, a small, dark-haired guy with a nervous twitch, had called in the Pennsylvania State Police and Internal Affairs. The now, happy to be at home, Rob Morgan was provided with a keypad communicator made for stroke victims. He was soon pounding out his side of the story.

Amanda Stone and Greg Morgan took him to Stone's warehouse out in the Cisco woods. They showed him proof that Stone had Maddy. He had her hair clip and her necklace. They told him he'd become obsessed with Maddy, like he was Ariel. That he was keeping her at a local hotel, tied up and drugged.

They assured him they were turning all the evidence over to the police, but first they'd take him to his daughter. They drove to the Econo Inn downtown. As soon as Rob walked through the door, Greg jumped him and Amanda stabbed him with a hypodermic needle. Their plan was to leave him for dead in what looked like an overdose during an affair. Rob didn't die, but their plan still worked. He looked like a vile cheat. He had no respect. No one to turn to. No one to care what he had to say.

Gloria cried at the revelation. Hard sobs wracked her skinny body and took the words from her.

Rob patted her arm.

"I'm sorry. I shoulda known. I shoulda trusted you, but oh my God, she was so beautiful. You always liked the pretty ones."

Rob sent her a message, *you are the pretty one.*

Gloria wrapped her arms around him for a bone crushing hug.

While Gloria and Rob had their moment, Tucker called Detective King. "How soon until you can check that warehouse? He may still have evidence in there."

"I'm on it. We have a warrant and a team of detectives over there now. We also have people meeting with Myers. I figure if he knows Rob Morgan is talking, he may want to share what he knows too."

Greg Myers was more than eager to talk, especially when he was told that the car he owned five years ago was just impounded by the State Police. It was time that vehicle was given a white glove check for evidence. Maddy Morgan's case was officially re-opened, this time as a homicide, not a runaway.

Greg Myers folded. He admitted he had been the one to dispose of Maddy's body, but it was Jeb Stone who killed her. He told them where they could find a video of Stone confessing to the murder. Meyers recorded Jeb when he explained to Myers how he killed the girl because she wouldn't shut up. She threatened to take Ariel away from him. Greg admitted he helped Stone cover up the murder to the police and Amanda. But Amanda was suspicious. She called Greg while Ariel was in the hospital.

She had the perfect plan.

Ariel would come home from the hospital. First chance Jeb got, he would approach the girl again. Amanda would catch him in the act and kill them both. She'd blame Jeb for Ariel's death, and she'd never be convicted for killing the bastard to save her daughter.

Meyer's admitted he wasn't keen on killing the girl at the time, but Amanda worried Jeb had made Ariel the heir to most of his estate, and she'd run to live with the trailer trash instead of her mother. Then where would Amanda be?

At the end of the interview, Myers told them where they could find Maddy's body. He'd wrapped the girl in plastic, took her out on Lake Erie, tied a large concrete lawn angel to the bag, and dumped her at Ferrel's Landing. Myers said he added the angel because he felt bad for the girl. She'd just been at the wrong place— running her mouth to the wrong guy— at the wrong time.

It only took dive teams one hour to find her and bring her up from her watery grave.

Jeb Stone accused Greg Meyers of trying to distract people from the truth—it was Myers and Amanda who killed Maddy. Some might have fallen for Stone's dispersion if the warrant hadn't revealed a hoard of evidence from the Cisco Warehouse. And, of course, there was Stone's video confession. Meyers wasn't dumb enough to transport and dump a body without proof he wasn't the killer.

When King stopped by the trailer at the end of the night, he pulled Tucker outside to update him. Tucker felt floored. So much changed simply by scratching the surface. If only the police had done their job five years ago, Josie would never have had to live in hiding. But instead of pursuing justice, law enforcement lined their pockets with Stone's money.

"So, it's over?" Tucker asked.

Detective King gave him a slap on the shoulder. "Pretty much all but the paper work. We're waiting on a new prosecutor to be appointed to file the official charges, since Rogers got fired. Good of Stone to keep such good records for us."

"So he was on the take?"

King nodded. "We have a ledger of payments to officials and cops. There are a whole lot of people in this town sweating tonight."

"I can't thank you enough."

"I wish I could have done more sooner. I was a new detective when I was assigned to Maddy's case. I never bought the runaway angle, but when I suggested foul play, my chief pulled me from the case. I knew something stunk, but I had no proof."

"Looks like you have it now."

"I sure as hell do. Now, you go and let them know this nightmare's about over. I'm going to go leak to the press that they're about to look like a bunch of dipshits. Again."

Chapter Forty Three

Maddy's official funeral was set to be a state affair. The governor even showed up for the occasion, though Tucker wasn't impressed. As far as he was concerned, they all picked the wrong side. None of them stepped up to help Josie, but now that the public was enamored with her, and poking their pitchforks at the cops and the elected officials…they were quick to show up with some pomp, circumstance, and crocodile tears.

As a line of dignitaries dressed in suits so perfectly pressed he couldn't spot a single crease or rumple approached, Tucker took Josie by the hand and walked in the opposite direction. He wasn't in the mood for small talk, especially at this fiasco of a funeral.

His family said good-bye last week, privately, in a boat service on the lake in the spot where Maddy's body was found. To him, this production was nothing but a waste of time. But it seemed to please Gloria, so for her, Tucker played nice.

Josie leaned close enough to whisper, "You're not worried, are you? About this morning?"

Tucker grunted and frowned. This morning hadn't helped his mood any. The doctor had told them no sex for six weeks, but Tucker caved. He was weak.

Josie gave him an ornery grin. "I didn't think men were ever supposed to regret getting lucky."

"I don't regret it. It's just that it's only been three weeks. What if—"

"It's fine. I know my body better than they do."

"They're doctors. They know things. We shouldn't—"

"Oh shush, Tucker Boone. You sound like an old woman."

Looking down at her, he shook his head.

She grinned, looking worry-free. "I needed that. It was like a stress reliever. I knew this day would be difficult. I think being relaxed is far more valuable than three more weeks of abstinence."

He still frowned. She shrugged and smiled back.

"There you guys are. You need to take your seats," Marlene said. "It's about to begin. I just got Hetty and Murray seated next to Gloria and Rob. I swear, getting all you people where you're supposed to be is like herding Gloria's cats."

Tucker and Josie followed her, taking their seats in the front row of the crowded church.

The local news put together a video to honor Maddy and her vibrant spirit. The air in the church grew thick and hard to breathe as images of the smiling girl moved across the screen. Then there were video clips. The place echoed with her voice, her laughter. Josie tensed; her nails dug into Tucker's hand. "She's gone," she whispered. "I can't believe that's all that's left of her…in that box."

Tucker tried to think of the right words to comfort her, but before his mind could come up with anything, Josie's hand went to her belly. He finally relaxed, feeling better about bending the rules. Josie had hope. And so did he. There were still plenty of miracles in this life: family, friends, and possibilities.

And there was justice. Jeb was back in jail, joined now by Greg Meyers, several cops, and the smug prosecutor.

And Rob was home.

Once the final prayer was offered, they followed the casket out of the church. Tucker helped get his dad into the limo as Gloria and Josie climbed in from the other side. They drove quietly along the road. Crowds gathered on the street, solemnly honoring the procession as it passed.

"If only Maddy could see," Gloria said, wiping tears from her eyes. "She'd feel like a superstar."

Rob took her hand and nodded.

Josie stared out the window. Police cars lined the entrance of the cemetery—their blue lights flashing. People crowded around the wrought iron fence that was piled high with flowers and stuffed bears. Josie broke down. Sobs escaped her. Tucker wrapped an arm around her and squeezed

her close. Gloria leaned forward and said, "She's all right, Josie. Call me crazy, but I know our Maddy's okay. I dreamed about her last night. She told me I wouldn't remember, but I do."

Josie nodded and smiled, dabbing the tears from her eyes.

"Look at that, will you?" Gloria said.

Josie and Tucker looked the direction Gloria pointed. Someone painted a glorious butterfly with outstretched wings and hung it from the entry arch. The purples and pinks of the creation seemed to reflect the sun and shimmer, as if it had life.

Gloria gasped. "It's gorgeous. I want to find who did that. And thank them. Maddy would—no, Maddy does love it. Fly free, baby girl. Fly free."

Acknowledgements

Thanks to CookieLynn Publishing for the opportunity to fly solo. Putting a book together and calling it done without the prodding of a publisher was both inspiring and terrifying.

I was beginning to wonder if this book would ever be done. I swear, like a bratty kid, this book didn't ever want to be finished. Bits and pieces kept not wanting to fit. I was about to chuck the story into the never-see-the-light-of-day file. Fortunately, I have friends. Thanks to them, they kept reading and reading, pointing out the strengths and flaws until FINALLY- this book felt done.

So, many thinks to the very best betas, editors, and proof readers. Thanks to Kelley Lynn for the content edit. Suzi Retzlaff and Melissa Maygrove for their most seriously awesome editorial skills. Thanks to Jo Wake and Susan Flett Swiderski for the proof reads (they read over all my many changes to catch butchered commas and vile homonyms).

As always, thanks to my beta readers whose feedback is always priceless! Kari Dinardo, Sonya Hedricks, Celeste Holloway, and Tammy Theriault. You ladies are awesome.

Special thanks to my husband for putting up with my distracted writer brain. Hopefully, forgetfulness is not grounds for divorce. And to Tina Longwell for her constant reminders that another book should be available soon.

I hope the final product is an enjoyable story. God bless.

About the Author

Elizabeth divides her time between her beach cottage and her scrupulously clean house in the hills of West Virginia. Ooops. That's fantasy Elizabeth. The real Elizabeth spends her days schlepping after her four boys (five if you count their father) and the assortment of pets they swore they'd take care of. She does live in West Virginia; the house is clean when the mother-in-law visits; and she does have serious dreams of living at the beach. Elizabeth is a Marshall University graduate with a degree in counseling. This has proven very beneficial when dealing with the make-believe friends she hangs out with all day (she calls this 'writing'). Follow her blog at: http://www.eseckman.blogspot.com

www.ingramcontent.com/pod-product-compliance
Lightning Source LLC
Chambersburg PA
CBHW031707170626
46808CB00005B/1638